'I can stop any time I want,' Henrietta replied, her face taking on a mutinous expression as she crossed her arms over her full bosom, highlighting rather than detracting from her curves.

'Prove it.'

'What are you suggesting, Mr Montemorcy?' Her carefully arranged curls shook with anger. 'I enjoy helping people. People need me.'

At last. She'd walked straight into his trap. 'I am suggesting a wager to demonstrate that you are addicted to arranging others' love-lives and you have no sense of discipline in these matters.' He watched her bridle at the words. He wondered if she knew how desirable she appeared when she was angry. Desirable, but very much off-limits…

AUTHOR NOTE

This book is set in one of my favourite villages in Northumberland—Corbridge. I had a great deal of fun walking through the streets, deciding where Henri and Robert lived and researching what would have been there then. The verger at St Andrew's Church was very helpful in answering my questions and allowing me to look around.

Special mention must be made of the hours I spent at the reading room in the Literary and Philosophical Library in Newcastle. The room dates from 1826, and there is a curved iron staircase that leads up to where the costume books are kept. There I discovered *The Woman In Fashion* by Doris Langley Moore (1949), a book full of authentic nineteenth-century costumes being worn by 1940s movie stars and ballerinas.

Henri has a special place in my heart, and I hope you will love her story as much as I do.

As ever, I love hearing from readers. You can contact me either via post to Harlequin Mills & Boon, my website, www.michellestyles.co.uk, or my blog, www.michellestyles.blogspot.com

TO MARRY A MATCHMAKER

Michelle Styles

All Rights Reserved including the right of reproduction in whole or
in part in any form. This edition is published by arrangement with
Harlequin Enterprises II BV/S.à.r.l. The text of this publication or
any part thereof may not be reproduced or transmitted in any form
or by any means, electronic or mechanical, including photocopying,
recording, storage in an information retrieval system, or otherwise,
without the written permission of the publisher.

® and TM are trademarks owned and used by the trademark owner
and/or its licensee. Trademarks marked with ® are registered with the
United Kingdom Patent Office and/or the Office for Harmonisation in
the Internal Market and in other countries.

First published in Great Britain 2011
by Mills & Boon, an imprint of Harlequin (UK) Limited,
Eton House, 18-24 Paradise Road, Richmond, Surrey TW9 1SR

© Michelle Styles 2011

ISBN: 978 0 263 21823 7

Harlequin (UK) policy is to use papers that are natural,
renewable and recyclable products and made from wood grown in
sustainable forests. The logging and manufacturing process conform
to the legal environmental regulations of the country of origin.

Printed and bound in Great Britain
by CPI Antony Rowe, Chippenham, Wiltshire

Born and raised near San Francisco, California, **Michelle Styles** currently lives a few miles south of Hadrian's Wall, with her husband, three children, two dogs, cats, assorted ducks, hens and beehives. An avid reader, she became hooked on historical romance when she discovered Georgette Heyer, Anya Seton and Victoria Holt one rainy lunchtime at school. And, for her, a historical romance still represents the perfect way to escape. Although Michelle loves reading about history, she also enjoys a more hands-on approach to her research. She has experimented with a variety of old recipes and cookery methods (some more successfully than others), climbed down Roman sewers, and fallen off horses in Iceland—all in the name of discovering more about how people went about their daily lives. When she is not writing, reading or doing research, Michelle tends her rather overgrown garden or does needlework— in particular counted cross-stitch.

Michelle maintains a website, www.michellestyles.co.uk, and a blog, www.michellestyles.blogspot.com, and would be delighted to hear from you.

Previous novels by the same author:

THE GLADIATOR'S HONOUR
A NOBLE CAPTIVE
SOLD AND SEDUCED
THE ROMAN'S VIRGIN MISTRESS
TAKEN BY THE VIKING
A CHRISTMAS WEDDING WAGER
  (part of *Christmas By Candlelight*)
VIKING WARRIOR, UNWILLING WIFE
AN IMPULSIVE DEBUTANTE
A QUESTION OF IMPROPRIETY
IMPOVERISHED MISS, CONVENIENT WIFE
*COMPROMISING MISS MILTON
THE VIKING'S CAPTIVE PRINCESS
*BREAKING THE GOVERNESS'S RULES

*linked by character

Chapter One

May 1848—Corbridge, Northumberland

Precise planning produced perfection.

Lady Henrietta Thorndike knew the saying from her childhood, and as she muttered the words for the two-hundred-and-forty-ninth time that morning, she was inclined to believe it. But straightening the peonies in the central floral arrangement for the third time, she wondered—had she done enough to produce the ideal setting for the wedding breakfast?

True, the bride was an exquisite combination of demureness and supreme happiness in her white silk and organza dress. The groom also seemed far more dignified in his burgundy frock-coat with its black velvet collar than the gossips in the village had considered possible, but something nagged at the back of Henri's mind as wrong.

Henri took a step back from the table where the peonies now stood upright. On the surface all appeared perfection. Even the notoriously tricky Northumbrian weather proved to be no deterrent to the festivities. Despite dire predictions to the contrary—most notably from Robert Montemorcy, and unremitting rainfall earlier in the week—the sun shone in a blazing blue sky.

But in the back of her mind she could hear her mother's strident tones, demanding she look again as she would never be good enough, that in her haste to be finished she always overlooked a glaring error. Henri took another sweeping glance at the scene, trying to puzzle out what she'd overlooked.

When the bride blushed happily in response to a remark from Robert Montemorcy, Henri realised and silently swore. Her mother's cameo brooch, the something blue and borrowed, lay on the chest of drawers in the front parlour where she had helped Melanie to dress. Nowhere near the bride.

In that heartbeat, despite the triumphs of the day, Henri knew she'd always remember her failure to ensure that the tradition about something old, new, borrowed and blue was followed through. If the marriage failed to thrive, she'd wonder if somehow it was because of the omission, an omission she had spotted and failed to rectify. She could well imagine Robert Montemorcy uttering pronouncements on the folly of putting credence in old wives' tales, but Henri knew she had to do something to make amends.

Plucking several of the blue forget-me-nots from the centrepiece, she strode over to the happy couple and tucked them into the bride's bonnet.

'Something blue, dear,' she whispered. 'No point in tempting fate.'

Melanie stammered her thanks and Henri withdrew, allowing the other well-wishers to offer their congratulations, safe in the knowledge that that particular crisis had been averted.

'Absolute perfection achieved,' she said in a low tone. 'I did it. I really did all of it.'

'Are you going to take credit for the bird-song as well? How did *you* manage to get them to sing so sweetly?' a deep voice laced with a hint of a Northumbrian burr asked.

'I find scattering bird seed is useful in attracting them,' Henri said in an absentminded voice as she concentrated again on the centrepiece. Was it her imagination or were the peonies leaning over to other side now?

'And what other tips do you give for achieving the weather, Lady Thorndike? How did you ensure sunshine? Even last night, the barometer was falling. It takes steely nerve to plan a wedding breakfast in the garden in May.'

Henri spun around and saw Robert Montemorcy regarding her with an amused expression. His immaculately cut black frock-coat and high-topped Hessian boots added a note of sartorial elegance to the affair and quite took her breath away. Not that she'd admit it to him. She'd sooner die than confess admiration for his form.

'Come, Lady Thorndike. What spell did you have to chant to guarantee perfect bridal weather?'

Henri took a steadying breath and readied her nerves for the coming battle of wits. Victory was going to be an altogether sweeter prospect if she ensured Robert Montemorcy was properly humbled.

'Weather is beyond anyone's control, Mr Montemorcy.' She made her voice like honey. 'I just hoped for the best.'

'I prefer to put my faith in science and observation. Cool logic.'

'Had you done that, you'd have been wrong.' She gestured towards the blue sky. 'Not a single cloud to spoil the day. I'll grant you that this spring has been wetter than most, but I just *knew* that today would be wonderful. But I did have an alternative venue to hand if necessary. Lady Winship offered Aydon Castle's hall. However, one must always consider the potential for her pugs to escape. On balance, the garden was a less tricky option.'

'Only you, Lady Thorndike, would consider planning a wedding breakfast in the garden during one of the wettest springs Northumbria has known easier than worrying about a few dogs escaping.' His dark brown eyes twinkled and the slight flutter at the base of her spine turned to a warm curl of heat. Henri lifted her chin and concentrated on breathing slowly. 'The generals in the British army could take lessons from your nerves of steel.'

'Lessons? No, no, I simply possess a happy talent for organising.' She made her face assume a studied expression of incredulity. 'In fact, this marriage would not have happened if I had not taken matters in hand.'

He raised an imperious brow, transforming his face into one of elegant scorn. 'You appear to entertain the notion that you had a hand in the marriage, rather than being the chief architect of its near-collapse.'

'Entertain, fiddlesticks. I *know*.' Henri nodded towards where the happy couple stood, receiving the good wishes of their neighbours. Mr Montemorcy needed to be enlightened. No matter how intensely that rich voice of his affected her, it didn't make his words true. 'This wedding only happened because of careful and strategic planning on my part. It was a close-run thing, particularly when Mr Crozier spoke of emigrating. To America. Thankfully he saw the sense in staying put and marrying the one woman who will give him lasting happiness.'

'It was Crozier's sense, not yours.'

Henri clenched her fists and struggled to maintain her temper. She'd slaved over this match, working hard to ensure that the bride and groom realised how exactly right they were for each other. 'Who else saw the potential in two lonely individuals? Who arranged the dinner party so that they sat next to each other and discovered a mutual admiration of Handel? Who hung back on the walk out towards the excavations so that there was a chance of the happy couple reaching a convivial understanding?'

'Who indeed?' he murmured, his eyes becoming hooded.

She glanced over her shoulder and lowered her voice to a conspiratorial whisper. 'Of course, with the actual wedding breakfast, I played a larger part. Dear Melanie can never organise anything.

And left to Mr Crozier, they would have eloped to Gretna Green and deprived the village of the chance to bestow their good wishes. Matters had to be taken into hand. I, for one, am well satisfied with the result. The entire village is here and Melanie has had the wedding she has always dreamt of. The memories of her perfect day will sustain her in years to come.'

'A wedding does not a marriage make. The new Mrs Crozier should remember today because of her groom rather than because of the setting.'

'But the setting helps. The perfect start to a marriage.'

'And this is what you base the right to usurp proceedings on?' Mr Montemorcy captured her arm and led her down the gravel path of her aunt's garden towards the summer-house. For a few heartbeats, intelligent thought fled and all Henri could think about was the pressure his fingers exerted on her elbow. 'A few engineered meetings of two people who had been near neighbours for years. This marriage would have happened without your interference.'

Henri dragged her mind away from the breadth of his shoulders and his sandalwood scent and back to the matter at hand. 'Years, Mr Montemorcy. Years without noticing that the perfect person lived a short walk away. That state of affairs would have continued indefinitely. Since arriving in Northumberland, I have facilitated three marriages, two reconciliations between estranged parents and their children, and one christening. It is altogether a brilliant achievement for sixteen months' work.' Henri crossed her arms. Mr Montemorcy had to realise how hard she worked for other people's happiness. She'd done this out of the best possible motives, and now she was about to see her aunt's eyes light up, if Mr Montemorcy didn't find some reason to wriggle out of their wager—a wager that, suspiciously, he had yet to mention. 'Who are you to say differently?'

'I'm urging caution, Lady Thorndike. Not everyone wants to be paired off in a manner that you deem fit. Nor do they want their lives ordered to suit your mood. What can you hope to achieve with such meddling?'

'A satisfactory result all around.' Henri clapped her hands together and rocked back and forth on her toes, and then revealed the true source of her happiness. 'And my aunt's purpose in life restored.'

'Meaning?' He arched one maddening eyebrow. 'You've lost me, Lady Thorndike. Your aunt is over fifty—surely you aren't going to try to pair her off with some unsuspecting retired military type?'

Henri took a deep breath and counted to ten, savouring the moment. Of all the satisfactions she'd expected to experience today, this was the one she had looked forward to the most.

'Don't you remember? We wagered, Mr Montemorcy, last New Year's. You didn't believe the groom could be brought up to snuff before hell froze over. I have done it in under the six months you specified.' Henri fluttered her lace-gloved hand towards where the happy couple stood giving each other besotted looks.

'Did you always enjoy ordering others' lives for them, Lady Thorndike? Or did it grow on you?'

Henri caught her bottom lip between her teeth, considering the question. Was it her fault that she could see solutions where others saw insurmountable difficulties? But ordering people about—surely he couldn't really think that's what she did? She might make suggestions, some stronger than others, but she *always* allowed people to decide for themselves. She wasn't like her mother, bitter and overly critical. She celebrated when people experienced joy. The challenge of improving people's lives gave her life meaning.

'I'm not overly domineering. My ideas are better than most and I simply possess a happy talent for organisation.'

His rich laugh rang out and Henri wondered if she was in fact being humoured. 'You do have a unique perspective on it.'

'It isn't my fault if the vast majority of people fail to see how problems can easily be solved. A cool head and a calm manner counts for much in life.' Henri gave a little clap of her hands before giving Mr Montemorcy a hard stare. 'Will you concede under the terms of our wager that you have lost?'

'On the balance of probabilities, I will admit defeat.' A smile tugged at his austere features, transforming his face for a heartbeat into knees-to-jelly handsome.

Henri thought once more what a good husband he would make, if only he'd allow her to find the right woman for him. But he'd expressly forbidden it and Henri wasn't prepared to take the risk and jeopardise their acquaintance, because his presence at any gathering made it all the more exciting. Often their exchanges ended with her pulse racing and her being filled with either a determination to prove him wrong, or the glorious bubbly feeling of being utterly right. And on balance, his being attached to some unknown miss would complicate those exchanges.

'Say the words, Mr Montemorcy.'

Golden sparkles flecked his eyes. 'Your aunt may excavate the Roman encampment. You have prevailed, Lady Thorndike.'

Henri clapped her hands. All night she had lain awake worrying. Would something happen at the last second and the marriage, with its garden wedding breakfast, have to be called off? Would Mr Montemorcy then renege on the wager?

For her aunt desperately needed an outlet for her energy. Ever since Henri could remember, her aunt had longed to excavate the Roman remains, and increasingly so since they'd been forced to sell the field to Robert. Whenever Henri had been about to give up with Melanie, she would think about her aunt's eyes shimmering with pleasure as she learnt that Henri had secured the excavation for her.

'There, it wasn't too hard to admit you lost. You are far from infallible, Mr Montemorcy.'

'Let me finish. It is a bad habit of yours—jumping to conclusions and overly complicating matters with emotion.' He held up a hand, silencing her. 'All social excursions to the site are forbidden. A scientific approach must be used at all times and your aunt must share all knowledge gained with me.'

Botheration. Henri worried the lace on her gloves. Mr Montemorcy had seen through her grand schemes and thwarted her after all! She had already had three picnics arranged in her head, complete with guests' list, menu and seating charts. They were going to be the centrepiece of her new campaign to arrange at least one more marriage before the summer had finished.

She'd even found bits of Roman pottery from her aunt's collection so that she could seed the site before the picnics took place. What could be more thrilling than a treasure hunt? Especially one where nothing was left to chance, where everything was perfect. And now this! Conditions from Robert Montemorcy about scientific approaches and the need to preserve the ground!

'Nobody ever mentioned conditions,' she muttered, scuffing the ground with her kid boot.

'I'm mentioning them now. Before you won, there was little point.'

'I don't see why you object to social excursions such as picnics.' She forced her voice to remain even. She would find a way around this new obstacle. There was a way around setbacks of this nature if she considered the problem hard enough. The happiness of others depended on it. 'They are a wonderful form of entertainment. And I promise they won't damage the integrity of the site.'

'And the encampment is a valuable piece of history. It is on *my* land now. Under *my* stewardship. If your aunt wishes to excavate, she may, but she follows *my* methods.'

Henri adopted a smooth placating smile. Robert Montemorcy was being stubborn. She could see it in his eyes and in the tightening of his shoulders. Very well, for now, she'd give way on the picnics, but he would eventually agree once he realised that no harm would come to his precious scientific method.

The selling of the land had been physically painful, but her late uncle's debts were far greater than even she had guessed. Her aunt had wept buckets. She hated letting anything go, but Montemorcy had paid a good price for the land and her aunt's financial difficulties were at an end. Or at least until her cousin made another one of his requests for money—but Henri had to believe that the last episode had taught Sebastian the importance of fiscal responsibility.

'I'm well aware of the debts my uncle incurred, but that is all in the past. My cousin is of an entirely different stamp. He plans to follow my advice for improving the remainder of his estate,' Henri said, trying a new tack.

Mr Montemorcy's brow darkened. 'Even you, Lady Thorndike, with all your skill at managing, have singularly failed there. Your cousin has garnered a reputation for debauchery. His debts will be worse than your uncle's in two years, if they are not already.'

'Society will gossip and all he needs is the right woman.' Henri forced the smile to stay on her face. It irritated her that Mr Montemorcy was correct in this one thing, if nothing else. Unfortunately, her aunt still was convinced that it was her late unlamented husband who had caused the problem and that her only son needed to be coddled and protected. Henri knew without her intervention, her aunt would be tempted to supplement her cousin's considerable income from her meagre widow's portion. She might not approve of everything that Sebastian did, but she refused to criticise him to others or let others judge him. He was family, after all, and one looked after one's family. 'You do Sebastian a disservice. He was shocked at the extent of debt.'

'Shocked, but he has continued to live his life with the same careless disregard.'

'Sebastian no longer indulges in such vices as gambling. He gave his mother his word. I also understand his current projects prosper.' Henri raised her chin, and hoped her words were true. Sebastian's last letter to his mother promised he'd mend his ways if she sent a little money until his latest scheme started to pay. 'And you know how it is with reputations—people are far more willing to believe a bad report than a good one.'

Mr Montemorcy's eyes became inscrutable. 'I'm delighted to hear it.'

'Is there anything else?' Henri asked, looking over Mr Montemorcy's immaculately tailored shoulder. She gave a nod towards Melanie so that Melanie could begin to cut the cake. Melanie blushed a deep scarlet and manoeuvred her new husband over to the splendidly tiered fruit cake. Silently Henri motioned to the vicar's youngest daughter to stand closer to the curate. They would make a charming pair, if a permanent post could be found for him, somewhere in Northumberland rather than becoming a missionary to Africa. The vicar would worry if his daughter went to Africa. She'd have to consider the matter seriously if the treasure hunt was forbidden. 'If not, I'll bid you adieu. Others require my attention.'

'Meddling in others' romantic lives has become a bad habit with you. I recognise that gleam, Lady Thorndike. Leave them alone.'

Robert Montemorcy put a detaining hand on Lady Thorndike's shoulder. Henrietta Thorndike wasn't going to wriggle out of this with a toss of her black curls and a soft sensuous smile from her full lips. Why was it that beautiful women caused more trouble than anyone else? Lady Thorndike appeared to think that with one sweep of her long lashes all her meddling and mischief would be forgotten. One light rap of her lace fan against his arm and she thought he'd indulge her passion for disruptive picnics. He knew her methods. She never gave in.

From Crozier, he knew what a near-disaster this entire episode had been and how close Henrietta Thorndike's machinations had come to failure. Crozier had been within a hair's breadth of leaving for America, all because Lady Thorndike had introduced him to the writing of James Fenimore Cooper and declared that Miss Brown had a *tendre* for men who behaved like Hawkeye in *The Last of the Mohicans.* 'Meddling is the passion that rules your life.'

'Meddling? I prefer to call it assisting two lonely people to find happiness.' Lady Thorndike waved an airy hand that only served to emphasise the way her dark purple silk dress caressed her curves. He struggled to ignore the rush of hot blood that coursed through his veins. Part of Henrietta Thorndike's arsenal was her latent sensuality, a pleasurable distraction that was apt to make men forget their train of thought.

She leant forwards and lowered her voice to a purr. 'You must understand that our new doctor, the curate and the butcher need wives.'

'You have forgotten the baker and the candlestick maker,' Robert remarked drily.

'No, the baker is happily mar—' She stopped and her cheeks turned a deep rose before she gave a small curtsy. 'I suppose you think the play on the rhyme amusing. And I tumbled straight into it.'

'I rest my case. Matchmaking consumes you and, if you allow it, it will ruin you.'

She flicked her tongue over her mouth, turning her lips a cherry-ripe red. 'Define *matchmaking.*'

'Aiding, assisting or otherwise seeking the advancement of marriage,' he said without hesitation.

'I have other passions. It is merely a pleasant pastime, helping others out. They have a right to their chance of happiness. After all, I had mine, even though it was cut short.' Lady Thorndike examined a bit of lace on her glove, hiding her face as she always did when she spoke about her late husband. 'And if anyone objected, I've never insisted. You, for example, have made it perfectly clear that you wish to choose your own partner.'

'If you ever tried to manipulate my private life, Lady Thorndike, it would be the end of our friendship.'

'I know the limits.'

She stared at him defiantly, her pointed chin raised in the air and her glossy black hair quivering with indignation. Robert returned her gaze with a steady one of his own. Clearly she had chosen to forget the first ball he attended in the neighbourhood, when she had attempted to pair him off with the new Mrs Crozier.

'All I can say is the late Sir Edmund Thorndike must have been a paragon of virtue and forbearance.' He held up his hand, stopping her outraged squeak. Someone had to save her and everyone else from her capricious nature. One day her little schemes would ruin some innocent. 'But we are not speaking about the past, Lady Thorndike, but the present. You are singularly unable to resist meddling in the matrimonial affairs of others. It is becoming worse by the day.'

'I can stop any time I want,' Henrietta replied, her face taking on a mutinous expression as she crossed her arms over her full bosom, highlighting rather than detracting from her curves.

'Prove it.'

'Are you seriously suggesting that the new Mrs Crozier would be better off if she remained a spinster, trimming hats and living on tea and snippets of hot buttered toast?' Two bright spots appeared on Lady Thorndike's cheeks and her eyes blazed sapphire. 'She has a bright future with a husband who loves her and a more-than-respectable income.'

Robert made an irritated noise. The new Mrs Crozier's figure proclaimed that she lived on far more than snippets of toast. 'Anyone with a half a brain could have seen the way the wind blew when Crozier took to visiting Miss Brown on the pretext of picking up his great-aunt's hats. You may have succeeded this time, but the next… You run the risk of destroying some innocent's future.'

'What are you suggesting, Mr Montemorcy?' Her carefully arranged curls shook with anger. 'I enjoy helping people. People need me. And this wedding breakfast will not run itself.'

At last. She'd walked straight into his trap—the reason he'd come to the wedding breakfast and engaged her in a battle of wills to begin with. 'I am suggesting a wager to demonstrate that you are addicted to arranging others' love lives and you have no sense of discipline in these matters.' He watched her bridle at the words. He wondered if she knew how desirable she appeared when she was angry. Desirable but very much off limits, and Robert never mixed pleasures of the flesh with his social duty. It caused complications. 'Unless you wish to admit defeat here and now?'

Her even white teeth worried her bottom lip. 'You make it sound like I have no self-control.'

'In recent months, you have lost whatever self-control you had in this matter.' Robert leant forwards, wondering how far he dared push her. But Lady Thorndike had to agree to the wager. Without it, his entire scheme for protecting his ward would fall at the first hurdle.

'What time frame do you suggest?' She smoothed the deep mauve of her gown and Robert knew he had won. She'd been unable to resist the temptation and had taken the bait. 'A wager is no good if it goes on indefinitely.'

'Until Lady Winship's ball in a month's time,' he replied.

'A month? I don't know whether to be flattered or amused that you do not think I can last a month. There are many other things in my life—visiting the sick, gardening and even doing needlework if I must.'

'A month will be enough to prove my point.'

'I will be delighted to prove you wrong.' Henrietta tapped her fan against his arm. 'And when I do, you will have to allow me to host a picnic at the excavations. And for added sweetness, the merest of trifles—you will dance a polka with me at the ball.'

Robert pressed his lips together—how had this happened? Despite all his precautions, Lady Thorndike had defined unacceptable terms. 'I don't dance.'

'I know. Everyone in the Tyne Valley knows.' She raised up on her toes and her eyes became the colour of a Northumbrian summer's morning. 'You avoided the dancing classes I set up for the village, pleading pressures of work. We were several men short. Even old Mr Everley came despite his aches and pains. The entire village's standard of dancing has been improved. All except yours.'

'It is good to know fewer bruised toes will happen at the ball thanks to your valiant efforts.'

'Your dancing will be a public declaration that I'm correct and you utterly misjudged the situation.' Her eyes took on a wicked glint. 'You are lucky that I am not insisting on you joining the next class.'

'And don't you want to know your forfeit, the consequences of failure?'

She gave a little deprecating laugh and he knew he had trapped her. Henrietta Thorndike's overweening confidence would be her undoing. He'd give her two days, a week at most, before she succumbed to temptation. But with the forfeit he had in mind, either way, his ward's reputation would be safe. 'I'm going to win, but what do you want, Mr Montemorcy, if I display a woeful lack of self-control?'

Robert forced his voice to be restrained, soothing. 'If you fail to do this, for the next six months you will have to announce whenever you arrive at a social gathering that you are a habitual matchmaker. You will also give up organising any social event for the period.'

The colour drained from her face. 'And what will I be doing with myself? I like to keep busy!'

'You can read my research and learn how the scientific method works and why it is appropriate for the excavation site.'

Lady Thorndike opened and closed her mouth several times. A flash of hurt crossed her features. Robert hardened his heart. Lady Thorndike needed to learn this lesson before she did serious damage to someone's reputation.

'Would you like me to wear a sign about my neck as well?' she asked, arching a brow. 'Just so that everyone knows? Matchmaking is something that is done with a subtle hand, Mr Montemorcy. If I declare my intention, all my schemes will be ruined.'

'That is rather the point, Lady Thorndike. You need to allow people to fall in love naturally and to attend social gatherings in the village without fear. Other people should have the opportunity to organise the events. How hard can it be?'

Henri raised her brows again, this time in amused disbelief—clearly Robert Montemorcy had no idea how hard organising social events could be! Suddenly she started to feel much more positive about the outcome of their wager. 'Would you like me to set this wager to paper, Mr Montemorcy?'

'If you wish. I'm quite happy to wager my dancing shoes against your declaration.'

'Make sure you attend the ball with your dancing slippers on.' Her eyes gleamed with mischief; she clapped her hands. 'And I shall invite you to my first picnic at the excavation. It will be a treasure hunt to end all treasure hunts.'

'You will lose, Lady Thorndike. I know you. The first time you see an opportunity you will have to grab it.'

Her deep blue eyes searched his face. 'Is there any particular reason why you have made this wager?'

Robert caught his upper lip between his teeth and briefly contemplated confiding in Lady Thorndike about his ward and her disastrous experience at the Queen Charlotte's ball, but decided that Lady Thorndike would be unable to resist offering unhelpful advice or spreading the news in an attempt to be helpful. Sophie had gone through enough without having to face that. No, until her enthusiasm for matchmaking was curbed, Lady Thorndike was positively dangerous and had to be held at arm's length.

'Your behaviour recently makes it necessary,' he said finally.

'I will not bother to answer that.' Lady Thorndike lifted her chin in the air, not quite disguising another flash of hurt in her eyes. 'Melanie has started to cut the cake and if she keeps sawing at it like that, the cake will crumble and nobody will get anything. I promised the vicar's daughters that they would each have a piece to put under their pillows so that they may dream of their future bridegrooms. Melanie agreed with me that it was a splendid notion.'

'Do you wish to end the wager already? No shame on either side.'

'Hah, you think too little of me.' Her dark blue eyes flashed defiantly. 'Remember, Mr Montemorcy. Practise your polka. I require a certain standard in my dancing partners.'

Chapter Two

Her wager with Robert Montemorcy was child's play, Henri reflected, slightly swinging the empty basket as she walked towards the circulating library several days after the wedding. All she had had to do was to become occupied with other things: visiting the various invalids in the parish with jars of calf's-foot jelly that was made to her mother's exacting receipt, making lists of things that needed to be accomplished before the ball, as well as events that would have to be held *after* the ball, deadheading the daffodils in the garden… She hadn't even had to resort to the dreaded needlework.

Robert Montemorcy was entirely wrong about her. She *did* have other passions in her life. It was simply that matchmaking was the most interesting. It brought the chance of happiness to so many people.

'Lady Thorndike, Lady Thorndike!' Miss Armstrong gave a wave from outside the haberdasher's. 'Have you heard?'

Henri composed her features and carefully avoided stepping on a crack in the pavement. 'Heard what?'

'Robert Montemorcy is going to be married! We'd all considered him to be *your* property, so it must come as a great blow.' Miss Armstrong adopted a falsely contrite face as the silk flowers inside the rim of her poke bonnet trembled with suppressed excitement. 'I know I shouldn't be spreading gossip but…I wanted to offer my condolences.'

Henri's stomach plummeted and she tightened her grip on her basket. 'Mr Montemorcy has never shown me any special favour, Miss Armstrong.' Hortense Armstrong was notorious for getting gossip ever so slightly wrong. Robert Montemorcy wouldn't do that without…without letting her know. Besides, he was far from being her property. They simply enjoyed pleasant conversations. 'How did you come by this intelligence?'

'Miss Nevin had it from her maid of all work who is best friends with the doctor's cook who steps out with the footman at the New Lodge.'

Henri breathed easier. Servants. There would be some truth to the rumour, but it would have been twisted and contorted even before it reached Miss Armstrong. And Montemorcy's admonition rang in her head. He wanted her to keep out of his private life. Was this the reason? An unknown visitor? An unknown visitor that did enjoy his special favour?

'Speculation never did anyone any good,' she choked out.

'The entire household is in an uproar. The lady in question, a Miss Sophie Ravel, arrived from London with her stepmother yesterday. You never saw the boxes and trunks. Even a pagoda-shaped birdcage with a canary. Like a…well…a pagoda—you know, one of those Chinese, foreign things. Two carts from the station, or so I heard. Miss Ravel was supposed to be the Diamond of the Season, but she has forsaken all for love.' Miss Armstrong gave a fluttering sigh and Henri found herself wanting to strangle her with a fierceness that was alarming.

'Two carts do not a marriage make.'

A frown developed between Miss Armstrong's brows. 'I've never heard that saying before.'

'Haven't you?' Henri smiled, and gave her basket a little swing. 'I think it is a good one. It is one of my own.'

'I imagine there will be a huge wedding. It will make the Croziers' wedding look quite countrified and provincial.'

'It is intriguing what servants hear…or don't hear.'

Miss Armstrong's face became positively unctuous, oozing with rumour and innuendo. 'Of course, the new Mrs Montemorcy will be expected to take her part in leading society. You will not have it all your own way any more, Lady Thorndike. The new Mrs Montemorcy might even agree with me about the necessity of having garlands at Lady Winship's ball.'

Henri gave Miss Armstrong a stern look. The conversation was fast becoming insupportable and beyond the bounds of propriety. She refused to think about any sort of wife that Montemorcy might take. She forced her breathing to be calm, even as a great hole opened up inside her. Robert Montemorcy couldn't marry. It would change everything.

Miss Armstrong's rosy cheeks became a slightly brighter hue. 'That is to say, Lady Thorndike, I hope the rumours are wrong. I merely sought to inform you so that you could make a reasoned judgement and not faint at any gathering.'

'Such considerations have never troubled me, Miss Armstrong. I never faint.' Henri put a hand to her chest and adopted her 'woman of sorrow' expression. It had held her in good stead for ten years whenever the prickly subject of remarriage was brought up. 'After all, a woman can only ask for one chance of happiness. And my dear sweet Edmund was gentle perfection. He never said a cross word or argued with me. He was quite simply irreplaceable.'

'You have always struck me as someone who enjoyed a good argument, Lady Thorndike. I fear I was mistaken.'

'Obviously.' Maintaining all the poise she could muster, Henri swept away from the infuriating woman.

As she entered the coolness of the circulating library, Henri stood for a moment and allowed the scent of leatherbound books and dust to fill her nostrils. There was something wonderfully calming about a library. Visiting one always restored her mood. And right now she needed to piece together the various bits of news and discover the truth. Robert Montemorcy had an unmarried female visitor—that much was clear from Miss Armstrong's testimony. But the precise nature and reason for the visit was shrouded in mystery. And she hated mysteries of this nature.

She hated the small spiral of jealousy that encircled her insides. Hated to think about him verbally sparring with this unknown woman. Would they wager as well? She clenched her fists and counted to ten.

Suddenly, down one of the aisles she spied a pair of broad shoulders encased in a form-fitting frock-coat: Robert Montemorcy. Who should have been at his desk in Newcastle, pontificating about the scientific method to his managers, or attending to his new guest, rather than causing innocent people's pulse to race and lose all power in their legs. Henri turned on her heel and started to tiptoe down the next aisle. Blindly she picked up a book and pretended to be reading.

She struggled to breathe and wished her corset was a smidgeon looser. It hurt far more than she thought that Robert Montemorcy had not bothered to confide in her, and the reason for the wager was now transparent. He was going to marry this unknown, and did not want anyone else encouraged to take an interest. But why the subterfuge—why hadn't he just told her? It was not as if she held any claim on him. She had thought they were friends. She could keep a secret and she wouldn't have interfered…beyond introducing the woman to society. She knew what it was like to be new and friendless.

'Lady Thorndike? Is something wrong?' Robert Montemorcy asked with a concerned note in his voice. 'You failed to acknowledge my wave. It is most unlike you. Preoccupied, yes, but never rude.'

'Go away. I'm reading.' Henri buried her nose deeper in the book and tried to ignore the way he towered over her. She wasn't attracted to him in the way Miss Armstrong suggested. Attraction was a gentle comfortable thing such as she had felt for Edmund. Robert Montemorcy always made her feel unsettled and determined.

'You will find it more edifying if you attempt to read right-side up, Lady Thorndike.' Strong fingers took the book from her unresisting ones. 'Allow me to assist.'

Henri's cheeks burnt and fury swamped her senses. How many people had thought him…her property? And was he truly going to marry this Diamond of the Season? A girl in her teens would be wrong for him. There was no way on God's green earth she could actually ask him. She had to banish all thoughts of such a thing or else…it would come out at precisely the wrong time. She squared her shoulders, forcing her mind away from Mr Montemorcy's matrimonial prospects.

'I wanted to look a point of information up,' she said quickly before she blurted out her real intention of regaining her composure after The Shocking News.

'Lady Thorndike, since when did you need to know about *The Good Husbandry of Cattle on the Yorkshire Moors*? Are you truly a secret bluestocking? Or is this in aid of some match that you intend to facilitate at some later date?'

'That is not what the book is about,' Henri said, putting a hand on her hip, trying to ignore the way his sandalwood scent enveloped her. 'You are merely seeking to discomfort me.'

He held out the spine. Henri read the title with a sinking heart. Of all the books she could have randomly chosen, it would have to be one that she had not the slightest interest in. She hurriedly replaced the book on the shelf. 'It simply proves why I couldn't find what I was looking for.'

'And here I thought you were trying to avoid me.' The richness of his voice rolled over her in delicious waves.

'Why would I want to do that?'

He gave a maddening shrug of his shoulders, emphasising their breadth. Henri forced her gaze upwards to his sardonic face. 'You know better than I. A guilty conscience? How are your attempts at keeping the wager going? Finding it difficult to stop playing Cupid? I hear the curate took the vicar's youngest daughter for a stroll after church last Sunday. Did you have a part in that?'

'I've kept to the letter of our agreement, which is more than I can say for you.' Henri gave him a stern look. How dare he insinuate that she was attempting to hide something! She had played the hand strictly according to Hoyle, not deviating at all, not even when Doctor Lumley had asked about the vicar's eldest daughter and whether she could sew a fine seam. He, on the other hand, had cheated. Manipulated her for mysterious reasons of his own and, what was worse, she had fallen for it. 'You attempted to deceive me. You procured our wager on an entirely false premise. It is only because I never go back on a promise that I'm even contemplating keeping it.'

He stilled and his cheeks flushed the slightest tinge of pink. 'What gossip have you heard, Lady Thorndike?'

'I've heard all about Miss Ravel's arrival. The village buzzes with the news.' And the impending nuptials, she thought with a pang. But she wasn't about to stoop that low and mention them! Robert Montemorcy had to reveal the news and then she'd make some withering retort, the perfect sort of response for when one with whom one's name has been inadvertently linked becomes engaged to another. Henri touched her little brooch that Edmund had given her for luck.

'News travels fast. Miss Ravel and her stepmother only arrived last night. I am attempting to choose some reading material for Miss Ravel as she has a preference for popular fiction, rather than the scientific tomes that populate my library. Do you think *Ivanhoe* will strike the right tone? Or would she prefer the latest Fenimore Cooper?'

He was searching the stacks for reading material for the unknown Miss Ravel. Henri hated how the knowledge hurt. 'If she likes such books, the young woman in question will have probably read *Ivanhoe*. And I believe Mr Crozier has the latest James Fenimore Cooper out. He might not be going to America, but he has developed a taste for adventure.'

'You are quite right. I will have to find another selection.' He stood there, looking at her, waiting.

'Why didn't you tell me that someone from London was arriving? With two carts full of trunks and bags. And a birdcage, general rumour has it.' Henri tapped her boot against the wooden floor as the words rushed out of her.

He gave her a level look with his dark brown eyes. 'Was it any of your business, Lady Thorndike? You would have given me a long list of things that needed to be done, people that she needed to meet and committees she needed to be on without ever having encountered Miss Ravel.'

Henri ground her teeth. Being new in a village like Corbridge was difficult. When she'd arrived, she had longed for someone to take her under their wing and provide some guidance. No one, not even her aunt, had, and she'd resolved never to allow that fate to happen to anyone else. She had organised the Corbridge Society for Hospitality, making Miss Armstrong her deputy, in part because of Miss Armstrong's ability to learn of new arrivals first, but also to keep Miss Armstrong fully occupied. 'Was Miss Ravel one of the reasons why you enticed me into this ridiculous wager?'

He was silent for a long heartbeat. Anger coursed through Henri. He was playing games with her. Nobody did such a thing. And it hurt all the worse that it was someone she liked and respected. She had thought he understood that she only wanted the best for people, and the fact he so offensively misunderstood her motives was deeply upsetting.

'I won't lie,' he said gravely. 'Miss Ravel's situation did have some bearing on my request.'

'Mr Montemorcy, you have treated me with contempt,' Henri ground out. Her insides ached. Robert Montemorcy hadn't trusted her enough to confide that his guests were expected up from London. He thought her so callous that she'd spread gossip or worse. And even now he kept the true reason for Miss Ravel being here hidden from her. 'I deserved better than that.'

'I had my reasons.'

'And they are…?' Henri asked in a low tone. 'Is there anything I should know? I have no wish to make any more *mistakes*.'

'That is Miss Ravel's business and not mine to tell.' A muscle jumped in his jaw and his face appeared more remote than ever. 'I will not have her become the subject of common gossip. I made her late father a promise and I intend to keep it.'

Henri took a step backwards and felt the books dig into her back. Her throat became dry. He had given Miss Ravel's father a deathbed promise. She'd rather thought her life was going to go on an even keel, but suddenly it was all change. She'd mistaken everything. Her blood fizzled. 'And you don't trust me with the truth. What are you afraid of, Montemorcy? What did you think I'd do? Shout the news from the top of the church steeple that you were about to be betrothed?'

'Miss Ravel is the daughter of an old and dear friend, Lady Thorndike, and my ward.' Robert attempted to contain his anger. How dare she stand there wearing a fierce expression and the ribbons of her bonnet trembling! His private life was private. And he certainly was not serving it up for her delectation, fetching bonnet or not. If he ever became betrothed, he certainly would not be informing Henrietta Thorndike first. Asking for her advice? The thought was unconscionable. 'Please choose your words with care.'

Her blue eyes opened wide. 'You have a ward? Why have you never divulged this information to me?'

'There are many things you do not know about me, madam.' Robert looked her up and down slowly, taking in the way her purple-and-white-checked day dress hugged her curves and then flared out into a full skirt. 'We are neighbours, rather than intimate companions.'

Two bright spots appeared on her cheeks. 'Having a ward is hardly a state secret.'

'My business, no one else's.'

'But pertinent to our wager. The fact remains—you manoeuvred me into that wager so that you could protect your ward from what you considered to be *my* unwarranted inference! I have *never* interfered when I was unwanted, sir! A simple request would have sufficed!'

Various other library patrons turned around and Robert winced. The gossip that he'd quarrelled with Lady Thorndike would be around the village in a matter of minutes. And it would only add to the speculation about his visitors and their reason for abandoning London. He should turn on his heel and walk away, but he quickly rejected the notion. If the village would talk, he'd give them something infinitely more interesting to digest than the suspiciously sudden arrival of his ward.

He placed a hand on either side of her, trapping her against the bookcase. 'I gave you the main reason at the wedding breakfast, madam. You are entirely too involved in your matchmaking schemes. You think of nothing beyond the next match. You dominate village social life with your musicales, picnics and dancing classes, which are all designed for one purpose: to facilitate matrimony, whether the parties involved are truly interested or not. Are you attempting to back out of our wager? You were so certain of victory. Do you wish to admit defeat?'

'No, sir, I'm not ready. I am no faint heart.'

Rather than seeking to escape, she held her head high and her being radiated hurt dignity. A vague sense of admiration filled him. He leant forwards so his breath would brush her cheek. 'I'm glad to hear it.'

'You are behaving improperly, sir,' she said as her breath came faster. 'In a public place!'

'Am I? How intriguing.' He fastened his gaze on her full red lips. 'Precisely what am I doing wrong, Lady Thorndike? Do tell. I wish to remedy my bad behaviour.'

The air between them crackled.

'I hope your dancing shoes are polished and ready,' she said with a husky note in her voice. 'I expect a polka worthy of the name after your underhanded behaviour.'

'My dancing shoes are in my wardrobe where they will remain. You will be unable to resist temptation, Lady Thorndike. We both know it. Admit defeat now and have done with it.' He leant forwards so that their foreheads nearly touched. Her lips were softly parted and he could see the pulse beating in the hollow of her throat. Silently he willed her to lean forwards and complete the tableau. 'Miss Ravel's visit is sudden. Her story is not mine to tell. But I promise you, if you attempt to ensnare my ward in any of your matchmaking schemes, you will regret it.'

Henri lifted his arm away from the bookcase as her eyes blazed defiantly. 'I have done nothing to facilitate or suggest any such match. Nor do I intend doing so in the near future,' she said in a furious undertone. 'You should have confided in me, instead of attempting this flim-flam nonsense of a wager to curb my behaviour. My behaviour, sir, has been exemplary in the extreme.'

Robert counted to ten and breathed deeply as the whispers grew in the library. The gossip would now centre on Lady Thorndike rather than on his ward. But he had not one twinge of regret. His ward's already fragile reputation needed protecting, which wouldn't happen if Lady Thorndike could not resist meddling. And the only way he could think of to ensure that had been the—deliberately provocative, he'd happily admit it—wager. 'You have several weeks to go. Temptation will get the better of you, Lady Thorndike. It always does.'

Henrietta Thorndike opened and closed her mouth several times, before twitching her skirts away from him. 'Good day, Mr Montemorcy. I believe we have entirely fallen out of civility with each other.'

'Were we ever in civility?' he murmured, his hand skimming her arm. 'Pray tell me when.'

'I have certainly tried to be polite, but I now see politeness is beyond you,' she snapped.

'Lady Thorndike, people are starting to stare. You are in danger of becoming remarked on.'

'Let them. This is a war of your making. I am through with being polite. Ponder on that.' She marched away, her purple-and-white gown swinging to reveal her shapely ankles.

Robert slammed his fists together as red hot blood rushed through his veins. Was there ever such an obstinate woman as Henrietta Thorndike?

Henri pressed her fingers to the bridge of her nose and took a deep breath, attempting to calm down after her run-in with Montemorcy. She hadn't been this angry in a long time. Serenity and a happy outlook on life were what she strove for, but really what she wanted was to run Robert Montemorcy through with a skewer. He'd tricked her into this idiotic and offensive wager. And now there was the problem of how his ward might fit into the delicate fabric of Corbridge social life.

She took a deep breath and twitched the folds of her dress so that they hung straighter.

When she was done, he'd be the one who was discomforted.

He would be dancing the polka and she would hold picnics at the Roman camp. 'I promise,' she whispered. 'I will do it.'

Aunt Frances's house with its gable roof and white-shuttered windows was as solid and welcoming as it had been when she arrived sixteen months ago, seeking to begin her life again. She forced air into her lungs. Robert Montemorcy had simply unnerved her. She hated quarrelling with anyone. Least of all a man she'd previously held in such high…regard.

'You've returned to home fires, sweetest of all the cousins in the entire world. Come share some cucumber sandwiches with me. We've much to discuss.'

Henri froze, her hand on the ribbons of her straw bonnet. The use of the phrase—sweetest of all the cousins—meant her cousin, Sebastian English, the fourth Viscount Cawburn, had returned to his birthplace and wanted something from her, something that would entail a great deal of trouble on her part with little thanks for her efforts on his. It was the very last thing she needed today, particularly not after her contretemps with Robert Montemorcy. All she wanted was a quiet turn about the garden to see if the roses had started to bloom, and a chance to calm her still-racing heart.

Was that too much to ask?

'The answer is no, Sebastian.' Henri's gaze focused on Sebastian's attire. His neckcloth was twisted as if he had struggled to tie it properly on the first try. Her heart sank. Further confirmation, if she needed it, that her life had taken a turn for the worse. She knew the signs. 'Definitely not.'

'You do not even know what I was going to ask!'

'It's something to do with a woman,' she said, setting her bonnet down on the entrance table and controlling her temper by taking her gloves off one by one. Sebastian's last adventure resulted in a furious former mistress, a cuckolded husband and a trio of pug puppies laying waste to the drawing room while Sebastian conveniently departed on a ship bound for Venice in the arms of another female. 'That much is perfectly clear.'

Sebastian's jaw dropped. 'How did you know?'

'Every time your stock and neckcloth are twisted in that particular fashion, a woman is involved. And if that is the case, you will be endeavouring to find a way out of the tangle you have created.'

'Nothing is wrong with my stock, is there?' Sebastian crashed his cup down and went to the mirror over the fireplace. He frowned and, with expert fingers, readjusted the stock. 'Henrietta, I'm worried that you've suddenly developed a suspicious mind. What is wrong with proclaiming your sweetness?'

'When you are in a normal frame of mind, you use Henri, and may I remind you that I'm your only cousin.'

'That makes you the sweetest one.' Sebastian wandered over to the plate of sandwiches, picked up one and resettled himself on the sofa. Before he bit into the cucumber sandwich, he gave one of his heart-melting smiles, the sort that had the débutantes and their mothers sighing in droves. 'It stands to reason.'

Henri motioned for the footman to remove the pile of cucumber sandwiches some distance away from Sebastian. 'You won't get around me that easily. And if you keep eating sandwiches at that rate, you will need a corset to fit into your frock-coats.'

'Gaining weight has never been one of my vices. You are far too young to become censorious.' He counted on his fingers. 'You're only twenty-nine. And do not look a day older than twenty-eight.'

'Twenty-seven next birthday,' Henri replied through gritted teeth. 'And not censorious, merely following my husband's deathbed advice. You're always trouble when you're besotted.'

Sebastian swirled the remains of his tea in his cup. 'I try hard to be good, but things happen. Edmund would've understood. Why can't you be understanding and considerate like he was?'

Henri pasted a smile on her face. 'We're speaking about your new love, not my late husband. She will be gone from your brain within a month.'

Sebastian adopted his injured-angel look. 'This time it is different, Henri. This time it is for ever. But how can I prove this to you, if you refuse to help?'

'Who is she? And, more importantly, does her husband shoot straight?'

'*Miss* Sophie Ravel is highly respectable. I resent the insinuation.' He leant forwards and his eyes were alight with an eagerness she had not seen since…since before Edmund's death. 'You'll love her, Henri. She is my other half. I swear it.'

Chapter Three

Henri's stomach dropped. Miss Sophie Ravel. Robert Montemorcy's ward. The one who had suddenly dropped everything in London to come to Northumberland. All for the sake of love. Miss Armstrong had it all wrong. Miss Ravel hadn't run towards love, but had been forcibly taken away from it.

And Sebastian had studiously avoided the *marriage* word. A cold chill went through Henri. Was it any wonder that Mr Montemorcy had kept the problem from her? He knew how staunchly she defended Sebastian, how she had assisted him out of difficulties in the past.

She tightened her grip on her teacup, sloshing the tea over the rim. She was far from blind to Sebastian's faults. Robert Montemorcy should have trusted her with the truth, explaining his concerns about her cousin as a suitor for his ward, rather than tricking her into a wager that she was now determined to win, whilst also finding out some way of making sure the situation did not become a disaster of immeasurable proportions.

Sebastian started on a long rambling explanation chiefly designed to convince her to help him.

She held up her hand, blocking his words. 'Sebastian, I refuse to assist, aid or otherwise participate in your quest for Miss Ravel.

Ruining a débutante is low even by your standards of behaviour. I am shocked and amazed that you could even contemplate asking me.'

Sebastian frowned and slumped back against the sofa, looking mortally hurt, as if she was the one to blame for his ill fortune.

'All I wanted you to do was to meet Sophie…and her stepmother.' His lips turned upwards into an angelic smile. 'Especially her step-mother. To show them how respectable my family is. How truly worthy we are. The stepmother wants occupying with projects rather than prying into her stepdaughter's innocent affairs. You are sure to find something for her to do!'

'Your complicated love life is your problem.' Henri glared at him and pointedly gestured towards the Persian carpet in front of the fireplace. 'I had to bring the pug puppies with me to Corbridge. Unlike you, I don't just abandon defenceless animals, even if I'm not fond of dogs. Your dear mama's carriage has never been the same. Travel sickness in a puppy is far from pleasant.'

Sebastian brushed the crumbs from his fingers. 'That is a bit unfair of you, Henri, bringing up the pugs. A huge misjudgement on my part, I'll accept that, but you rose to the occasion magnificently. One couldn't ask for a better or more loyal cousin.'

'It took me an age to get rid of them.' Henri struggled to keep her voice steady. Sebastian knew how she felt about dogs, even such little ones as the pugs. 'Lady Winship was reluctantly persuaded to give them a home.'

Sebastian put his hands behind his head and stretched out, a particularly pleased smile on his face. 'And how is dear old Nellie? I have not seen her in an age!'

'Lady Winship has become devoted to the pugs,' Henri admitted. It had been one of her better ideas, getting Lady Winship to take the trio. And her mind shied away from why Sebastian addressed Lady Winship in such familiar tones. Some things were best left to the imagination. 'By the middle of next week, you will have forgotten

Miss Ravel's name, Sebastian, and those sandwiches were for Aunt Frances.'

'Cucumbers give Mama indigestion. I'm doing her a favour.' Sebastian made a show of dusting the plate down before carelessly placing it on the table. Henri reached over and straightened the plate.

'Sebastian!'

'I saw Miss Ravel silhouetted in the evening light, just as she was getting out of a carriage to attend the opera, and I knew that she was the woman for me. I will never forget her or the way the last rays of the sun lit her hair. She is an angel set on this earth.' He cleared his throat. 'I worship the ground she walks on. The *M* word entered my head.'

'Marriage? You?' Henri stared at him in disbelief. Sebastian, who had successfully avoided so many marriage traps, was actually contemplating marriage to Miss Ravel. 'Then what is the problem? Women normally fall at your feet. And despite your various misdemeanours, the best houses in London still welcome you.'

'Her family, or more specifically her guardian.' Sebastian clasped his hand to his breast. 'Robert Montemorcy is the sort of man whose library is entirely filled with books from *The Gentleman's Manual to Libraries*. He probably has never been outside England.'

'Robert Montemorcy was educated in Edinburgh, at the Sorbonne in Paris, and studied chemistry in Germany,' Henri replied evenly, disliking Sebastian's curled-lip sneer. She might be upset with Mr Montemorcy, but it didn't mean that others could abuse him. 'He has a wide range of business interests, including an ironworks that makes most of the steel and iron for the railways. And he is a highly accomplished chemist. He is a great believer in the "Scientific Method" and a stalwart of the Lit. and Phil.'

'You mean he makes money, but what clubs does he belong to? What titles has he inherited? Who were his ancestors?'

'Sebastian, is that really important? What matters is that Mr Montemorcy purchased Chestercamp field.'

'Montemorcy purchased that field!' He clapped his hand to his head. 'It all makes a sickening sense. I'm undone. Why is Fate so cruel?'

'He kept you out of debtors' prison.'

'Spare me the village gossip, Henrietta. It was never going to come to that. I was simply short of a few readies to pay Papa's bills. You should never have suggested to Mr Montemorcy anything different and now…'

'You're being obstinate.' Henri crossed her arms. Montemorcy had been all sympathy when she encountered him out on a walk and she had given up hope of selling the field. They had fallen to discussing Romans. It had been the start of their enjoyable conversations. Her throat tasted like ashes. Maybe it would have been better if they'd stayed distant neighbours.

'Mr Montemorcy bought the field because he is interested in bringing a scientific method to excavating Roman remains. Aunt Frances is terribly excited about the prospect.'

'More to the point, Montemorcy has caused Sophie to be moved to Northumberland under the pretext of broadening her education. As if the biddies who control the Season could not see through that threadbare excuse.' Sebastian snapped his perfectly manicured fingers. 'Northumberland? Why not Italy or France? I wrote to Sophie that she should make sure he took her abroad, but the note was returned…unopened with the injunction never to contact her again.'

Henri went cold. Sending Sebastian's letter back was a mistake of the highest order if Robert Montemorcy had wanted to dissuade Sebastian. If only Robert Montemorcy had asked her advice, she'd have explained. Sebastian was easily handled as long as he thought the idea had emerged from his own brain. Sebastian always pursued the unattainable until it became attainable and then he lost interest.

And he'd never ruined a Diamond. He never would. He knew where society's lines were drawn. Robert Montemorcy should have had more sense. He should have sought her advice; now, she had a lovelorn Sebastian to contend with.

'What did you do to Miss Ravel to have her removed from London? She should be enjoying the Season.'

'Nothing.' He held up his hand and his face became utterly angelic. 'I swear to God, Henrietta. We were only talking…in the library with the door closed. I wanted to know if a heavenly creature like her could ever love a sinner like me, but her stepmother happened in and had an attack of vapours, which led on to unprecedented hysterics.' A distinct shudder went through him. 'It was ghastly. I suggested Miss Ravel dose her stepmother with water to bring her to her senses, but Miss Ravel flat out refused.'

'Sebastian, if you are trying to flannel me about your debts, I will never forgive you.'

'I love Sophie, Henri, truly I do. Her dowry means nothing to me.' He snapped his fingers. 'I would run away with her in an instant… even if she was a pauper. It is her infuriating guardian causing all the problems. He has no right to control Sophie's life and impose restrictions on mine.'

'If the lady is truly your love, you will find a way. I did with Edmund. I was the one who proposed, remember?' Henri tapped her fingers against her thigh. Sebastian would have to understand. This time, she was not going to get involved. 'You have to believe, Sebastian. And you do not need me.'

'Is that your final word?' His eyes narrowed and flashed.

'Yes. I facilitate matches for no man. Not any more.' Henri fluffed out her skirt, making certain the top flounce fell correctly, and reached for the bell to summon Reynolds. She had won. She had proved that she could remain aloof from Sebastian's schemes. Success. Robert Montemorcy was completely wrong. She did know when to stop. 'And in a few weeks, you will have forgotten all about this Sophie Ravel.'

'Have you ever forgotten Edmund? Have you thrown away his letters or do they remain in that box—waiting to be read one last time? If you can't forget him, why do you think I will forget the love of my life?'

Henri closed her eyes. Edmund's strawberry-blond hair and regular features swam in front of her. Her breathing became a bit easier. She did remember. And there was no point in opening the box; she knew what it contained. Someday she would, she would reread every letter, but not today, not at Sebastian's insistence.

'That was low. You should call on Miss Ravel directly and discover the true state of affairs for yourself. I don't see why you are being such a namby-pamby sensitive poet about this. Mr Montemorcy will hear your request politely. Our family does have a certain standing in the neighbourhood.'

She waited for Sebastian to fall in line with her wishes. Sebastian's face took on a crafty expression and he began to fiddle with his stock.

'Say that you will meet Sophie and report back to me. You know you will call. You always do your welcoming bit. All I want to know is how she fares and if I stand a chance. That will give me the courage to face him and do battle for my darling girl.' Sebastian knelt before her, catching her hand. His eyes became pools of blue. 'You know what happens to people when you insist on them doing things they fear. Think about what you did to Edmund. Your insisting on the elopement surely hastened his death.'

'Sebastian.' Henri bit her lip, hating the guilt that swamped her senses. She had been the one to insist on eloping when her parents had refused permission. Her intentions had been so good—it had all been so that Edmund could be properly nursed and looked after. Edmund had agreed with her reasoning. She hadn't realised exactly how ill he was until after they were married. She'd never have allowed him out in the rain that night of the elopement if she'd guessed he had another cold coming on his chest.

She forced her mind away from the past and towards the uncomfortable present. And did she want an open breach with Montemorcy, if he did do as Sebastian had suggested and cut him dead? It would make the situation worse and potentially disrupt her standing in the village.

Discretion. A quiet sounding out rather than a full-frontal assault would win the day.

Besides, family duty meant she owed it to Sebastian to discover what had really happened with Miss Ravel. And it was only polite to call on Miss Ravel and her stepmother and welcome them to the neighbourhood. As chairman of the Corbridge Society for Hospitality, it was expected of her and it would annoy Robert Montemorcy no end. This had nothing to do with matchmaking and everything to do with clarification. Henri gave an inward chuckle. She did look forward to seeing Robert Montemorcy's face when he finally had to admit defeat and dance to a tune of her choosing.

'I'll meet Miss Ravel, but I will not plead your case for you.'

'Henri, you really are the sweetest of all cousins and I mean that this time, truly I do. Someday soon my angel and I will be reunited.'

Robert attempted to put yesterday's quarrel with Lady Thorndike from his mind and to concentrate on the pressing problems of revitalising the long-neglected estate. He had spent far too much time on that woman as it was. Henrietta Thorndike should understand that he had acted in the best interests of his ward. Dance the polka indeed. He wasn't going to think about holding Henrietta Thorndike in his arms or how her hand would feel against his shoulder as they circled the Winship ballroom...

As his tenant cleared his throat and touched his cap, Robert forced his mind away from the wager and asked his tenant farmer for the explanation behind the poor state of the stone walls.

A sudden ear-piercing shriek drowned out Giles Teasdale's stuttering reply. Muscles tensing, Robert turned and stared in horror as Teasdale's dog lowered its head and charged at the woman who had fallen to the ground, pulling viciously at her skirt.

'Get that dog away from that woman, Teasdale!'

'Bruiser don't mean no harm,' Teasdale bleated, catching Robert's arm, rather than going after the dog. 'He just has an eye for strangers. He'll stop if she does. He ain't never bitten anyone yet, like. The post-coach to Jedburgh is about due, like. He wants her out of the road. He's trying to help.'

'The highway doesn't belong to him.' Robert shook the tenant farmer off and started for the dog. His fingers caught the dog's metal collar and yanked him away.

'Go on. Back to your master! Now!'

The dog snarled, but Robert clung on, giving the dog an abrupt shake. 'Let's go, Bruiser, let's get you back to where you belong. It's the Queen's highway, not yours.'

'He thinks it is,' Teasdale called from where he stood beside the gate. 'You be careful, Mr Montemorcy, sir.'

The dog bared its teeth and lunged towards the prone woman. Robert braced his feet and pulled again. This time, the dog turned, snarling at him. Its fangs were inches away from his wrist. Robert shook the dog, throwing it to the ground. It lay there, stunned, then looked up at him with big eyes, before tentatively licking his hand in a gesture of submission and whining. Teasdale's bleats about how it was not his fault filled the air.

'Go on. Back to your master, Bruiser.' Robert kept his grip on the collar and led it back to Teasdale. Teasdale fastened a rope about its collar, striking the dog violently about the head.

Robert shook his head in disgust. Teasdale would sell him the dog before the day was out and Teasdale's dog-owning days would be at an end. The man could forget any future work, too. A man who struck a dog in that fashion would be more than willing to strike a man or a boy on the slightest of pretexts. It was one of the few things that Robert agreed with his late father about—such behaviour was the coward's way.

Controlling his anger, he turned his attention back to the poor woman who had been the victim of Bruiser's attack. She had made no move to uncurl from the tight ball. Her straw bonnet was covered in dirt and tiny stones, but remained on her head, hiding her identity. He had reached the dog before it bit her, hadn't he? He knelt down at her side and saw the torn lace petticoat rucked up over the sensible boots. Blood trickled from her shin, but without a thorough examination it would be difficult to tell how badly she was injured.

'You are safe now. The dog is under control. Can you get up? Did you hit your head when you fell?' Robert asked in a soft voice. A doctor should be sent for, but he didn't trust Teasdale. 'We need to move you and get you out of danger. The post-coach stops for no one.'

The woman gave a low moan and shook her head.

Robert gently turned the woman over. Her face was white against the darkness of tangled curls. Henrietta Thorndike, but a Lady Thorndike made suddenly vulnerable and without her fearsome expression. He softly swore as his blood sizzled. An added complication. She'd probably blame him for this as well as everything else. Her earlier words about how they had fallen out of civility haunted him. Was she coming to apologise or merely doing her duty visiting tenants?

'Lady Thorndike, it's Robert Montemorcy,' he said quietly, attempting to control his body's unexpected reaction to a glimpse of her slender leg. 'The dog has gone. You are safe. You will be looked after. I promise you that.'

Henrietta Thorndike moaned incoherently as she screwed up her eyes tightly in pain.

He tried again. Civility be damned. 'Lady Thorndike, are you all right? Give me a sign you understand what I am saying. Did the dog bite you anywhere besides your shin? Lady Thorndike, you are ruining a perfectly serviceable bonnet. We need to move before the post-coach comes through.'

'Call me Henri. Hardly anyone ever calls me Henri these days,' she murmured, her long lashes fluttering. Dark against the pure cream of her skin. Utterly delectable.

Robert drew in his breath, sharply, and struggled to control the hot rush of blood to his nether region. Right now, she needed assistance. He scooped her up and carried her to the side of the road as the post-coach thundered past.

'Please. Am I going to die? Is my face ruined? My leg aches like the very devil.'

Robert gave a short laugh as the air rushed from his lungs. How like a woman to be worried about her looks, rather than exclaiming about how narrowly the coach had missed the both of them.

'Henri, then. Your face is as ever it was.' He knelt down beside her and supported her shoulders so she could sit up. Her body relaxed against his and the pleasant scent of lavender rose about him. Her bottom lip held a glossy sheen and trembled a few inches below his.

'Please tell me the truth,' she whispered, lifting a cool hand to his face. 'Are you are keeping something from me? If I am horribly scarred, people are going to turn away from me…'

Giving into temptation, he bent his head and brushed his lips against hers. The tiniest of tastes, but firm enough to make his point clear. Her long lashes fluttered and a long drawn-out sigh emerged from her throat.

'Do I look like a man who would kiss a woman with a ruined face?'

Chapter Four

Do I look like a man who would kiss a woman with a ruined face?
The words echoed around and around in her brain. Henri lay on the
side of the road with Robert Montemorcy's arm about her shoulders
and his body supporting hers, far too stunned to move. Her lips
ached faintly from the kiss. And what was worse, her entire being
demanded more.

The world swayed about her. Her entire being was aware of his
arm about her shoulders, the thump of his heart and the way her
body curved intimately into his as if they were a perfect fit. It would
be easy to stay here for the rest of her life, safe.

She wanted him to kiss her again. Properly this time. Long and
slow.

The thought shocked her to her core. She was supposed to be
beyond such things. Her heart was buried with Edmund. In any
case, she had read St Paul's letter to the Corinthians in the bible as
a young girl and her nurse had explained *charity* was another word
for love. Love was supposed to be patient, gentle and kind, bearing
all things, and she had decided that was how she wanted love to
be. It was what she had felt for Edmund. What she felt now was a
red-hot rush of blood and desire. An insidious curl of warmth that
kept calling to her, making a mockery of her ideals.

She struggled against the weight of his arm, pushing her traitorous thoughts away. 'Let me go. I'm out of danger.'

'Henri?' The warm tone enticed her to stay, but she forced her body up to a sitting position and his arms fell away.

'No, I'll be fine. I'm always fine. There's no need to be concerned about me.'

She shrugged slightly, hoping the languid feeling would go. The horrifying moments of the dog attack were over, and Robert Montemorcy had seen her in an embarrassingly weak moment. Kissed her even. She curled in her hand in frustration. Lying in this man's arms was the last thing she desired.

She hated this hot unsettled feeling. With Edmund, she loved him with a pure devotion. But now she'd enjoyed a kiss with another man. And, what was worse, wanted to be kissed by him again.

'My muscles are akin to jelly. That's all. I had a momentary lapse.'

'It is the shock. It will pass.' He gave her shoulder an awkward pat. The heat from his hand jolted through her.

'I will live,' she said, frowning as she suddenly became cold. Fate must be laughing. She was now beholden to Mr Montemorcy for saving her when only seconds before the attack, she had been filled with such righteous anger about how he'd treated her and her cousin that she'd failed to notice how close she was to Mr Teasdale's house and that dog.

How could she be angry with a man who risked his physical safety for her? She'd seen him wrestle that beast to the ground, the act of a true hero.

'The dog savaged your leg. It will have to be seen to.'

She half-closed her eyes and again saw the beast's jaws, coming ever towards her, and then how it had turned to attack Robert Montemorcy. The world turned black at the edges.

Henri gritted her teeth. Whilst she despised her own weakness at being so cripplingly afraid of dogs, she refused to faint. She never fainted. It was a point of principle. Fainting was for people like her late mother who had nothing better to do and wanted attention.

'You shouldn't have risked yourself for me,' she said, concentrating on the stones in the road. 'I fell and became winded. It could happen to anyone. That coach would have missed me.'

'Why would I walk away from a person in trouble, particularly someone I consider to be a friend?' he asked in that lilting Northumbrian accent of his. 'And I refuse to allow my friends to be crushed under the wheels of a coach.'

'Shall I fashion you a halo? Your Good Samaritan credentials are impeccable,' she said, trying to move her ankle; waves of pain crashed over her. Perhaps she'd been overoptimistic in thinking she could make her way home. Her ankle seemed to be insistent on aching. Of all the stupid accidents, to try to run but instead to trip and turn her ankle. And then the dog had sunk his teeth in, pulling at her. It might hurt, but there wasn't much blood. That had to be a good sign.

She would be willing to guess that Robert Montemorcy had had a good glimpse of her petticoats. She tried to remember if she was wearing her lace-trimmed one or the more practical flannel one or, worse still, the one that needed mending.

'Your humour was unaffected and that is a start.' A dimple flashed in his cheek. 'Henri.'

She looked up into his piercing amber eyes. Her insides did a queer sort of leap that had nothing to do with her ankle. 'Are you really going to call me that? You've always called me Lady Thorndike before.'

'You said I might as I saved your life.' He leant close and his breath fanned her cheek. 'Who am I to deny a beautiful woman? You may call me Robert if you desire.'

'Not that. I'm just…well…me.' Henri squashed the faint sense of giddy pleasure that ran through her. Not even Edmund had considered her beautiful—striking, maybe, but not a beauty. Her nose and mouth were too big for her face, and her figure a bit too angular. 'My colouring and figure are all wrong to be considered fashionable.'

'You're far too modest, Henri.' The lines about his eyes crinkled and made him appear younger, more approachable. 'And here I thought you didn't care a jot for fashion. You have your own unique style.'

She stared up at the blue sky, trying to gather her wits about her. She knew what he was doing—speaking of inconsequential things until she had recovered. She wished they weren't quite so personal. She needed to change the subject quickly or that unsettling ache in her belly would grow. She needed to get up and be on the same level as he. Then she could take control of the conversation and keep it away from potentially troublesome personal details. If he was a gentleman, he'd never refer to the kiss again. It was an aberration brought on by the dog attack.

Henri attempted to stand, then sat back down again as throbbing pain shot from her ankle. She hugged her knees to her chest.

'A dangerous dog like that should have been chained. It savaged my leg without provocation,' she said, attempting to control the pain. Mind over body. Once she started to walk, she'd shake off the pain. 'I expect I need to arrange a talk for next autumn on the correct care of dangerous animals. The last one obviously had no effect whatsoever.'

'The dog is not to blame. The owner is.' His dark brown eyes burned. 'And as I'm the man who pulled the dog away from you, I'm not the one who needs the lecture. As attempts to deflect attention from your injury go, that was pretty pathetic. I'm concerned about *you*, Henri, not what caused the accident. The causes can be remedied later.'

He'd seen through her ruse. With an effort she turned her head. The world tilted slightly and if anyone else had been standing beside her she would have given in to the darkness. Here she was berating Robert Montemorcy and he had saved her. Tears pricked her eyelids.

'I give you my promise. It will be sorted out. And, Henri, you know you can depend on me keeping my promises. I have always kept them.'

'Give me a moment to compose myself and I shall be on my way. I've only slightly twisted my ankle. I used to do that frequently when I was in my teens and it never lasts long. And the bite on my leg looks worse than it is,' she said and forced her body to be upright. Sharp pain shot through her ankle, sending a wave of dizziness crashing through her. It might take a little longer than she first considered to shake the pain off. She'd worry about the blood later, rather than put Robert out by asking for help. Other people always needed it more than she did.

'How far do you think you will get on that ankle?' He hovered near her. His hands brushed her elbow. A jolt went through her and she was intensely aware of him standing behind her, ready to catch her if she fell.

'I should make it back to my aunt's. This little incident has inexorably altered my scheme for the afternoon.' Henri looked at him. She was in no fit state for visiting. Her skirt had a great tear and she also wanted to keep her wits about her when she met Miss Ravel. She had to tread carefully. She wanted to keep both her promise to Sebastian and to Montemorcy.

Henri risked another excruciating step and felt the sweat begin to gather on her brow. She hated to think about walking all that way home, particularly as a fine drizzle had started and a Northumbrian drizzle nearly always turned into a full-blown rainstorm. But Henri knew she could not stay in the road or, worse still, rest at Mr Teasdale's. The man was a disgrace to the neighbourhood.

Mr Teasdale, having secured the dog, advanced towards them, whining about how this was not his fault. Robert waved him away, telling him to go and fetch the doctor.

'I'm going home,' she announced in a loud voice.

'You won't make it, not on that ankle,' Robert said, turning back to her. His face darkened as she took a hopping step. 'Henri, you are a danger to everyone else. What will happen if a cart or carriage comes along the road? I give you a half-dozen steps before you have to sit down again.'

'Is this another one of your idiotic wagers? How far can Henrietta Thorndike walk before she gives up? Let's see, I will wager that I can walk further than you think!'

'A statement of fact. You have no need to play the martyr.'

'You know nothing about me and my strength of character, Mr Montemorcy. I have a strong constitution.'

'I do not doubt your spirit, but your flesh.'

Henri took a cautious step. The pain went through her in agonising waves. 'See, I can do it. You should have more faith in me. My mother was strict about my upbringing. She hated weakness in anyone but herself.'

'Are you always this stubborn? Dark humour doesn't change your injury.'

'I find it helps.' Henri hated the way her voice caught in her throat and looked down. Her stomach lurched again, and she finally gave in. 'My ankle hurts…Robert…oh, I want it to stop.'

He held out a hand. 'You don't have to do this on your own, Henri, simply to prove a point to me. If I apologise for not telling you about my ward, will it help? I do regret that you took the news in the wrong fashion. I made a mistake. There, now can you accept my help, rather than fighting me every inch of the way?'

She shook her head, hating the lump that formed in her throat. Why did he have to start being pleasant? 'You will observe the stern stuff I am made of. I persevere.'

She took a third step and wished she hadn't. More than anything she wanted to give way and accept his arm.

'You delight in taking stubbornness to new heights. It will take you hours.'

'I'm pleased you see the sense in what I am doing.' Henri concentrated on taking the next step.

'I only see nonsense.'

Her foot slipped. And, somewhere, the dog began barking again. She reached out a hand and encountered his stiff shirt front. She clawed at it.

'Falling. Dizzy,' she mouthed as the humiliating blackness threatened to claim her. 'Dogs frighten me. Always have. Help me, please, I don't want to be a weak-willed ninny. Want to be strong. Have to be.'

'Allow me. Now, hush.'

He scooped her up, holding her against the broad expanse of his chest. Henri turned her face so that she could not hear the steady thump of his heart and took deep steadying breaths. There was something reassuringly safe about his arms and the way he walked with firm steps. She could allow herself to be carried for a little way and then, when her ankle hurt less, resume her journey.

'Where are you taking me?' she asked. 'Mr Teasdale's front room?'

'To my house.' He lifted an unyielding eyebrow. 'It is no more than a few hundred yards. You need medical attention. I would not send a dog to die in Teasdale's front room. The man lives in squalor not even fit for a pigsty.'

Henri struggled against the bounds of his arms. 'Don't you think you should ask me first?'

He stopped in mid-stride and seemed amazed that she could possibly object. 'You will be quite safe there. The doctor has been sent for and my man Fredericks will alert your aunt to your whereabouts.'

'You've thought of everything.' Henri leant back against his arms. The wind tousled his hair slightly, highlighting his strong jaw and the way his mouth was bow-shaped. 'But I don't want to trouble anyone.'

'Suffering from a dog attack is no time for missish behaviour,' he said, covering the ground with rapid strides as if she weighed no more than a feather. 'Miss Ravel and her mother will be pleased that you are calling, even if in an unorthodox fashion. She has heard of you and your romantic past. She was asking about you this morning at breakfast. I haven't bothered to enlighten her that you are the least romantic person I know.'

A small shiver went down her spine as she examined his hawklike profile. She didn't know which was worse—that Robert thought she was unromantic or that Miss Ravel had spoken of her. She needed to discover Sophie Ravel's side of the story before she decided on her course of action. 'My fame precedes me. How stupendous.'

'You grow pale, Henri. Is your ankle bothering you that much?'

'I have finished fainting for the day.' Henri attempted to keep her teeth from chattering. 'I simply twisted it. It will be better in a few moments. You should leave me to rest at the side of the road.'

'Stop being a hero. You've gone grey with pain. But we will allow the doctor to decide.'

'The doctor will agree with me. It is a twisted ankle and the bleeding has stopped.' Henri held her body slightly away from his. She was intensely aware of the way his chest muscles rose and fell underneath his frock-coat, and the way his stock was a bit undone, revealing the strong column of his throat. And the way her heart had started to thump. 'And I've no intention of fainting again.'

'A lady who declines to faint. Will wonders never cease? My mother had it down to a fine art. She swore it was useful in ending arguments.'

'The force of the argument should hold sway rather than a dramatic gesture. Any fool knows that.'

A light flared in his eyes as a half-smile tugged at his mouth. 'You're definitely not most women.'

Henri frowned. A compliment couched as an insult or the other way around? Her head spun as her body shifted slightly in his arms.

'If I get too heavy, you must put me down. I dare say I can hop.'

'Hopping doesn't come into it. And you will have to obey me for once.'

His arms tightened about her, pulling her more firmly against his body. His chest hit hers and she forgot the correct manner of breathing. It was as if she had been encased in ice and had suddenly come out in the sun. If she turned her head only slightly, her lips would brush his neck.

She screwed up her eyes and tried to conjure up Edmund's familiar features. Annoyingly they were indistinct, like a miniature that had spent far too long in the sun, and were growing more indistinct. The memory did help to curb her impulse, but it also frightened her. If she failed to remember his exact features, what else had she forgotten? For so long it had been a part of her, but it was slipping away.

'My duty is to ensure you are safe and keep off your ankle, Henri,' Robert Montemorcy said, bringing her back to her current predicament. 'And I do endeavour to do my duty. Always.'

Henri gritted her teeth and tried to keep the world from turning dark. She glanced up in his eyes and noticed they were not solidly brown as she'd thought, but full of a myriad of colours. 'And that is what I am—a duty?'

'Why are you out this way?' he asked, not replying to the question.

'I wanted a stroll,' she said too quickly. How could she confess without explaining everything?

'Indeed. All the way out here. Were you going to call? Apologise?'

He gave a cynical smile. 'It is far too much hope for. The great Lady Thorndike has no need of apologies.'

Henri knew her face flushed. Perhaps she had been a bit high handed at their last meeting, but he had been as well. 'What I was going to do is of no import now. Everything has changed.'

Robert sat in his dark oak-panelled study, contemplating the glowing embers of the fire Dorothy Ravel had insisted was necessary to ward off the chill of a Northumbrian summer. But instead of seeing the embers, he kept seeing Henri's pale face and remembering how her body felt curved against his, how her lips had touched his for one glorious instant.

The vulnerability in her eyes when she claimed that she could cope tugged at his heart-strings. And her determination to make good her promise.

What was he going to do about her? She was an added complication that he didn't need. Beautiful headstrong women were always trouble. He'd seen it when his father remarried, and how his father had changed, particularly after his stepmother ran away with her impoverished but titled lover. His father had been unable to take the rejection and had taken his life. Later still, he had his own experience with changeable women and had learnt to trust facts rather than emotions.

What was her destination? Here? And if yes, why—to apologise? Henrietta Thorndike never apologised for anything. Was she trying to do her duty as she saw it in welcoming the Ravels to the neighbourhood or did she have an alternative plan?

She had singularly neglected to answer his question about her cousin. He curled his fingers about his pen. He'd view any attempt to open communication between her cousin and Sophie as a clear breach of their wager. And he'd inform her of that.

'The doctor is here, sir,' Davis the butler intoned.

'Show him into the green drawing room. The upstairs maid is sitting with Lady Thorndike,' Robert said.

'Is it true, Robert?' Dorothy Ravel burst into the room. Her Belgian lace cap was slightly askew. 'Have you brought that man's cousin here? I will not have my girl getting upset again!'

'Dorothy,' Robert said evenly, looking at the woman who had helped to bring him up, 'Lady Thorndike is a friend. She had a mishap. The New Lodge was by far the most sensible place to bring her.'

The woman's ribbons quivered and she tightened her layers of shawls about her shoulders. 'I'd hoped and prayed that it had all ended, but I worry so. Sophie must make a good match. Her father longed for it.'

'And I'm well aware of the necessity. I did promise James on his deathbed. No rogues, rakes or rascals. I intend to keep my promise. Sophie will marry a man who is worthy of her and her fortune.'

'I suppose...there is no hope—you and Sophie? You could always move to a warmer climate... London would welcome you... You are thirty-three and it is high time...'

Robert recoiled from the unspoken request. 'You, better than most, know my history, Dorothy. Sophie deserves someone she loves with her whole heart and who is closer in age and temperament. I've known Sophie since she was in her cradle.'

'I curse that stupid woman.' Dorothy Ravel rolled her eyes. 'What she did to you was less than kind. You had a lucky escape, Robert. And your father was an old fool to marry that...that short-heeled wench. Mr Ravel told him to his face when he remarried. No good comes of lust and indulging spoilt women's whims. He attempted to add her to his collection of beautiful objects and paid the ultimate price. But that was his shame and not yours.'

'I know what my father did. I choose to remember him for other things. The way he was before it happened.' Robert focused on the fire. His father might have felt compelled to commit suicide after his stepmother deserted him, but he'd learnt to trust facts rather than his instincts where women were concerned. He'd learnt that long ago. All relationships were governed by logic and scientific method. It was the only way.

'And Daphne Smith—do you know what she was?'

'I understand Lady Alderney is quite happy living abroad in Italy. I go down on my knees nightly, thanking God that I was saved from a fate worse than death. And logic should rule the heart rather than the other way around.'

Robert pulled at his cuffs. He had been far too young then and far too ready to believe the lies that sprang from beautiful titled lips. Daphne had seemed to be an angel set on this earth and he had worshipped the ground her dainty foot trod as only a lovesick youth could do. He'd naïvely believed her protestations that she could care for him, if only her parents would allow her to. Her refusal of his proposal and her subsequent mockery after she had secured Viscount Alderney's hand had made him even more determined to succeed and to follow his father's injunction that a rational approach was the only way. And succeed he had, until one day he realised that success had a sweetness all of its own and the refusal was no longer the spur it once was. Thereafter he'd been very careful to take his pleasure only from sophisticated women who expected little in return—always ending the affair before his emotions were fully engaged rather than risk the hurt.

'Do you think that Lord Cawburn sent Lady Thorndike as a spy? Does she know what he tried to do to my darling girl? The wickedness he had planned? I have heard stories, terrible stories. Why he remains accepted in polite society, I have no idea!' For the second time in as many days, Dorothy appeared to be on the brink of hysterics as she fumbled for her handkerchief.

Robert put a calming hand on Dorothy's ample shoulder. There was no need to inform her of his wager with Henri and their quarrel. Dorothy might read far too much into it. 'Lady Thorndike's reason for being in the neighbourhood will be entirely innocent. She is well-known for her generosity and she always calls on visitors. She has started some society or other.'

'I do hope you are right. I worry about my little girl and that… that monster. The women he has ruined. And rumours of his gaming…'

'Trust me to handle it,' Robert said grimly. 'It is why you came to me in the first place. Nothing will happen to Sophie under my roof. She is safe here with trusted servants to watch over her. And when we know she is sensible, then she can go out into society again.'

'You are so good to us, Robert.' Dorothy dabbed a handkerchief to her eyes. 'My nerves…the very thought of having to meet that man again is enough to make me take to my bed.'

'I will explain it to Lady Thorndike. She won't want to embarrass you or your stepdaughter. She may be many things, but she's not cruel and she is a strong upholder of society's virtues.'

Dorothy Ravel twisted the handkerchief about her fingers. 'I find that society goes out the window when family are concerned. And Sophie is at such an impressionable age…'

'I give you my word, Dorothy. Cawburn will only ruin Sophie over my dead body. Trust me on this.'

Henri lay on the dark green damask couch and gazed up at the ornate ceiling. Robert Montemorcy's house with its highly polished wooden floors, plush Persian carpets and various clocks and other mechanical items whirling smelt of wax polish and other chemicals. It had puzzled her at first and then she remembered Robert kept a small chemical laboratory for experiments. He'd even created a new type of white paint for Melanie Crozier when she complained of the old one streaking and ruining her watercolours.

A variety of clocks started to strike the hour, reminding her that time was fleeting. Henri shivered and pulled the soft wool blanket up around her chin, wrapping herself in a cocoon against the world.

For once Robert was correct. She would never have made it home. But she'd leave as soon as her aunt's carriage arrived. It puzzled her why Miss Ravel and her stepmother hadn't greeted her and had left the nursing to a junior maid. But then not everyone was comfortable around invalids.

Henri moved her ankle and, despite the laudanum the doctor had forced her to drink earlier, it throbbed with a dull ache. Henri wrinkled her nose. One more fallacy. She had always thought laudanum took away all physical aches and pains. Edmund in his gentle reproachful way had always sworn it did when she enquired.

'Lady Thorndike?' Mr Montemorcy stood in the door, filling it. The light filtered in behind him and prevented her from seeing his face. 'I regret to inform you that you will need to remain here for a week, two at most. Doctor Lumley requests it.'

Henri concentrated on a particularly fat cupid, trying to conquer the inexplicable urge to weep. She was not sure which was worse— that Mr Montemorcy had begun calling her Lady Thorndike again or the fact she was not to be moved. To be looked after as a matter of duty, rather than out of love and affection. She wanted to be home, surrounded by familiar objects. At least there the servants were friends. 'Surely my aunt—'

'Doctor Lumley fears infection and wants to make sure you are kept quiet with your leg raised. Until you have fully recovered.'

Infection. The word stabbed at Henri. It was a horrid way to die and there was little anyone could do once it had taken hold. Edmund used to fear it far more than the lung fever that eventually killed him.

'But the bite was washed clean.' Henri hated the way even the mention of infection sent an ice-cold chill down her spine.

'Dog bites are notorious for infection. And your ankle is badly sprained. He doesn't want you moved until the swelling goes down.'

Tears of frustration pricked her eyelids. He didn't understand.

She wasn't going to get an infection. Infections happened to other people. She was always sensible about such things. She took care, but there were so many things that had to be attended to. 'I can rest at home.'

'Doctor Lumley wants you to be nursed properly.' His tone was warm, but commanding. He expected to be obeyed, Henri realised with a start. It wasn't open for negotiation. 'I understand from Doctor Lumley that your aunt is not entirely well. Staying here is the only solution. Unless you wish to risk an infection...'

Robert's words flowed over her. She trusted Doctor Lumley and he wanted her in this house, being looked after. He had cured her aunt's fever last winter when everyone despaired. What wasn't she being told? She took a deep breath. 'I...I...'

'You have gone green, Lady Thorndike.'

'I know what infections can do,' she said in a rush.

'As I do, Henri.' He turned his head towards her, throwing his features into sharp relief. 'My mother died from one when I was ten.'

'My late husband...used to fear them.' She hated the way her voice quavered and stopped. She should have more control after all this time. It had to be the laudanum. She tightened her grip on the blanket, concentrated on the flocked wallpaper rather than on Robert's mouth and regained control. 'He'd seen his father die from a splinter of wood, but Edmund died of...of other things.'

'It is awful to lose someone you love.'

Henri glanced up at him and saw the tenderness in his eyes. He understood without her having to explain about Edmund's death and the agony he had experienced. Why did he have to be the one who did?

'Did...did the doctor say anything? Does he think I might—?'

'Right now, it is time. Everything that can be done is being done. But if you do not rest, I will not be held responsible.' He patted her shoulder. 'The village would never forgive me if I lost you.'

Henri wrinkled her nose as relief flooded through her. Somehow it made it easier to think that Robert was there with her, even if it was just words. 'Hardly that. I keep bullying people into things they don't want to do.'

'Like dancing lessons.' A heart-melting smile crossed his face. 'And it will be strict rest. Doctor Lumley insists. He said something about last winter…'

Henri made a face. Doctor Lumley would have to remember how last winter, she had suffered a chill and had been far too busy to rest—the Ladies' Aid Society had needed to make up the baskets for the poor. She could think of a dozen pressing problems and a half-dozen more minor crises that required her attention. And then there was the vexing problem of Sebastian and how he had conned Aunt Frances out of the housekeeping money that last time he was up here. Could she direct the house even if she was lying on a sofa with her foot raised? 'I can't remain here that long. I have responsibilities. My aunt depends on me.'

'You wish to get well. The entire village can exist without your interference for a few weeks. In next to no time, you will be arranging people's lives again.' He gave a crooked smile that lit up his face. Henri tightened her grip on the coverlet as her heart started doing crazy flips and she found herself watching his lips. 'Think of it as a way to win our wager.'

'But a few weeks…the ball…people will forget about it!' Henri's body started to tremble. Suddenly the entire room tilted. She concentrated on the china ornaments and gradually the giddiness left her. It was a reaction to her predicament rather than to Robert Montemorcy's nearness.

'You do people a disservice.' His smile became liquid honey. 'Catch up on your reading. My library is well stocked, but someone can always be persuaded to go to the circulating library and get out the guide to better cattle, if you require.'

Henri smiled back at him. Relief flooded through her. Seemingly their quarrel was over. They could even laugh about it. With Sebastian, such things festered and lingered for days. 'Being here will demonstrate to you that I have other passions in my life besides matchmaking. If I succeed, you will be dancing the polka.'

'On that ankle?'

'Did I say with me?' Henri pressed her fingertips together. It had to be the laudanum. The thought of dancing with Robert sent another warm giddy thrill through her. She frowned. She'd never been given to giddiness, not even with Edmund. 'I will watch with approval whomever you decide to dance with.'

'But first you have to win the wager.' He leant forwards and a myriad of colours lit his eyes. A woman could spend a lifetime studying those eyes and never be able to name all the colours. 'I fully expect you to give in to temptation.'

'I shall delight in proving you wrong.'

His shoulders relaxed slightly, but there remained a guarded wariness about his eyes. 'That is more like the Henrietta Thorndike I'm used to.'

If only life was that simple. He wanted something more, she was sure of it. The unspoken request hung in the air.

'I owe you an apology,' she said into the sudden silence.

'An apology? What have I done to deserve that?'

'I made a mistake, Robert. You were trying to do what is best for your ward.' She held out her hand. 'You were worried. Hopefully next time, you'll trust me with the full truth before embarking on a madcap wager.'

He took her hand and raised it his lips. The briefest touch was enough to send her heart thumping.

'There is no need for an apology—as long as we understand each other now.'

She lifted her chin and stared straight back at him. Gathering intelligence wasn't wrong. She wasn't actually doing anything with it. And she wouldn't meddle until she knew the full story. 'Yes, we do.'

He turned towards the door. His eyes lit with a sudden flare. 'I will hold you to it.'

Chapter Five

'Henrietta? May I call you Henrietta? I feel like I already know you.' A blonde head with dishevelled curls and pale slightly protruding eyes peeked around the door, waking Henri from an uncomfortable sleep on the sofa. The young woman was clothed almost entirely in flounces and impractical Belgian lace. The dress appeared to be more suited to a London ballroom than a rainy afternoon in Northumberland. 'You're awake. Please say you're awake. I've longed to meet you.'

Henri struggled to sit up straight on the damask-covered sofa as the torrent of words rushed over her. She glanced at the small clock that was now shrouded in gloom.

Two hours since Montemorcy left her to sleep. Two hours of sleep. She never slept during the day. Naps were for invalids.

Her ankle throbbed, reminding her that her activity would be curtailed for the next few weeks. She had to hope that no one took pity on her. She'd had enough pity, concern and being treated like she was made of spun-glass after Edmund died to last several lifetimes. 'I'm awake. And you are the Miss Ravel that everyone in the village is speaking about.'

The young woman gave a tiny curtsy. 'In the flesh.' Her cheeks flushed bright pink. 'Is everyone speaking about me? Truly?'

'The village was much intrigued by your canary and its pagoda-shaped cage.'

'Robert gave it to me last birthday as I expressed a wish for it. He always gives the most splendid presents.' Miss Ravel glanced over her shoulder to the right and then the left. 'I wanted to see you before they forbade it.'

'Why would they forbid it?' Henri tilted her head to one side.

'Everything new or interesting is forbidden these days.' Sophie gave a dramatic sigh. 'Even walking on my own or with a maid, which I used to love. My stepmama…feels that I am incapable of being sensible…after the débâcle in the drawing room. Earlier this week I opened the canary's cage because it must hate it, but it just looked at me and pecked a few more seeds. I don't understand it. I'd be out of the cage in a flash if I were that bird.'

'I'm sorry to hear it.' Henri frowned. It was wrong to keep someone caged like a bird. It encouraged rebellion. She could remember just before she had insisting on eloping and how her mother's attitude had contributed to her need to escape. Edmund had understood and she'd never gone back to the house where she grew up after Edmund's death.

Sophie clasped her hands together; the bright coral bangles on her wrists crashed together. 'I've longed to meet you ever since Sebastian first told me about you and your romantic life. It's all so wonderfully tragic. I wept buckets.'

Henri clenched her jaw. Pity again, and from someone who never even knew Edmund. Sebastian had no right to tell her the story or to imply that Henri was some sort tragic heroine. 'What did he say?'

'How you had eloped and then your husband died tragically a few months later.' Sophie adopted a soulful look. 'I thought it all terribly romantic. To be that in love and then to have it dashed from your lips as it were at such a young age. You have never remarried?'

'Edmund was ill for a long time before and after the marriage.'

Henri kept her eyes on the ormolu clock. Had she ever been that young? This Ravel person made it sound as if she was languishing for a lost love. She wasn't. She had a fulfilled and busy life, useful. She helped other people and didn't have time for maudlin thoughts. 'I've never found the right person to replace him. Never wanted to.'

'Yes, I know.' Miss Ravel put her hands to her chest and gave a long drawn-out sigh. 'I thought it the most romantic thing in the world to marry someone who was suffering and to seek to relieve their pain, and should I have the great misfortune to ever be in such position, I shall follow your lead. After all, once you give your heart, it is given.'

'How well do you know Sebastian?' Henri asked, determined to steer the conversation away from her private life and towards things of far greater interest—namely, how Sophie Ravel saw Sebastian. This might be their only chance to speak privately if Miss Ravel was to be believed. 'I understand there was a contretemps.'

'We've only spoken in snatches. He was in the process of telling me about your tragic life when Mama happened in the room. He had just put his arm about my shoulders as I was weeping... And then quite suddenly and without warning, I was whisked up here. I'm forbidden all contact with Sebastian, which is a shame as his outrageous comments made me laugh. How can anyone take him seriously?'

'Miss Ravel, do you know my cousin's reputation?' Henri asked gently.

'He's much older than me and far more experienced. But his face reminds me of an angel's face. A true Exquisite, everyone says so.' Sophie paused, fiddling with the tie on her black silk apron. 'But he told me that he worshipped the ground I walked on. Mostly people ignore me, but Sebastian—I mean, Lord Cawburn—keeps saying how he'd like to make violent love to me in the most inappropriate places. He doesn't mean it, of course, but it is flattering.'

'He's the sort of man who is not safe in carriages,' Henri said, making a sudden decision. As much as she hated to admit it, she agreed with Robert. Any match between the pair would be a disaster. Sophie Ravel was not the sort of person who would hold Sebastian's interest for the longer term or who could take a firm line when Sebastian started to commit his little misdemeanours.

If there was an alliance, it would be an unhappy one, but Sophie had to think that she had come to the conclusion on her own. Henri tapped her forefinger against her chin, considering. She wouldn't directly meddle, more…suggest and allow the conclusion to come naturally.

'Not safe at all. And he means precisely what he says,' Henri said. 'It's part of his charm. He never lies. He simply says things in such a manner that people discount it.'

'I know all about the value of a sharp elbow.' Sophie gave a proud toss of her head. 'A true gentleman like your cousin wouldn't do anything that I didn't want him to do. He said so. All I had to do was to say the word *cease* and he would. We were about to practise when Stepmama burst in.'

'Sebastian can be remarkably hard of hearing,' Henri said drily. She gathered Sophie Ravel's hand between hers and was surprised how small and delicate it was. 'I doubt an elbow would deter him. You might have to use a frying pan to get your point across, should he ever entice you into a carriage, and you might need to hit him more than once.'

Sophie's blue eyes widened to the size of saucers. 'A frying pan, truly?'

'If you can find one to hand… Very useful things, frying pans—cook your breakfast on it as well as dispatch unwanted advances.' Henri hit the side of her head. 'Whack on the side of the head. It is the only method he'll understand.'

'I'll keep that in mind, but I'm sure you are funning me.' Sophie Ravel's bottom lip stuck out slightly. 'Sebastian is simply the most thrilling thing to have happened to me. And I'm certain you are mistaken about him. He only says things to amuse.'

Mentally Henri sighed. 'Edmund was the same age as I. Sebastian is rather older than you. He will be thirty next birthday.'

'It isn't the age that matters, but the feeling. In any case, he isn't as old as Robert, and dear Stepmama is hopeful…' Miss Ravel put a hand over her mouth. 'Here I go, telling tales again. Robert says I spend too much of my allowance and whoever gets me had better have enough money to keep me. Does Sebastian, as I won't get my fortune until I am twenty-one or I marry?'

Henri hated the small curl of annoyance. Robert Montemorcy would be bored within moments if he married this chit. She sincerely hoped that Robert had more sense, but then she had discovered in the years since Edmund's death that men seldom had sense where women were concerned. They had a tendency to overlook the perfect woman and develop a *tendre* for someone unsuitable…much as Sebastian had done with Miss Ravel. It was why matchmaking became so important for everyone's peace of mind.

'I suspect you will discover that the marrying bit must be someone your guardian approves of or there will be no money. It is how matters work.'

'Always?' Sophie Ravel's eyes widened with shock. 'But Robert would never…or would he?'

'Always,' Henri answered steadily. 'And then it will be up to your husband to decide, but you will be able to guide him. But if you marry without your guardian's permission, you will have to wait…'

'Oh, bother! I hadn't considered that. Robert hates it when his will is crossed,' Miss Ravel cried, putting her hand to her mouth. 'I'm sure Sebastian will wait for me if his heart is true. I quite like the idea of having a man such as your cousin wait for me. He'd said he'd do it as long I didn't take too long. And until I'm twenty-one isn't awfully long, is it? Not if his heart *is* true?'

'It is best to discover his true intentions. You ought to write to him and explain the situation. It is what I would do,' Henri said as a wave of tiredness swept over her. Everything was going to be sorted out. Sensibly. All it needed was a firm hand and a steady nerve. Once Sebastian read the letter, he'd be off to find an heiress whose family approved of him. Problem satisfactorily concluded. Men like Robert overcomplicated things.

A single lamp shone in the drawing room and the only noise the scratch of a pen. Robert frowned. The room should have been filled with the sound of soft breathing.

Henri was sitting up, sucking the end of a pen while various pages of notes and lists surrounded her. Her black hair had come loose and a single curl touched her neck, emphasising its slenderness and pointing down towards where her breasts swelled. The whole tableau was intimate and private. It was all too easy to imagine Henri with her dark hair spread out over a pillow. What her skin would taste like and how her curves would feel against his. There were also reasons why becoming involved with Henrietta Thorndike was not going to happen.

Robert forced his gaze from her, steadied his breath and examined the chaos.

'What are you up to now? I don't think it is what the good doctor would call rest,' he said softly.

She glanced up and he saw her right cheek was covered in a blue-black ink smudge. It gave her an endearing look. He wet his handkerchief in the jug of water that stood on the chest of drawers and held it out to her. 'You've an ink blot on your right cheek.'

Her skin flushed rose and she scrubbed away with his handkerchief. 'It always happens when I get absorbed in things.'

'Doctor Lumley said "rest", not "direct the entire village from your bedside".'

'I haven't moved my ankle.' She gestured towards where her foot rested on several pillows. 'How can I sleep when I worry? There is the ball, where loads remains to be done, and after that a concert. I was planning on writing to a variety of professors to see if we can get a lecture series organised for this autumn.'

'The cemeteries are full of people who had little time to rest.'

'Oh, please!' She slapped her hand against the papers.

He leant over and twitched the paper away from her. It was covered in neat diagrams about how the flower arrangements should go, as well as a plan for the most expedient receiving line. Underlined and with exclamation points was the admonition that under all circumstances, the pugs must be restrained and not allowed on the dance floor.

Her lavender scent tickled his nostrils. He concentrated on breathing slowly, becoming more certain with each passing moment that he'd made a mistake earlier in giving in to temptation.

'Henri, you should allow people to do things on their own. Is all this correspondence for the ball?'

She gestured towards another pile. 'Those are for the ball. That lot over there is for the Ladies' Aid Society as we were planning a whist drive and other entertainments to raise money for a fountain, and finally my instructions to my aunt on how to economise while I'm indisposed. If Aunt Frances is allowed, she'll burn seven candles a night.'

Robert gave a low whistle, impressed at the sheer energy Henri possessed. 'Why did you do it?'

'To take my mind off my ankle and the possibility of infection. I have found if I'm doing things for others, then I've no time to think about my own predicament. It is by far the most effective remedy.'

'Physical pain doesn't go away if you bury yourself in work.'

'What would you know about it?'

'I've had my share of broken bones.' He gave her a dark look.

'Engineering and chemistry are not exactly safe occupations. Experiments can go wrong.'

Henri put her pen down and stared at him expectantly. 'Continue. You have never said.'

'They happened a while ago when I was younger. What other instructions have you sent your aunt?' Robert picked up a page from the 'home' pile. He stilled as he read the injunctions to keep Sebastian away from the cucumbers as cucumbers were far too dear and under no circumstance was her aunt to pay any of Sebastian's tailoring bills. 'Has your cousin returned to Corbridge? When the Season is in full swing? I had understood he never returned here.'

'Yesterday.' She challenged him with a steely-blue gaze. 'The gossip will have it that he is let in the pockets or some such nonsense, but you and I know differently. Sophie Ravel came to see me earlier. You kept the full story from me.'

Robert cursed under his breath. Sophie had foiled Dorothy's scheme to keep the pair apart until he had extracted a promise from Henri, a promise she was sure to give as she wanted to win the blasted bet. To keep Sophie safe, he would dance and he would even sanction a picnic at the ruins. But now, it would be a fumble-fingered approach. 'You should have told me about Cawburn's arrival. It changes everything.'

'And as you singularly failed to confide in me about Sophie and her predicament, why should I consider the need to tell you anything?' she remarked, a smug smile playing on her lips. Henri was up to something. It bothered him that he hadn't worked out what it was, but give him time and he would. 'Sebastian is a cross I have to bear.'

'You do remember our wager?'

'Surely you are not suggesting that I would play matchmaker?' Her eyes widened, but Robert wondered if it was a studied look. 'Despite the provocation, I'm doing nothing of the sort. In fact, I wish to call an end to the ill-conceived idea. I do understand why you did it, but given that I'll easily win being cooped up now… where is the fun in that?'

'Where indeed?' he murmured. 'Very well. We will call a truce, Lady Thorndike, until you have recovered. I've no wish to make it easy for you. The wager is abandoned.'

She gave a brisk nod, but the tiniest of smiles played on her full lips. 'Did you think Sebastian would remain in London? You should have known that he'd scamper up here once you removed his love.'

'I misjudged the situation,' Robert admitted reluctantly. 'I'd not considered his devotion would be so great. You have always claimed that he'd rather be dead than north of the Humber.'

'Now that's a first—you admitting you're wrong.' Henri pressed her hands against her gown. First the handkerchief to clean her face and then Robert admitting that he'd made a mistake and readily agreeing to a truce. A lock of hair had fallen over his forehead. Her fingers itched to smooth it away. She struggled to breathe normally and wished her stays were looser.

'Sophie wrote a letter to your cousin this afternoon. Her maid handed it to me. I suspect she was hoping to have it posted along with your notes and then have your aunt post it onwards, but now I realise she knew he was here.'

'I know nothing about it,' Henri replied truthfully. She sat up a bit straighter and lowered her lashes demurely. 'But Sophie Ravel strikes me as a very determined young lady. Something that is forbidden gains in value. Have you read the letter? Or did your spies simply inform you of its existence?'

'An expression of piety does you no good.' Robert's laughter filled the room. 'I know you'll be involved somehow. But having met Sophie, do you truly think she is the correct person for your cousin? Can't you resist meddling for once?'

Henri put her hand to her head and tried to think clearly. 'You do me a disservice. Before I meddle, as you called it, I do seek to make sure the couple in question are compatible.'

'Out with it, Henri. What is the trouble? What do you have against Miss Ravel? Why don't you think this is a good match? I'm interested to hear your reasoning.' His eyes danced.

'Do you intend to marry Miss Ravel?' she asked in a careful voice. Her insides tightened, waiting for the response. If she knew he was spoken for, maybe this intense physical awareness of him would vanish.

Instantly he sobered and put the paper down. His brows drew together. 'That, Henri, is none of your business. You are teetering on the brink of asking a question that could be construed as matchmaking and interference in my private life.'

'It is a natural enough conclusion. The entire village has remarked on Miss Ravel coming up here when no one knew of her before. They believe she has fled towards love, rather than running away from ruin.' Henri kept her gaze fastened over his shoulder. With each breath she took the tight fluttery place in her stomach became tighter and more noticeable. She refused to think about the kiss they had shared earlier. Would he have kissed her if he was promised to another? Her cheek burnt. There was no way she could even refer to the kiss.

'As it happens, village gossip is wrong. I've no plans to marry the chit.' He turned towards the roaring fire, hiding his face. 'I've known her since she was a babe in arms and I made a promise to her dying father. I'll be glad once she has settled into a good match and is no longer my responsibility. I pity her poor husband, whoever he is, as she will lead him a merry dance. She was the apple of her father's eye and he only married her governess so that Sophie would have a mother…after her mother died. It would be cradle robbing and my tastes are more mature.'

Henri discovered she could gulp air again. Robert Montemorcy had no plans to marry Sophie Ravel and liked women closer to his age. He sought to honour a promise to Miss Ravel's father. It shouldn't be important, but it was. 'I can understand that. Miss Ravel is awfully young. It is one of the reasons I suggested that she write to Sebastian with the suggestion that they wait until she reaches her majority. It is good her father thought so much of her.'

'And furthermore, my dear Henrietta Thorndike, I have no plans ever to marry. I am far too busy with my work. I'd make the worst sort of husband and who would put up with my temper?' He turned back around and gave her a burning look. 'You may keep me crossed off that matchmaking list, the one you are preparing to resurrect after our wager is finished.'

'I have no such list,' Henri replied truthfully—she kept her best ideas in her head rather than written down.

'And I would take it as a personal favour if you did not include Miss Ravel's name either.'

'How many times must I say that no such list exists?' Henri squared her shoulders and stared defiantly at him. 'Most people marry eventually.'

'I'm far from most people. Have I asked you why you have never remarried?'

She shifted uncomfortably on the sofa. He was hitting below the belt. Her reasons were private and certainly not something she would discuss with a man whom she had shared a kiss with. Edmund was irreplaceable. No one else had ever had that lovely gentle smile, which made her feel so content. She couldn't explain about the awful loneliness after he had gone without seeming somehow needy.

He leant forwards, so their breath was intimately laced. The shifting colours of his golden-brown eyes mesmerised her and all she could do was to stare at them and hope.

'It is a private matter,' she whispered.

'As are my reasons.' He moved away from her. 'Shall we keep it that way? No attempts at matchmaking on either side. And now, it is time to take you to bed and prevent you from doing any more work. Shall I carry you up?'

The words conjured up an image that she had tried to bury. She focused on the ormolu clock and forced her breathing to be even. 'I could lean on a stick. I can get up the stairs on my own if I take it slowly.'

'Sometimes, Henri, you have to let other people take care of you. Allow me to keep you safe.'

Safe. She hated to think how long it had been since anyone offered to look after her; even Edmund had needed her to look after him. She watched how the fire highlighted the planes of his face and the darkness of his eyes seemed to swallow her up. He was going to kiss her again. Her entire being quivered with anticipation.

Suddenly the clocks began whirling and chiming, breaking the spell and calling her back to reality.

'I think I'm overtired,' she whispered, clutching the blanket to her chest. 'Please allow me to stagger. You've done enough. I've inconvenienced you for far too long today.'

'I will call the footmen. They can make a chair to carry you up. Pleasant dreams.' He turned on his heel and left the room.

Henri stared after him and the loneliness inside her ached worse than before.

The dreams came thick and fast, a result of the laudanum Sophie had insisted Henri take when she came to bid Henri goodnight.

Henri struggled to sit up, sweat-drenched and heart pounding.

In her dream, Edmund watched her with a thoughtful expression and then whispered goodbye before fading to nothingness. She had screamed for him to return, but instead, in a swirl of mist, Robert Montemorcy had appeared, taking her in his arms and kissing her. His lips explored hers, taking their time, slowly but thoroughly, sliding over hers and delving deep. The searing intensity jolted her awake. Edmund had never kissed her in that possessive manner. Edmund's kisses had always been wistful and sweet.

In the grey dawn light, Henri's fingers explored her aching mouth. She struggled to control her racing heartbeat. A large part of her wanted to sink back into the dream, but the more sensible part of her told her to stay awake and to try to think about things.

As she reached for the lucifer matches, her hand knocked the candlestick, sending it crashing to the floor.

'Are you all right, Henri? Do you need assistance?' Robert's voice echoed throughout the room.

Henri sharply drew in her breath. She had hoped that Sophie or one of the servants would be sitting up, but her bad luck continued to hold. He would have sat up, wouldn't he? She pressed her fingers against her temples and bid the traitorous thoughts to be gone. His voice was a laudanum-induced hallucination.

'Lady Thorndike? Answer me.'

'I'm all right,' she called out and hoped it would satisfy him. The thought of encountering him when dressed in a borrowed nightdress with her hair about her shoulders and soon after her explicit dream made everything worse. 'Truly, I'm fine.'

'You sound far from fine. You sound in pain. Martyrdom is an unattractive quality.' He came into the small invalid's bedchamber, carrying a candle. His shirt was undone and the golden light of the candle highlighted the shadowy hollow of his throat. The shirt moulded to his chest, leaving little to the imagination.

Against all reason, Robert was here, looking after her instead of delegating the task to a servant. And in a state of semi-undress, carrying the single source of light, a light that highlighted his masculinity, demonstrating how deficient her imagination truly was.

Without saying a word he reached down and retrieved the errant candlestick, placing it on the wicker chair beside her bed.

'Sorry I woke you. My dreams were...very vivid.' Her hand played with the ribbons of her nightdress. 'Normally, that is to say…I rarely remember any of my dreams. I must have lashed out in my sleep. A nightmare.'

She stared at him and dared him to say differently. Far better that he think it a night terror rather than some mad longing to be kissed by him.

'The laudanum.' He used his candle to relight the one beside her bed, bathing the room in a soft light that did nothing to lessen the feeling of intimacy. 'It gives strange dreams. I avoid it except when strictly necessary.'

'You must be right. It can do strange things.' Henri pulled the blanket higher until it reached her chin. 'I regret disturbing your sleep.'

'Someone needed to watch over you.'

'I would've thought one of the servants. Miss Ravel's maid?'

His eyes crinkled at the corners. 'My mother always insisted it needed to be a family member who watched anyone who had laudanum or was seriously ill. Everyone had to take their turn, even my father. He complained, but he did it.'

'She didn't trust the servants.' Henri tried to concentrate on his words rather than on his nearness. She could almost reach out and touch the hollow in his throat. Her fingers tightened about the blanket. His looking after her had nothing to do with Miss Ravel and everything to do with his upbringing. It was something he'd do for anyone under his care.

'Not to look after invalids. It had to be done properly.' A wistful smile crossed his face and Henri knew that his mother must have been very important to him. She wished she had had a mother who encouraged people to look after family, rather than demanding attention all the time and telling Henri that she was a shamming and ungrateful daughter when she complained of an aching head. 'Mother was very insistent on such things. To be nursed by her was truly to be taken care of. I only wish I could do the same.'

'It was very kind of you, but I wouldn't have minded if a servant sat with me.'

'But I would have.'

Henri closed her eyes, thinking of what he'd said earlier about his mother dying of an infection. From an early age, she had learnt to accomplish things for herself because no one else would. Her needs were less important than her mother's, or later Edmund's or, later still, a host of other more deserving people. Far easier to help out than to be overlooked. But in the middle of the night with her ankle throbbing, the thought he was there, watching her, filled her with wonder. Intellectually she knew he'd do it for anyone in his care, but she did enjoy that brief instant of feeling special. 'Men hate nursing—a fact of life.'

'If the patient is asleep and quiet, it becomes a pleasure.' His lips quirked upwards and he held out two books—one on chemistry and the other on archaeology. 'Someday I'd like to find a way to extract aluminium cheaply, but I haven't been able to find one yet. And I also want to know more about the latest advances in archaeology. I feel a more thorough approach rather than treating it like treasure hunting would work.'

'Then I apologise for being restless. Far be it from me to interrupt an inventor at his work.'

'You were a welcome distraction.' He repositioned the pillow under her ankle and then straightened the blanket, tucking her in like a child. Henri's heart panged. She hated to think how long it had been since anyone did something like that for her. Even Edmund had wanted her to look after him, rather than looking after her. It was only a little thing, but meant a lot. Someone cared enough to make certain she was comfortable.

'I promise to be good and not to knock over any more candles.' Henri concentrated on retying her nightcap, acutely aware of his long fingers and the way they had brushed the blanket. 'You can go back to your post. I'm fully recovered.'

He remained next to the bed. The candlelight highlighted the planes of his face and the mysterious hollow at the base of his throat. Henri attempted to ignore the way her pulse leapt.

'You may keep me amused for a little while. Your eyes are far too bright.'

He had noticed her eyes. He understood without her saying that she had no desire to sleep. Henri's insides trembled with a warm unfamiliar ache.

She raised herself up on her elbows. 'Miss Ravel has a tender heart. She brought the flowers up before I went to sleep. Thank you for relenting and allowing her to visit me openly.'

He placed his hand on her shoulder. A warm pulse went through her at his touch, but she held her body absolutely still. 'I spoke with her stepmother and explained. There is little to be gained in actively encouraging Sophie to rebel. I am not so old that I can't remember how much fun I had with rebelling.'

'And her letter to Sebastian?' Henri asked, seeking to distract her mind from the way warm ache seemed to radiate from his hand. 'Will you allow communication?'

'I will deliver it personally to your cousin. Unopened. We need to speak as he has returned. I can hardly forbid him visiting you. The gossips throughout Northumberland would be working over-time. Sophie came up here to protect her reputation, not provide for speculation.'

She stared at him in astonishment. 'What caused the sea change?'

'He ran like a redshank up here after Sophie left. It is impressive. I want to know why so I can better assess the situation. I take a pragmatic view on these things. Like you, I do gather intelligence.' He tilted his head. 'A calm rational approach. Logic.'

Henri clamped her mouth shut. The temptation to crow about her victory nearly overwhelmed her, but she'd be generous in victory. Someday soon, he'd admit the errors of his ways. But she'd wait and allow him to discover it on his own. 'The scientific method in operation.'

'It is far better than the methods you employ, Henri.'

'There is nothing wrong with my methods. They bring results. Instinct and intuition. Precise planning produces perfection.' She moved her ankle and searing pain shot through her. A groan escaped her throat as she clawed at the coverlet.

'I know you don't like it, but maybe you should have some laudanum to dull the pain.' He put out his hand and Henri clung on to it tightly as she shook her head. Somehow, his strong fingers made it more bearable. 'Being a martyr never helped anyone. You do not have to do penance.'

She smiled up at him, forcing her hand to let go, and when it did a great feeling of loneliness swamped her. What did Robert Montemorcy know about her need for penance? She did have to make amends for her sins. She bit her lip and hoped he would consider her grimace was from the pain rather than the knowledge. 'It'll pass. It already has.'

'Liar.' His smile lit up the room, but he allowed her hand to fall to her side.

Henri knew her cheeks flamed and hoped that he would think she was frightened about reliving the experience rather than dreaming about him again. And she was aware suddenly that she was in a thin lawn nightgown. 'Sleep cures all ills.'

'I should go.' The unspoken request was there—*unless you want me to stay?*

And she did. Her body wanted his arms about her. In another moment she would beg. Henri swallowed hard and reached for her paper and pen. 'I am perfectly fine. I've recovered...from my dream.'

'If you need me, call. Dream well.'

Henri sucked the end of her pen. Pleasant dreams indeed. The last thing she wanted was to dream as she'd only dream about his mouth moving over hers. What was required were lengthy notes on the correct order for the dances at the ball, the correct positioning of the floral pieces and plans for several future events that would better the lives of the villagers rather than considering how Robert's lips might feel against hers again.

Chapter Six

Anger simmered through Robert. Left to kick his heels in the faded glory of Dyvels' entrance hall like some lackey or servant instead of being shown to the drawing room and given the respect due to a neighbour. He found it hard to believe that any relation of Henri's could be so lacking in manners.

'It is far too early in the morning for such an unwelcome visit, Montemorcy.' Cawburn gave an exaggerated yawn and stretched.

'I have been up for hours.' Robert hooked his thumbs in his waistcoat. After his encounter with Henri, all desire to sleep had fled. He'd done the decent thing and left, rather than giving in to his desires and taking her into his arms. Kissing Henri again, properly this time, would lead to complications. And he preferred to keep things simple and logical. He valued her as a friend too much to risk her reputation. Or losing her. But the memory of her mouth against his and the way her nightdress had revealed her curves had played havoc with his sleep.

'As it is, three meetings will have to be postponed,' he said. 'I've missed the late-morning train to Newcastle.'

'We obviously keep different time.'

In the fierce morning sunlight, Cawburn's overly smooth face showed slight puffiness. In a few years' time, Robert could well imagine how Cawburn's looks would be ravaged if he did not stop his hard living. Robert tried and failed to see anything of Henri's stiff backbone in Cawburn.

When Dorothy had first alerted him to the potential disaster, Robert had been tempted to ignore Cawburn's interest in Sophie as he reckoned it was only a matter of time before a new woman who was far more sophisticated than his ward entered Cawburn's life. But Cawburn had gone beyond the bounds of propriety, and brought the affair to a head by trying to seduce Sophie in a public place.

Faced with a series of hysterical letters from Sophie's stepmother, he'd adopted the only sensible course of action and removed Sophie up here. But Cawburn had followed. Very well, if he wanted to be Sophie's suitor, then he courted her properly and in the open. Cawburn would not ruin his ward.

'It's eleven in the morning,' Robert said, glancing at his pocket watch.

'Practically middle of the night but then I suspect you have been up since before dawn beavering away like a good little factory owner or whatever it is you do.'

Robert allowed the deliberate insult to flow over his head. 'I have a letter for you from my ward.'

'Since when have you taken to reading others' post, Montemorcy?' Cawburn smirked. 'Such a thing must be beneath even you and your limited pretension to gentility.'

'I've not read it,' Robert replied between clenched teeth and after he had counted to ten. He refused to give Cawburn the satisfaction. 'Nor did I dictate it.'

'You haven't.' Cawburn snorted. 'I don't believe you. You are one of those people who are not content until they can control everything. Always twisting facts and circumstances to suit your purposes.'

'As you would see, if you took the time to examine it, the seal remains intact.'

Robert tossed the letter in the air. Cawburn snatched it.

Cawburn turned the letter over, tested the seal and frowned. 'What made you change your mind?'

'Your cousin,' Robert replied shortly. 'Lady Thorndike convinced me that your intentions are honourable. I'm giving you the chance to prove it. Abide by Sophie's wishes. Keep her in the bosom of her family.'

'Good old Henrietta! I knew she wouldn't let me down.'

'You asked your cousin to intercede? To play matchmaker?' Robert gave a silent laugh. Henri had succumbed. She had been unable to resist matchmaking, but she also had sought to hide the slip from him. Was it any wonder she wanted a truce?

Cawburn blanched slightly. 'Entirely innocent, old man. Could I ever live it down if Henrietta arranged a match for me? Good God, man, I know what my cousin is like! She'd never let me forget it! I merely wanted to know if there was any chance for me…after what happened. To know Miss Ravel's state of mind. And now, my angel has written.'

Robert's shoulders relaxed slightly. Cawburn's word tallied with Henri's.

'Your cousin suffered a mauled leg while carrying out your *innocent* errand. We are awaiting the doctor's verdict to see how badly sprained her ankle is.'

'Henrietta has a knack of looking after herself. She hates a fuss.' Cawburn gave a little wave of his hand, dismissing Henri's injury. 'And I thank you for the letter. It is most unexpectedly decent of you. Not the sort of thing I'd have thought a Cit capable of.'

'If you wish to court my ward, you pay court properly.' Robert crossed his arms.

'Properly?' Cawburn picked at his cuff. Robert detected a slight fraying of the cuff and the stock. He knew that he had put pressure on Cawburn's lenders, but had not seen any sign until now. The man was short of funds and saw Sophie as an easy mark. And it was his firm belief that any woman Cawburn married would be bled dry.

'You apply for my permission first as I'm Sophie's guardian. I am more than happy to give it to anyone, even you, if certain conditions are met. Otherwise you will have to wait until Miss Ravel obtains her majority. Are you prepared to wait that long for funds, Cawburn?'

'Why should love be dependent on whether one's friends and relations approve?' Cawburn shook his head in mock despair. 'It is not the way I do things, Montemorcy. I believe in liberty and freedom of expression. One cannot dictate where or when love will happen.'

Robert retained a leash on his temper. The only creed that Cawburn believed in was the pursuit of pleasure. He knew nothing about responsibility or living within his means. His estate was mortgaged to the hilt and he had recently lost heavily on the gaming table. Once he'd learnt of Cawburn's interest in Sophie, Robert had made it his business to buy up some of the debts as they had potential for a bargaining chip.

'Have you found a way around your debts? You have an estate that is entailed and mortgaged beyond prudence. You spent the money not on improvements, but on the games and women.'

'Miss Ravel is well provided for. The extent of her dowry was much discussed in London.' Cawburn gave a lazy smile. 'There will be no problem in meeting my debts.'

'And will you give up your mistresses?' Robert asked. His entire body tensed. The man could no more give up his mistresses than stop breathing. But it would be a start, a statement of his intention towards Sophie.

'There is no reason to get personal.' The tips of Cawburn's ears turned pink. 'I never discuss the intimate details of any lady.

Can I help it if some women are possessed of an overly generous nature?'

'Precisely why I intend to protect Sophie from men like you,' Robert ground out. 'I was prepared to give you the benefit of the doubt, but your answers have decided me—until you sort out your debts, I refuse to give you permission to court my ward.'

'Is that all you came to say? Keep away from Sophie or else? Sophie is a grown woman, she should be allowed to make her choice. It happens all the time.' Cawburn curled his lip. 'If that is your last word on the subject, then so be it. I won't ask you again for permission, Montemorcy.'

Robert grabbed the lapels of Cawburn's jacket. 'And use another go-between. Keep your cousin out of this.' He tried and failed to see something of Henri in Cawburn—her lively intelligence or her kindness or even her smile. Nothing. If it was war Cawburn wanted, Robert would give it to him. After all, he did know where more of Cawburn's debts could be obtained.

'Montemorcy, you know my cousin will never develop a *tendre* for a vulgar man like you.' Cawburn made a mocking bow. 'She prefers men with—how shall I say it?—more aristocratic temperament and refinement.'

The jibe hit Robert in the stomach and he struggled to keep his face blank. 'We were speaking of you and my ward.'

'A friendly warning. Getting ideas above your station can be bad for you. Fatal.'

Robert ignored the well-aimed barb and marched away from Cawburn. A further reminder, if he needed it, that kissing Henri again would be a mistake. It was important to keep the boundaries in his life intact. Putting his faith in facts rather than giving in to emotion and allowing it to cloud his judgement as his father had done had kept his heart for many years. He'd learnt his lessons. Wanting and acting on his desires were two separate things, particularly where a woman like Henri was concerned.

In his haste to be away from Cawburn and his poisonous innuendos, he nearly bowled over Miss Armstrong, who stood there with a jar of calf's-foot jelly and her mouth open, watching the entire proceedings. He ground his teeth and hoped that Miss Armstrong had heard very little, otherwise the Corbridge gossip machine would be working overtime. 'Miss Armstrong.'

She turned a sort of purple-pink and the flowers on her poke bonnet jiggled. 'I'm trying to find Lady Thorndike. I heard she was unwell. But no one will tell me anything. I've brought her favourite remedy—calf's-foot jelly.'

'Lady Thorndike is convalescing at my house,' Robert said. The stench of the noxious substance filled the street.

'At your house!' Miss Armstrong put her hand over her mouth and flushed scarlet. 'I hate to say it, but isn't that most improper?'

'My ward is there, as is her stepmother. They are visiting from London.'

'If I can be of any assistance, I will be. Lady Thorndike has named me as her assistant on the Corbridge Society for Hospitality. I would adore the chance to show Mrs Ravel and her daughter true Corbridge hospitality. It would really make me feel like I was doing something to assist poor dear Lady Thorndike.'

He paused. Miss Armstrong could be excitable, but she was a strong upholder of society values. Henri would have a reason why she had asked Miss Armstrong to be her deputy. It seemed to him that Henri did so many things herself that she forget others could do them if given an opportunity. This would be a way of demonstrating to Henri that village life continued without her—that she was allowed to take the time to recover without worrying frantically about organising everything.

'I would look on it as a great honour if you could take Miss Ravel and her mother under your wing,' he said, making a bow. 'They are strangers and are in need of friends.'

'I shouldn't want to step on anyone's toes... Lady Thorndike...'

'Lady Thorndike is indisposed and likely to remain that way for some time.' He lowered his voice. 'She has badly sprained her ankle. The doctor is hopeful that it is not too severe, but time will tell.'

'You mean she won't be able to make the ball?' Miss Armstrong's eyes widened. Her hue went a violent shade of pink. 'And here I thought she'd be dancing the first quadrille. And who will supervise the hanging of the garlands now? We do live in interesting times.'

'Indeed we do.'

'Oh, I'd be honoured to be Miss Ravel's chaperon.' Miss Armstrong gave a trilling giggle. 'Lady Thorndike will have to admit that I can do things as well as she can, particularly when a gentleman like you requests.'

'You're far too kind.'

Robert gave a nod to where Cawburn stood glowering, following the whole exchange. He hoped so as much had been for his benefit. Cawburn knew enough about Corbridge to know that Miss Armstrong would be an entirely different duenna to Henri. Calm cool logic over the unfettered emotion.

Every available surface of the small sickroom room was covered in small tokens to help her recover. Henri had lost count of the number of jars of calf's-foot jelly that had been delivered to the New Lodge since late morning. Even if she could abide the stuff, one jar was far more than sufficient. But they kept arriving with little notes saying that they had been made to her exacting receipt. The stench was enough to turn even the most ironclad stomach. And Henri knew she'd have to eat every mouthful as one never refused a gift.

And then there was the letter from Lady Winship, which had accompanied her offering. Lady Winship was dreadfully sorry about the accident and Henri must concentrate on getting well, rather than worrying about the forthcoming ball. Lady Winship understood completely if Henri wished to withdraw from the first quadrille on the grounds of ill health. And Miss Armstrong had offered to step into the breach with the hanging of the garlands from the chandeliers. The pugs sent their love.

'Bother!' Henri exclaimed and threw the letter down on the bed.

Tears of frustration came into her eyes. All she wanted to do was to forget about her late-night encounter with Robert and the way her thoughts increasingly revolved around him. She'd even gone to the trouble of dressing in a simple mauve gown, rather than staying in bed like an invalid in case he decided to continue their conversation in the morning light. But he'd left without saying goodbye.

Everybody at New Lodge seemed intent on treating her as if she was made of spun glass and liable to break. Mrs Ravel had banned all the well-wishers on the grounds that they were likely to make her overtired and so her mind kept going over and over her various encounters with Robert.

'Is everything all right, Henri?' the man in question asked as he came into the room, carrying another jar of calf's-foot jelly. Annoyingly he had not grown two heads or developed some hideous deformity. Instead he was as handsome as ever and her heart did a little jump at seeing him. 'Mrs Eastwell stopped me on the way home from the station. She remembered how you brought her some when she was ill last winter and how you proclaimed that it was the perfect thing for anyone who was under the weather, and she wanted to make certain that you had sufficient. She hopes you recover very quickly.'

Henri flopped back against the armchair, grateful for the excuse to distract her mind. 'Another one! And an extra-large one at that. Botheration.'

'How many?'

'I stopped counting after ten. I always used to bring calf's-foot jelly to invalids, but that was because I didn't actually have to eat the concoction.' Henri put her hands on top of her head and tried to concentrate on the brown jug rather than the way Robert's coat moulded to his form. 'It is gratifying that so many are concerned about my well-being but…did they all have to bring the same thing?'

'A first. Henrietta Thorndike admitting that she might have been mistaken in her approach.' His brown eyes danced. 'Calf's-foot jelly is supposed to be excellent for building up strength.'

'There is no need to give my lecture back at me.' Henri shuddered. 'The very thought of calf's-foot jelly turns my stomach. Do you think Cook might be able to do something with it? I shall have to eat it all as people gave it as a gift. Could it be put in pies?'

'Then I won't tell you that more is on the way. Several people stopped me. They want you well and were concerned for the future of village society. I assured them all the entertainments would take place, but others would have to help. There was no shortage of volunteers.'

Henri covered her hands with her eyes. 'I've only sprained my ankle. I'm hardly at death's door. Why are they treating me like this? Why are they punishing me?'

'Hardly punishing. They are concerned about you and are only taking your advice. You should be proud.'

Henri felt her shoulders relax. It would be so easy to start to depend on Robert. But that was not how her life plan went. She'd learnt the hard way that depending on people only led to heartbreak. 'It will be a lesson to me to try to be more inventive in the future with my gifts to the sick.'

'I saw Miss Armstrong earlier. She enquired after your health. She has also agreed to take Sophie and her mother under her wing while you are indisposed. She is your deputy in the Corbridge Society for Hospitality. Apparently she has very little to do and wishes to fully take up the mantle of her office.'

'How kind of her.' Henri's heart panged slightly. She liked doing that sort of thing. And Mrs Ravel was the sort of person she knew could be moulded to help out. She debated if she should warn Robert about Miss Armstrong and how easily she misconstrued things, but decided that such a warning might be construed as meddling and against the spirit of their new-found friendship. Robert could learn for himself why Miss Armstrong was given honorary titles with very little to do. 'She will take her duties seriously, I'm sure. You should consider having a supper party before the ball.'

He gave her a puzzled look. 'A supper party?'

'It will make Mrs Ravel and Sophie feel more at ease before they go to Lady Winship's. I can…help with the plans.'

'No.'

Henri looked at him in dismay. 'But why not? It is the perfect solution.'

'You're to get well and rest. The reason you are here rather than at your aunt's is so that you will rest. Plotting supper parties is hardly resting.' He picked up a small woollen blanket and tucked it around Henri, a little meaningless gesture, but one that brought a lump to her throat.

'Mrs Ravel will be able to manage adequately without me,' she said quickly.

'She will?' His eyes widened as he swallowed rapidly. 'And you will let her?'

'I've every faith in Mrs Ravel. Mrs Ravel and I had a long discussion this morning and I learnt what an accomplished hostess she is. They give her headaches the day after, but I've explained that she will be fine as the air is much better in Corbridge.'

'The air?'

'She is looking forward to visiting people in the neighbourhood,' Henri continued, warming to the theme and beginning to enjoy seeing Robert unsure and off balance. Mrs Ravel, except on the subject of her stepdaughter's matrimonial prospects, seemed to be very sensible. She simply needed confidence, and hosting a dinner party would give her that. 'I assured her that Sebastian hates At Homes with a passion, and in any case my aunt refuses to have an At Home without me.'

'And you promise not to be involved with the supper party.'

Henri shook her head. 'I'll forgo that pleasure.'

'It is settled then.' He put the calf's-foot jelly down and held out a small bouquet of forget-me-not flowers from behind his back. 'I brought you these. They reminded me of you.'

Henri bit her lip and the room swam in front of her eyes. She attempted to take small calming breaths. All she had to do was to hold out her hand and her fingers would brush his linen shirt front. She focused on the tiny pearl buttons of his shirt front. Time stood still.

'Henri?' he asked softly. 'Have I brought the wrong sort of flowers?'

'They're my favourite. Nobody else thought to bring them. I adore flowers.' She bent her head quickly and inhaled their sweet scent. She wanted them to remind her of Edmund's eyes, but her mind went back to Robert on the day of the Croziers' wedding and their wager. She put her hand to her mouth and held back a muffled sob. 'Truly I do.'

He gently squeezed her shoulder. 'They were supposed to cheer you up, not make you cry.'

Somehow it made it worse, his being concerned. She put the flowers down and gave a shrug. 'I could say my ankle hurts far too much, but that is self-evident. Everyone is rallying round and making it easy and that is most unexpected. I help people, but I didn't expect people to...well...help me.'

'What are you afraid of, Henri? What is so wrong about accepting help? With admitting sometimes you need to put yourself and your health before others? That the village can continue without you?'

Henri thought of the box that sat gathering dust under her dressing table. She had promised herself that if she was ever not busy, she'd open it and take the time to properly read the letters and truly say goodbye. Over the past ten years, she'd successfully avoided looking at the box, but now it appeared the good intentions of everyone meant that she'd be left with no alternative. She'd have to face it and the grief. At the time, the grief had been all-consuming and now she worried that it wasn't there. And if it wasn't there, did that mean she hadn't loved him enough? Was that why he had refused to fight the illness any more, despite her finding other possible remedies? Why Edmund sent her out of the room when he knew that he was going? But she refused to explain that to Robert. The words stuck in her throat and the tears continued to slip down her face.

'Henri, it is more than the flowers.' He took the small bouquet from her unresisting fingers and laid it on the table. Then he silently passed her a handkerchief. 'I can fix what is wrong if you tell me.'

She wiped the tears from her face. She had to give him some reason for her tears or otherwise she'd be in his arms again. 'After Edmund died, everyone tried to be kind and I hate a fuss being made. But I was so used to looking after him that suddenly there was nothing for me to do. For a long time, I sat staring out of the window and then I saw a beggar woman collecting sticks for her fire. I knew I couldn't do much, but I could help that woman. I could do things like visiting and taking baskets around. So I started helping and people stopped treating me like I was an object of pity. And now today there is every sort of fuss. Stupid to cry. I haven't cried since Edmund died, not like this. It must be the laudanum.'

'Only the laudanum?'

'Has to be.' She lifted her chin, and forced her lips to smile. She tried to ignore how warmth infused her being. 'All better now.'

Robert tilted his head to one side, regarding Henri's defiant face with concern. A sheen of tears still shone in her eyes. The flowers had unnerved her far more than she wanted to admit. He had wanted to make her smile and instead he'd caused her to cry. He'd thought her a specific type of person, but now he discovered that she was very different, far less secure than he had considered. 'There is only a fuss because people are concerned about you. People do not bring jars of calf's-foot jelly to just anyone.'

A watery smile crossed her lips. 'I suspect it was sheer curiosity. The Ravels will be a source of much fascination. And I suppose to gloat that I have hurt my ankle. I've proclaimed the dangers of being unaware often enough.'

'You hold yourself in too little regard, Henri. And there is nothing to be ashamed about. The dog slipped its chain. You were unfamiliar with the dog and it happened.'

'Even so, I handled it poorly.' She raised her shimmering eyes to his. Robert clenched his fists to keep from dragging her into his arms. She was a neighbour and that was all. 'I keep thinking about… the attack. I dislike being a bother and now everyone is making me rest and trying to take burdens from me. I want to use my mind.' She held up a hand. 'And, no, I don't want to read *Ivanhoe* or a Minerva Press novel. Or even the latest Fenimore Cooper. Sophie has already suggested the possibility, but they hold no attraction. I want to do something with my mind. Something useful.'

Robert tapped a finger against his lips. Yesterday he'd seen the softer side of Henri Thorndike and found, to his surprise, that he enjoyed it. He wanted to explore the woman behind the façade of efficiency, the one who wasn't always standing, being capable. He enjoyed puzzles and Henri had secrets that she wanted to keep hidden. All he had to do was to keep her off balance. He didn't want the new softer Henri to be subsumed back into the fearsome Lady Thorndike.

'Do you dislike numbers?'

'I can do arithmetic…well enough.' She tilted her chin in the air. 'I manage the accounts. My aunt is hopeless. And I'm much better than Sebastian. It infuriates me when men proclaim women can't add up. We can. I am better than most. But I won't read about the scientific method and archaeology despite our truce. A woman must have her principles.'

'Another project of mine.' He returned in a few heartbeats with a huge sheaf of papers and put them in her lap. His hands brushed her shoulder. Her flesh quivered under the gentle touch. 'Make yourself useful and sort out my research on aluminium. Find where I've gone wrong. Aluminium is one of the most abundant minerals on the planet, but in its pure form it is worth a king's ransom. If a process can be found, it could change the world.'

Her brow knotted. 'I know how rare aluminium is. It is worth more than gold if you can get it as a metal, but I know nothing about such things. Seek someone else to make sense of it and find a flaw in your reasoning.'

'But you can learn. You have a quick mind. It would be a great help to me. Of course, there's always sewing.'

Henri screwed up her face as he guessed she might. Henri might have started the Ladies' Aid Sewing Circle, but he'd never seen her with a needle in her hand. 'Sewing and I are nodding acquaintances only.'

'But I thought you gave lectures on the importance of needle-work? You have organised classes for the lasses from the factory.'

'Telling other people that it is a good thing and actually enjoy-ing myself are two separate things. My threads always tangle and I have a habit of pricking my thumb. I leave it to the experts.'

'Either you can wallow in self-pity about your ankle and con-template the amount of beef jelly being delivered, or you can do something productive and help me. Your choice.'

She folded her hands in her lap and her face took on a mulish expression, which was far better than her earlier broken-hearted one. 'And you trust me with your research, but not with the Roman encampment?'

'Find a hole in my logic, and we will discuss the treasure-hunting picnic.'

She was silent for a long time, her neat white teeth worrying her full bottom lip, turning it a luscious red. 'It is tempting, but...'

'No buts, just do it.' He leant forwards so their foreheads nearly touched. 'Prove a woman is just as good as a man at such things, Henri. Prove to me that there is more to you than unadulterated self-pity.'

Chapter Seven

Henri scrunched up a piece of paper and threw it on the study floor. Two days into her helping Robert to sort out his research and she found she actually was beginning to be interested in the scientific method. She could see how he'd started, how some experiments hadn't worked and how other ones had. She could see how it could be applied to the excavation. She also had learnt that Robert Montemorcy had a habit of making notes in the margins. She might not be able to calculate as well as he could, but she certainly could organise.

'You are downstairs.' Robert came into the room. Henri's breath caught slightly. His hair curled at the ends as if he had been caught out in the rain. 'How did you keep your weight off your foot when you came down the stairs? Cane or banister? If you'd called, I'd have been happy to carry you.'

'I leant on Sophie's arm. We made slow but steady progress. Doctor Lumley is certain that the ankle is only sprained and there will be no lasting damage.' Henri forced her breathing to be even. The sudden image of Robert carrying her, her breasts flattened against his chest and her mouth turned towards his, flooded her brain. In the cold clear light of morning, she knew she could control this unsettled feeling. 'And I can rest as well down here as up in the sickroom. And the pies Cook makes with the calf's-foot jelly are unexpectedly delicious. I shall have to get the receipt and recommend it. I shall have gained weight by the time I've finished, but it is the way to eat the stuff.'

His dark eyes danced. 'I shall have to call you Pie.'

'Pie?' Henri jabbed the pen down, making a hole in the paper. 'What sort of name is Pie?'

'Henri-ate-a Pie or Pie for short. It suits you and your propensity to eat pies rather than jelly.'

'That is an unworthy pun.' Henri knew her face flamed. It had been a long time since anyone had given her any nickname, let alone one as ridiculous as Pie. Edmund had often made up nicknames. Some she had liked better than others. But with Robert, Pie made her feel as if she was his younger sister and that wasn't precisely how she felt about him. 'You may cease and desist. I prefer Henri. I've always preferred Henri.'

'Point taken. I shall remember to call you Henri from now on… or perhaps Thorndike.'

Henri ducked her head as the room suddenly seemed to grow small. He wanted to have a special name for her. They were becoming friends. 'Here, you should see this.'

His eyes widened as he picked up the paper she was working on. 'You started…'

'Self-pity never solved anything,' she said briskly. There was no point in explaining that she'd resorted to it to keep her mind from the explicit dreams. Sometimes during At Homes, other women had confided about their vibrant sex lives with their husbands, and Henri had wondered why they went on about it. With Edmund, it had been pleasant but not earth-shatteringly magnificent. And after last night's dreams, she started to wonder if it had been him rather than her, and she hated how disloyal it made her feel.

'You admit the scientific method has merit,' he said and his eyes became the colour of molten caramel.

'For scientific things, yes.' Her stomach did a funny sort of a flip at his look. She closed her eyes and steadied her breath.

His eyes narrowed. 'Did Lumley give you permission to be up? Your cheeks have become flushed.'

'He says the ankle is healing satisfactorily and complimented Sophie on her bandage-tying skills.' Henri forcibly turned the conversation away from her health and her reason for her discomfort. 'Sophie turned beet-red. It is a pity that she remains confined to nursing relations. Her skills are wasted.' Henri twisted the soft wool of the shawl about her fingers. Keeping her mind on Sophie was far better than contemplating the length of Robert's fingers.

'Ah ha, you will have to admit—you can't resist matchmaking and meddling, particularly when it means you don't have to discuss your health. Very well, I will assume your ankle is better, Henri, but you will remain in this house for a little while.'

'It is hardly matchmaking to mention that your ward is good at nursing. Doctor Lumley's marital status has no bearing on this conversation. Trust you to lower the tone.' Henri adopted a pious look, but it unnerved her that Robert had guessed her reasoning. 'I think you only wanted to have a truce so that you wouldn't have to dance with me at the ball.'

'As if I would try to get out of dancing with you...' he murmured, his lilting voice sliding over her skin. 'You would not have found me deficient in that regard.'

'Sophie agreed with Doctor Lumley that being downstairs is the best place for me.' Henri kept her eyes straight ahead. 'And, between the village's offerings and the bottles of various potions, there was no room to spread out your notes. I think I'm beginning to understand your approach, but it seems awfully complicated.'

'What if I like my current system?' His eyes crinkled into a heart-melting smile, sending a warm tingle coursing throughout her. She found herself focusing on the curve of his upper lip rather than on the figures.

Henri put her head to one side and assessed him. She'd been certain that it was only the intimacy of the sickroom that made her aware of him, but down here in the drawing room, the same sort of intense fire filled her. She had cause more than ever to regret the kiss. Perhaps there was a logical explanation. Something about not being in close contact with a man for ten years and suddenly finding oneself in the arms of a highly attractive desirable one. And, what was worse, wanting to be there again. She'd always despised those widows who were desperately searching for another man to replace their lost husband. But Robert was completely different in temperament to Edmund, unsettling and more inclined to want his own way.

'If you liked your current system, you would never have asked me to sort out your notes. And I fail to see any scientific method in the order in which you arranged them. Experiments are jumbled with cuttings, raw data with published,' she said, tapping her pen against the stack of paper.

'Where are the Ravels?' he asked, changing the subject.

'Miss Armstrong does take her responsibilities seriously and called for them in her carriage. She can be overexcitable and inclined to exaggeration, but she is a strong upholder of virtue.' Henri sat up straighter and reached for the lists of experiments. Robert should've been aware of unintended consequences. Miss Armstrong had appeared bedecked in bows and ruffles and her face became like thunder when she discovered that Robert was not at home. 'About these experiments…'

He gave her a searching look. 'Miss Armstrong is more than capable of introducing Sophie and her mother to the neighbourhood. Or is there something else you wish to deflect my attention away from?'

Henri's stomach tightened. Miss Armstrong had little love for Sebastian after Sebastian had been rude to her and she had an overly developed sense of propriety. And she had gone on and on about how girls had to show that they could be trusted out in society. How would Sophie fare under such a chaperon?

'Mrs Ravel is a very determined lady,' Henri said quietly, wondering how she would drum it into his brain that he was risking alienating Sophie. 'A mother bear intent on protecting her cub, but… My mother suffered from the same outlook. The strictures she put on me chafed and I eloped—'

'Sophie is on trial, Henri.' He waved an impatient hand, cutting off her words. 'We both want to see how she acts and if she has learnt her lesson.'

'And if Sophie hasn't…learnt her lesson, what are you going to do? Forbid the ball? Wait to see if she becomes wiser?'

'It has been discussed,' he admitted, his eyes sliding away from her. 'The last thing anyone wants is for Sophie to ruin her chances of a good and secure marriage.'

'You're approaching this scientifically? Experimenting with little events like At Homes? Sophie is a flesh-and-blood person, not a test tube of chemicals. You need to think about her feelings.'

'Sophie needs to prove herself, to prove she can be sensible.'

Henri leant forwards and caught his hand. He looked at her and she found she could only concentrate on his mouth. She forced her gaze upwards. 'You must listen to me. Allow Sophie to go to the ball. Allow her to have some fun. People will watch out for her. She'll not be ruined.'

He curled his fingers about hers and held her there. 'Sophie will prove equal to the task. Small social situations to allow her to regain her confidence. Have faith. Is there something wrong with believing, Henri? You worry too much. Trust me.'

She forgot how to breathe, forgot everything and simply looked up at him with parted lips. Her fingers longed to smooth away the lock of hair that had tumbled down over his forehead. His mobile mouth hovered inches from hers. All she had to do was to lift her face ever so slightly and wrap her arm about his neck. Her fingers longed to bury themselves in his damp hair…

A distinct rumble of carriage wheels sounded, breaking the spell. Henri allowed her hand to drop by her side. Her face flooded with heat. She had been about to kiss him! It wasn't Sophie that she had to worry about, but *herself.* All of her mother's dire predictions about what was going to happen if she didn't learn to curb her passions flooded back over her.

'I do believe I hear a carriage,' she said and hoped it sounded bright and cheerful. 'It'll be Sophie returning, full of tales of the various At Homes.'

'I do believe you are right, Thorndike.' His exact tone of voice mimicked hers. 'We shall have to continue this entirely interesting conversation another time. And we will finish it.'

Henri put her hand to her aching mouth and tried to wish away the disappointment. When she closed her eyes, the only face she saw was Robert's sardonic one, rather than Edmund's placid features. Her insides trembled. Edmund's memory was supposed to be with her for ever. If she forgot him, she'd cease to be Lady Henrietta Thorndike, and she wasn't ready to be anyone else.

'Keep still, Henri, or I won't be able to get your profile done properly.' Sophie spoke from behind her easel and Henri wondered how the young woman knew that Henri had just flexed her good foot. 'Be good. Concentrate on the canary.'

Henri tried to ignore the itch that had started on her chin. It had seemed like a good idea when Sophie suggested a portrait three mornings ago, a way to keep out of Robert's study and stop thinking about him. It gave her the excuse she needed to stop sorting out his research, but she had never thought it would involve such a large amount of time motionless and giving her mind time to contemplate the precise curve of Robert's mouth and how his frock-coat hinted at the hard planes of his chest.

'May I see the sketch?' Henri held out her hand and dragged her mind away from the rapidly developing daydream about Robert. She hated to think about the last time she had been given to dreaming her life away.

'I haven't got your mouth quite right.' Sophie gave a pretty frown and shut the drawing book. 'When it is finished, then I will show you. This is going to take me all day and most of tomorrow, maybe on into the evening.'

'Shouldn't you be getting ready for the ball tomorrow? The At Homes have gone well, according to your stepmother.' Henri tried to keep the wistful note out of her voice. She had spent the entire night waking from dreams where Robert had grabbed her about her waist and danced her around the room. A proper polka rather than a staid waltz.

Sophie toyed with her pencil. 'It depends on if I'm going. Mama hasn't decided yet. I've performed well at the various At Homes and have managed to keep from blotting my copybook but…am I ready? Have I learnt my lessons? Mama keeps saying it is my choice, but…'

'You must go. The ball is sure to be tremendous fun. Everyone will want to meet you.'

'There are always other balls. I want to be able to go and not have everyone watching me and whispering about the awful tangle I make of things.'

Henri's stomach tightened. Sebastian was wrong to have abused Sophie's *naïveté* in that fashion. She deserved an opportunity to prove that she had learnt her lesson. Robert risked destroying her spirit.

'Besides, you must be my eyes and ears. Your guardian has promised to dance a polka. You must make sure he does.'

'Robert never dances. He thinks it is frivolous and far from logical.' Sophie bit her lip. 'Or at least he hasn't for a long time. He used to when he was younger. I can remember peeking down at a dance once and he was there, waltzing with a distant cousin of mine. They were such a handsome couple. Her blonde looks set off his wonderfully. Everyone thought they were going to marry, but nothing came of it and she married an elderly earl. She has two little boys now. Robert has never danced since. Stepmama warned me about it.'

Henri kept her face bland as silently she urged Sophie to continue. She'd never considered that Robert must have been disappointed in love. It explained his cynical edge. And she wasn't going to think about the blonde who had made him stop dancing.

'He'll dance tomorrow night,' she said with a decisive nod. 'If you ask him.'

'Why?'

'We had a wager and he agreed that, if he lost, he'd dance with me.'

'You had a wager with my guardian. How tremendously thrilling.' Sophie put down her pencil. Her eyes gleamed. 'You must tell me everything, Henri.'

'The substance of the wager isn't important as we now have a truce, but he was willing to dance.' Henri concentrated on keeping her head still and her expression rigid as Sophie reopened her sketch book. She wasn't going to explore the hurt and betrayal. She could better understand his misguided motives now. Sophie was awfully young and easily led. 'It would be right and proper for him to dance with you. Otherwise there might be speculation.'

'He won't like that. Will you ask him for me?' Sophie added a few more rapid strokes of her pencil. Her eyes danced with mischief.

'If you like… I should have thought of it before. It is the best way to shield you from comment. Far better than forbidding you to go.'

'Are you sure you won't come as well, Henri? I know you have agreed to stay for the supper party, but you could come to the ball and see my triumph. See me dancing with Robert.'

Henri clapped her hands. It was as if a great weight had been lifted from her shoulders. She had undone some of the damage that Sebastian had wrought. Sophie wasn't frightened of going to a ball. 'My ankle still pains me, so I shall expect a full report.'

'Robert can't stand simpering ninnies. And far too many women simply look into his eyes and see his bank balance. You should hear Mama on the subject.' Sophie sucked the end of her paint brush, making it come to a point. 'Is there any chance…of you and Robert?'

'Put the matchmaking thoughts from your brain, Sophie. It doesn't become you. I've no intention of remarrying. One does not seek to replace perfection.' Henri knew her cheeks reddened slightly. The sooner she left, the sooner she could get back to her old life. There must a half-dozen people who needed her assistance. And when she returned to that life, all desire for Robert would vanish.

'I think perfection must have been very difficult to live with. I know I'm far from perfect.'

'The entire village will be expecting to see you at the ball.' Henri attempted to move the conversation away from the dangerous shoals of her relationship with Robert. 'They will have been debating for hours on the nature of your dress. Miss Armstrong is sure to have worked various old ladies into a veritable frenzy with her hints and little remarks.'

'Miss Armstrong is only being pleasant to me because Robert is unmarried. She fancies herself as Mrs Montemorcy.' Sophie looked over both her shoulders and lowered her voice. 'Stepmama is certain that Robert will get a title for services to industry. It is only a "matter of time".'

'Sophie, repeating gossip is seldom attractive.'

'But if gossip is true, what is the harm in repeating it?' Sophie fluffed up her curls. 'Miss Armstrong underestimates me. She thinks because I'm only seventeen, I'm completely brainless and do not see through people. I learnt long ago to judge between the genuine and those who sought to use me. However, her excessive civility impresses Stepmama.'

Henri stared at Sophie in astonishment. Clearly there was more to Sophie than she had first considered. She might be young, but she did notice things.

'Is there some problem?' Robert asked, coming in. He placed his top hat down on the table. 'Sophie, moderation. Your voice could be heard halfway to Corbridge, if not Hexham. What are you two discussing with such vigour?'

'Henri informs me that you'd best dance with me if you want to keep speculation about my past to a minimum. I've been explaining why you don't dance.'

Robert's eyes assessed her and deepened to a molten caramel. Henri's breath caught in her throat.

'Does she, indeed?' All warmth drained from his face. 'And Henri knows best.'

The air crackled between them. Henri was the first to drop her gaze.

'On things like this, I do,' Henri remarked as steadily as she could. 'I dare say that you can dance the first quadrille with your ward. It's for Sophie's sake, rather than mine that I ask. It'll serve to introduce her properly to the village. Your duty, Montemorcy.'

'And you know my duty?'

'Yes. This dance with Sophie.' Henri knew she lied. She wanted to dance with him and spend a few moments in his arms. But the more she thought about it, the more she knew she was correct. Robert needed to dance with his ward. He needed to lay his ghosts to rest.

He sketched a bow. 'I'll take the matter under consideration.'

Henri hated the way her stomach hurt and how much she wanted it to be her whom he danced with. 'It is good to know that you will consider it.'

'Then I am going to the ball and dancing.' Sophie clapped her hands.

'Henri appears determined that you will go.'

'Sophie believes that she needs to stay here with me and I protested.' Henri reached over and rearranged the coverlet that was protecting her skirt. 'I believe she needs to be seen and what better way to be seen than to dance the first quadrille. If you'll not dance with her, then you must nominate someone else. She mustn't be a wallflower.'

'You've expended considerable thought on this.' Robert's eyes travelled slowly down the black round gown and returned to linger on her lips.

'Just as you are determined to have me embrace the scientific method.' Henri gave him a hard look. 'And Lady Winship is sure to agree about the arrangement. Miss Armstrong always muddles her figures, going to the left when she should be circling to the right.'

'You do Miss Armstrong a disservice.'

'I think not. I've seen the damage she can work on an innocent dance. Ask Lady Winship about the Harlequin incident from last autumn.'

'Isn't my portrait of Henri good, Robert?' Sophie handed it to him with brilliant smile. 'I really think I captured her. Why she's been allowed to remain a widow all this time, I have no idea.'

'Perhaps because I want to be one,' Henri muttered under her breath. She could see what Sophie was attempting to do—arrange a match, despite her earlier protests. The approach was far from subtle. But, honestly, the thought of a match between her and Robert was ridiculous. Both were entirely set in their ways. Neither wanted marriage. She curled her fingers and refused to think about her intimate dreams about him or…the kiss she was supposed to forget, but kept remembering at the oddest of times. She'd never lingered over Edmund's kisses. And now she struggled to remember a single one.

He looked at the picture and then at Henri. The furrow between his brows deepened. Henri craned her neck, trying to get a glimpse of the portrait. She had seen some of Sophie's other work and thought it quite good, in particular a portrait of Robert where his face was relaxed and smiling. There had been something about the eyes.

'It is a passable likeness, but you have not got her mouth quite right. Thorndike's is more bow-shaped.'

'Just passable?' Sophie tried to snatch the picture from his fingers but Robert held it away from her. 'I want it to be perfect. Give me it so I can destroy it. You're a beast, Robert.'

Robert calmly folded the portrait and put it in his frock-coat pocket. 'I'll keep it safe. You may draw Henri another one, one with a bit more accuracy.'

'And I did not even get to make a judgement?' Henri asked, putting her hand on her hip in mock indignation.

'In my experience most women hate pictures of themselves.' The dimple flashed at the corner of his mouth. 'Sophie will show you when the new one is ready.'

'Am I expected now to sit for more hours?' Henri collapsed against the back of the chair.

'Is that a problem?'

'I believe I deserve a chance for fresh air before Sophie becomes a slave driver again. Is it any wonder I'm longing to dance when all I do is sit?'

'Are you longing to dance?' he asked, his eyes turning speculative.

'Yes!' she cried. 'I adore dancing. It is one of the few bonuses of being a confirmed widow. You're able to dance with those whom you choose. I was looking forward to the ball. It's for the best I'm staying here as I doubt I would've been able to resist the temptation.'

'We want your ankle to be completely healed before you leave here!' Sophie cried. 'Robert, make Henri understand. She must stay longer.'

'There has been enough posing for today,' Robert declared. 'Henri can burn off some of her energy by coming for a walk into the stable yard and you, young lady, had best get your ball gown out. You do not want to suddenly discover that you need to alter the dress, the way you did an hour before you first went to Almack's.'

'And it was far from my fault that the ruffle was wrongly placed on that dress.' Sophie rushed off to her bedroom, leaving Henri with Robert. He held out his arm.

'Is this your way of saying that I'm recovered and should consider returning to my life, despite Sophie's desire to continue playing nursemaid?' Henri asked in alarm as they walked out into the stable yard.

She had hated her first few days here, but she had come to enjoy the unaccustomed feeling of peace and tranquillity. And what if he did wish to be rid of her before the dinner party? What possible reason could he have for that? She tried and failed to imagine Robert and Miss Armstrong together.

Her footstep faltered. Instantly his arm came around her waist, holding her upright. Her entire being hummed from the contact. 'Are you certain?'

'Stiff muscles,' she said and kept her gaze straight ahead.

'You are looking very serious suddenly,' he said as they made slow progress towards the stable. 'A day or two more will hardly be a hardship. You seem to be a steadying influence on Sophie.'

Henri forced her brow to clear and her face to become a bland social smile, but her stomach knotted in disappointment. She'd half-hoped that he wanted her there for himself, but he wanted her for his ward. It was also none of her business whom Robert became involved with. She had given such things up. She was content being a widow. And if she kept telling herself that she'd believe it. 'I'm trying to puzzle out why I need to come to the stable yard, rather than taking a turn about the garden.'

'There is someone I'd like you to meet, Henri. Someone who wants to apologise.'

'Mr Teasdale wishes to apologise?' she asked, keeping her eyes firmly down on the flag stone rather than glancing up into his face. She knew her cheeks flamed. 'It has taken him long enough. It has been over a week.'

'I had to wait until I could trust him, but here he is, contrite and sorry.'

Henri turned towards where Robert pointed. There in the yard stood a mastiff dog, its head tilted to one side, tail slowly wagging. Her knees turned to jelly. She reached out and clung to Robert's arm. If she could, she'd run back to her room, but as it was she could only stand.

'That is the dog that attacked me. Mr Teasdale's dog. Why is he here?'

'My dog now.' Robert put a protective hand on her shoulder. 'Teasdale was not a fit keeper for such a magnificent beast. It is astonishing how quickly he calmed down. All Boy wanted is a bit of care and attention.'

'I will...I will take your word for it.' Henri silently measured the distance between the yard and the house. If she walked very quickly, she might make it back safely. But now every waking moment would be filled with dread. 'Was there any need for me to meet this creature? I could have happily gone for the rest of my life never encountering it again except in my nightmares! He savaged my leg!'

'Knowing the dog better, I think he was trying to rescue you after you fell. He wanted you off that road. He saw you fall and thought to rescue you from the post-coach.'

'He did?' Henri didn't attempt to hide her incredulity.

'I thought once you'd met Boy properly, you would cease to be afraid,' he said quietly, holding her elbow in an unrelenting grip. 'It is no good going through life being scared—you must confront your fear head-on.'

'And you accuse me of being high-handed!' Henri shifted uneasily. Robert had no right to do this to her. 'It might attack me again.'

'I'm giving you the opportunity to overcome your fear. I don't want you to become a prisoner in your house, afraid to go out of the house for fear of meeting a dog.'

Henri tried to ignore the perspiration breaking out on her forehead. All she could see was the dog's jaws. It was unfair of Robert not to warn her. Now she'd have to confess about her fear and he'd laugh. 'I am not overly fond of dogs, it's true. Can I go back in now? It is a bit much for my ankle. It is throbbing. I think I need to sit down. Yes, that's it. My ankle is poorly.'

'Any dog frightens you?' He spun her around so he was looking directly into her eyes. 'Why didn't you tell me before? You can admit weaknesses, Henri. It means people are less likely to make mistakes and errors of judgement.'

'It is hardly something one brings up in casual conversation.' Henri took a steadying breath. It was far easier now that she was looking at Robert rather than at the mastiff. She had to hope that he did not think her a complete ninny and mock her like Sebastian always did.

Haltingly, she continued, 'I even had to get rid of the pug puppies Sebastian left the last time. They nipped and jumped up. One drew blood. And travelling up to Corbridge was a nightmare. My aunt loved them, but the thought of having a dog in the house, particularly those ones as they tended to throw up... I had to persuade Lady Winship to take them.'

'Puppies sometimes nip if they are overexcited or not trained properly.' His eyes shone amber, but there was only concern. 'Is there any particular reason you don't like dogs?'

She took a deep breath, hating how childish she was going to sound. 'Sebastian once dared me to walk along the high ridge by the hounds when I was about ten. Sensibly I refused. He enlisted Edmund in the scheme. They both walked along the high ridge without a problem. They both kept on and on at me until I tried. I missed my step and fell in. The dogs tore at my skirt and I screamed.' Henri bit her lip. She risked another quick glance at the dog. Instead of jumping about like he had done, the dog had settled down with its large head on its paws. 'Sebastian thought it would be amusing to see what would happen if he left me there to fight them off alone... The more I screamed for help, the harder he laughed, and the more aggressive the dogs became. I tried to run, but one of the hounds knocked me down. Edmund rescued me when he realised that the dogs were about to tear me limb from limb. And I loved him for it.'

His face became thunderous. 'Did they get in trouble?'

'Sebastian swore us to secrecy. After that, Edmund decided to become my protector.'

Henri looked at her hands and waited to hear his scornful laughter. It was such an inconsequential fear. Sebastian sometimes teased her about it.

Robert continued to look at her with concern.

'It was a long time ago,' she said into the silence. 'And I *do* hate still being afraid.'

'Will you meet Boy or is it too much?' He pointed towards the dog. 'See, he is trying to be as inconspicuous as possible.'

Henri turned round, ready to refuse. But the dog put his paws over his nose, hiding his face. The effect was so comical that Henri struggled not to laugh.

With Robert standing next to her, the dog could hardly harm her. Henri risked a breath. She trusted Robert to look after her.

'I will meet him, but only to show you that I am not paralysed by fear.'

Robert whistled and the dog instantly trotted up, looking far more like a small horse than a conventionally sized dog. At Robert's signal, the dog dropped down on its haunches and held out its right paw.

'If you would just take his paw.' Henri screwed up her eyes and held out her hand. Robert's strong fingers curled around it and held it tight. 'Look at me, Henrietta Thorndike. Not the dog, at me. There are tricks you can learn to show a dog you are the master. It is all in how you approach the dog and the tone of your voice.'

Slowly Henri opened her eyes and found herself staring into his.

'I want to do this, but…'

'The only way to stop being afraid is to conquer your fear. Once you have done it one time, it becomes easier.'

'How do you know?' Henri asked.

Shadows invaded his eyes. 'I do. When I was young, after my mother died, I used to be afraid of many things. But I learnt how to overcome them. My father insisted that I ignore my emotions and put my faith in cool logic. People depended on me to make the right decision with the foundry and my other businesses. I learnt and it became easier. Trust the facts, not the fear, Henri.'

Afraid of many things. She found it difficult to imagine Robert ever being afraid and, more to the point, to be willing to admit it. 'Even dancing?'

His face became remote. 'I've never been afraid of dancing. I simply choose to forgo the dubious pleasure of having my feet stepped on while candle wax drips on my head.'

'Sophie said you used to be a marvellous dancer. She used to watch you dance when she was a little girl.'

'Sophie has altogether too loose of a tongue. It was a long time ago.'

'You should get used to it again. If I can meet a dog, you can dance. It would mean a lot to…to Sophie.'

'The two matters are unrelated.'

'Are they?' Henri crossed her arms. Trust the facts, indeed. 'They seem to be the same thing. You want me to do something I fear, but at the same time you wish to avoid something you fear.'

'Your view differs from mine. I'm not afraid of dancing. I simply no longer have time for something that frivolous.'

She gave an uneasy glance at Boy's teeth and the way his tongue lapped at them as if he were sizing her up for another meal. 'If I meet Boy, will you at least dance with Sophie?'

His amber eyes blazed at her. 'Prove it to me first, Henri.'

Henri drew in her breath. 'I can't make any promises, but I will try.'

A small light of respect came into his eyes and a great bath of warmth infused her body. She wasn't going to do this for anyone. She was going to do this for herself.

'Crouch down and hold your hand out palm upwards. Remember he has fears as well, but he wants to be your friend.'

Slowly Henri advanced forwards until her hand touched the dog's velvet nose. The soft swoosh of breath tickled her palm, but the dog made no move towards her.

Behind she could sense Robert; even though he made no move to touch her, she knew he was there, willing her on.

With a hesitant finger she touched the dog's ear and saw the massive eyes soften. 'I accept your apology, Boy.'

The dog gave a low woof and it was all Henri could to keep upright and not run.

'He is saying that he is pleased.' Robert put his hand on top of hers. 'Stroke his head. A firm but gentle touch.'

She reached out a hand, hesitated. She fumbled for her reticule and its good-luck charm, wincing as she realised that it was lying up in the sickroom. 'I'm not sure about this. The omens aren't good.' The words seemed feeble.

'Omens? You don't need to rely on any superstitious nonsense.

One thing more. Allow him to become your friend.' There was something in his eyes. 'Please.'

'Why? I think it would be better if we discussed Sophie and the ball. Have you made a list of eligible men who could partner her for the first dance if you will not?'

'No.'

Henri blinked. 'No? I'm certain if you sent word to Lady Winship, she'd be more than happy to help.'

'Every time you want to divert attention, you start on about someone else's problem. Your problem, your fears.'

Henri opened and closed her mouth several times, trying to think of the appropriate response. 'That is preposterous nonsense.'

Robert reached out a hand, but she ignored his outstretched fingers. He was asking her to do far more than meet the dog. He was asking her to change her life and put her past behind her—to stop caring for others and start looking to her own happiness. And she knew in that heartbeat that she wasn't ready to take the risk. What if she lost her heart to him? Could she live with that? She looked into his eyes and saw pity at her hesitation.

'Is it so very hard to do, Thorndike, to let go of your fear?' he asked softly.

'You are asking far too much of me.'

Without waiting for an answer, Henri turned and fled back to the house, running with an unsteady gait.

Robert allowed his hand to fall back at his side and knelt down beside the dog. Boy nuzzled his hand.

'I did it wrong, Boy. I misjudged it,' he said. 'I pushed her too hard.'

Chapter Eight

The next morning, leaning on a cane, Henri knocked on the door to Robert's study. She had spent most of the night thinking about the incident with Boy, going over it in her mind. She had been wrong to fling those accusations at Robert. She had read far too much into his words. She had gone beyond the bounds of propriety and had behaved like a spoilt child, not much older than Sophie, taking to her room and refusing to come down for supper as her ankle hurt too much.

'I wanted to apologise for my behaviour in the stable yard yesterday,' she said, concentrating on the way his long fingers grasped the fountain pen rather than on his face.

'Think nothing of it.' His warm voice rolled over her. Somehow, his making light of it made her feel worse. She wasn't asking for favours from him. 'It happens. I asked too much of you. Your fear is real. It was wrong of me to discount it. I will remember that for the future.'

Henri stood still, shocked. She'd been prepared for scorn and Robert appeared to be understanding. She clenched her fist.

'I want to try again. I gave in to the fear. Running away solved nothing.' She smoothed the folds of her skirts, hating the way her heart skipped a beat. She wanted to see the regard in his eyes rather than pity. The thing she hated most of all was pity. 'Please can you help? Can you give me a second chance with Boy?'

His face became a wreath of smiles. The tension in Henri's shoulders eased.

'There's no shame in asking for help. It's what friends are for.'

'But I hate doing so. Asking for help makes you weak.' She licked her dry lips. Henri thought about her mother and how she kept demanding attention all the time. 'The last thing I want to be is a clinging vine.'

'*Clinging vine* are not exactly the words that spring to mind when I think of you.'

'Oh, what—*obstinate* and *stubborn*?'

'Possibly.' The dimple in the corner of his mouth deepened. 'Stop fishing for compliments!'

'Only you would understand what a compliment *obstinate* is!'

He offered her his arm, but she refused, gesturing with her stick. 'We people of independent mind walk under our own power.'

'You're determined to prove your point.'

When they reached the yard, Boy clambered to his feet the instant she saw him. He strained slightly against the chain. But this morning, Henri could see he was only excited, rather than trying to hurt her.

Slowly she edged her way towards him, holding out her hand. She wanted to lay her fear to rest, rather than hug it to her. She could change. Her past didn't have to be a prison.

Gingerly she touched the dog's head. The fur was silky smooth under her fingers. The dog settled down at her feet. 'Pleased to meet you, Boy, again. I hope we can be friends now that you have been tamed.'

'He wanted a bit of understanding and to know what the rules were,' Robert murmured, his breath tickling her ear. Henri's pulse started to do strange things.

'Back to your rules.' She struggled to breathe normally. 'You're only comfortable when you're setting them.'

'They do help keep things in order. Boy reminds me of my first dog, Jack. Jack was a faithful dog, always following my footsteps until he died.'

'Were you upset when he did?'

'Utterly distraught, but my mother gave me another dog for my birthday. And I found that I loved him because of Jack.'

'So the dog wasn't a replacement?'

'I wanted a dog in my life. There is something about having a dog to come home to. And the risk of losing it was not as terrible as not having a dog.'

Henri studied the pattern of the cobblestones. What he said might be true for dogs, but not for people. She'd never wanted an abstract husband to share her life with. Just any man wouldn't do. Edmund was irreplaceable. And losing him had hurt too much.

She liked Robert. Anything more would be complicating things and the last thing she needed in her life was more complications, more possibility of being hurt.

'I will take your word for it,' she breathed.

The dog lifted its paw and placed it on her knee, breaking the spell. 'How did you tame him so quickly?'

'After a fashion, but I fear he has not learnt all his manners.' Robert gestured and the dog lay down at their feet. 'He has left a dirt print on your dress.'

Henri started to rub it, but it seemed to get worse. A tiny cry of frustration escaped her lips.

'Allow me.' His fingers moved hers away and, with a few deft strokes, the patch of dirt was gone. Where his fingers had touched her gown, it seemed a warm sensation grew within her. He stood, unmoving. The gentle breeze ruffled his dark hair. 'You're free from blemish.'

'Would that everything was so easily solved!' Henri gave a smile and turned back towards the house. Her limbs trembled. It would be so easy to turn into his arms and lift her lips to his. This time she wanted a proper heart-stopping kiss, rather than a gentle brush. But with all the stable hands and gardeners about, it would be madness. One simple locking of lips in public and her entire reputation could be in jeopardy.

'The best things are worth waiting for.' He kept step with her slow pace. Her entire being was aware of him. She wished she dared lean on his arm, but instead concentrated on moving steadily.

'Has Sophie sorted out her gown?' Henri asked when they had nearly reached the door. 'Will she dance with whomever she wishes? With Sebastian? Or will she be forced to cut him dead?'

'It is up to Sophie whom she dances with. Cawburn has not had the courtesy to answer her letter. Neither has he visited you here.'

Henri kept her shoulders steady. 'He hates sickrooms. Always has. He never visited Edmund once he found out how ill Edmund was. Edmund forgave him, of course, so I had to.'

He shook his head. 'That doesn't excuse him. He should have.'

'No, it doesn't.' Henri regarded the brass door handle of the front door. Faced with Robert's concern, she found no easy lie sprang to her lips. Sebastian and her aunt's not visiting did hurt, but she understood what they were like, and once she returned home, she knew they would react with concern. There were other more important topics to discuss. 'Have you spoken to Sophie?'

'You told me to listen to Sophie and I have.' He looked at her with a steady eye. 'Yesterday. After you walked away. I needed to know the truth about what happened with your cousin.'

Henri started. Robert had spoken with Sophie and, what was more, believed her. Her work here was done. As soon as she could find a good excuse, she'd go before the supper party. And then her world could go back to how it was. The only trouble was that she wanted to be here with him. She drew a deep breath. 'What is your conclusion?'

'She has done nothing to be ashamed of. I can trust her judgement. She needs to be properly fêted at the ball. I will make the sacrifice and dance, Thorndike.'

'And you are coming to the ball, Lady Thorndike?' Miss Armstrong asked with a faint frown as the servants finished serving the dessert. Throughout supper she had kept peering at Henri and finally it appeared Miss Armstrong's curiosity had the better of her manners. 'Lady Thorndike, I have always said that you had the potential to lead fashion if only you'd give up your devotion to mauve. The dress is distinctly—'

'I like mauve,' Henrietta said between gritted teeth. Potential to lead fashion, indeed. She *set* fashion in Corbridge. She gave advice on fashion. Her enforced absence from the social scene had obviously given some people ideas. And mauve was practical. She had simply exchanged the day bodice of her mauve skirt for the evening one with a décolleté neckline trimmed with a profusion of lace.

'I myself am attempting a negligent attitude with a Grecian scarf worn over a Spanish bombazine and a Cossack petticoat. It is the very essence of this Season's cosmopolitan style,' Mrs Ravel confided in a stage whisper. 'What influenced your dress?'

'Northumbrian weather,' Henri said firmly.

She heard a sound of choked laughter from Robert's end of the table.

Mrs Ravel's brow puckered as the remark appeared to sail over her head. 'But will you change your mind about the ball, Henrietta? We do have room in the carriage.'

'My ankle will give way if I stand for a long period, so I've sent my regrets.' Henri practised perfecting the bland society smile. 'Doctor Lumley confirmed this view earlier this afternoon.'

'However, Lady Thorndike insisted there was no need to cancel our little supper party,' Robert interrupted, an urbane smile on his face. 'I'm very pleased that she decided to grace the table with her wit and charm.'

'Quite sensible to give the ball a miss. One must always follow the good doctor's instructions. You were kind to ask the dear doctor.' Miss Armstrong gave a decided nod, making the trio of feathers on her headdress sway. Her hair was distinctly more yellow since the last time Henri encountered the woman and her gown's décolleté neckline bordered on indecency, even if Miss Armstrong did keep it hidden underneath a lacy shawl. 'I know I value his advice, but he is terribly busy with his practice. So many patients to see, so little time for anything else.'

Henri kept her mouth shut and exchanged an amused glance with Robert. Did he remember about how Miss Armstrong had feverishly pursued the good doctor last spring? Or he had forgotten?

'I never planned to go against the doctor's wishes, but they did coincide with mine.' Henri inclined her head. 'I'm looking forward to hearing all the doings. Sophie has promised that she will tell me every detail.'

'I am sure you had a hand in her decision, dear Mr Montemorcy. Lady Thorndike is well-known for her stubbornness and her lack of regard for her personal health. She goes out visiting the poor in all sorts of weather.' Miss Armstrong fluttered her lashes and her voice rivalled treacle for its sweetness as she toyed with the few final bites of the pudding. 'After all, how could she refuse you such a simple request? You did play the Good Samaritan. I suppose, in the circumstances, it was necessary.'

'Robert has always been very good to those less fortunate than himself,' Mrs Ravel said.

'I rather think it was how fortunate I was to have Lady Thorndike grace my home. She has provided the Ravels with interesting conversation.' Robert inclined his head and his gaze lingered on Henri, travelling slowly down her neckline. 'There is nothing unfortunate about Lady Thorndike.'

'I agree wholeheartedly,' Sophie called out from where she sat between two elder statesmen of the village. 'Lady Thorndike does add a certain lustre to the supper.'

Her stepmother gave her a quelling look, but Sophie appeared to be unrepentant.

Henri forced her attention on to the flickering candles, rather than looking at Robert. Miss Armstrong's insinuation that somehow she had caused Robert to rescue her and that she was imposing caused her blood to boil!

The only thing she was waiting for was for Doctor Lumley to inform her that it was safe to return home. She had no desire to be here at this dinner party, making small talk when she was incredibly aware of the man sitting a little way from her. Robert Montemorcy had a knack of complicating her life.

'I was lucky Mr Montemorcy happened to be there,' she said, adopting her best social voice.

'Some people seem to have a way with accidents,' Mrs Ravel said. 'I'm dreadful. I never know what to do. Far better to let cooler heads take charge is my philosophy.'

'People rarely plan to have an accident, Mrs Ravel.' Henri gripped her fan a bit tighter. A little over a week being looked after and everyone appeared to forget that she was extremely capable. She'd gone back to the intolerable cotton-wool. 'I actively try to avoid them.'

'But Mr Montemorcy was certainly a hero in rescuing you.' Miss Armstrong's feathers bobbed in agreement. 'Corbridge is lucky to have someone like you, Mr Montemorcy.'

'And I didn't act the hero either. I simply grabbed the dog's collar and prevented anything else happening,' Robert said smoothly. 'Doing what is right takes little thought. Had Mr Teasdale paid attention to Lady Thorndike's earlier suggestions, it is doubtful if the dog would've ever escaped.'

Henri exchanged glances with Robert and a warm glow infused

into her being. He understood. It had been a long time since anyone had understood her in that way.

'Was the dog destroyed?' Miss Armstrong gave a small shiver and pulled her lace shawl tighter about her shoulders while simultaneously letting it drop at the front to reveal the depth of her décolleté. 'I would've demanded the dog be destroyed if it had attacked me. You would have done that for me, wouldn't you, Mr Montemorcy?'

Henri's stomach clenched. Miss Armstrong seemed determined to stake her claim to Robert. Whereas the situation would have amused her a few weeks ago, now she wanted to make a cutting remark.

'Would you, Miss Armstrong?' he said, gesturing towards the hall. 'It's fortunate for Boy that he attacked Lady Thorndike as she possesses a much more forgiving nature.'

'You mean the animal remains alive!' Miss Armstrong gasped. 'I have need of my smelling salts.'

'Mr Montemorcy has taken ownership of the dog,' Henri said and watched Miss Armstrong flush further in indignation. 'He is training it. The dog has entirely changed.'

'But…but…dogs like that are not to be trusted,' Miss Armstrong cried. 'You must be mistaken, Lady Thorndike. Mr Montemorcy, please tell Lady Thorndike to stop her funning.'

'Mr Montemorcy has worked miracles with the dog.' Henri pushed back her chair and stood. She gave a perfunctory curtsy towards the assembled group. 'We've become friends. I believe Boy was attempting to rescue me rather than trying to eat me.'

'You have made friends with the dog?' Miss Armstrong screeched. 'But I thought you hated dogs, dear Lady Thorndike. It's why Lady Winship had to take all the pugs…'

'All Boy wanted was a kind word and a full belly.' Henri ignored Miss Armstrong's interjection. Lady Winship *had* wanted those pugs in her life. She simply hadn't realised it the first time she encountered them. 'Mr Montemorcy is its acknowledged master now. And he assures me that the dog was trying to rescue me from the post-coach.'

'I should have considered that Mr Montemorcy would be masterful. He is like that.' Miss Armstrong fluttered her lashes and allowed her shawl to slip. 'I'm most impressed on how the house has been improved. It was never like this in the squire's day.'

Henri ground her teeth, holding back a swift retort. She would not sink to Miss Armstrong's level. 'The one thing I shall miss is seeing Mr Montemorcy dance this evening.'

He gave her a startled look.

'Have you forgotten? You are to dance with Sophie.'

'And with me as well, I hope,' Miss Armstrong cooed.

At least she would be spared Miss Armstrong's triumphant look when she led Robert out on the dance floor. Henri looked from Miss Armstrong to Robert in his immaculate evening clothes, which fitted his form precisely, highlighting the breadth of his shoulders and the elegant curve of his calf. Everyone would whisper when the pair took the floor and say what a charming couple they made. And the words would be passed from gathering to gathering in the weeks to come and she would have to endure it with a smile. She froze, listening to her sour thoughts.

She was jealous. How had that happened? She had sworn that she'd never look at a man again, not in that way. What was wrong with her? Henri put her hand to her head and tried to regain her balance. She might feel friendship for Mr Montemorcy, but nothing more. Her heart remained buried with Edmund. It had to be. Edmund was the love of her life. She'd known that when she was twelve, and she was steadfast. If her heart was changeable, what did that say about her? Her mother had always sworn that, unless she was careful, she'd become a flighty scatterbrain with no more consistency than a flea. Until now she thought she'd avoided that fate. Her hands shook.

'If you'll excuse me, I shall leave you to go to the ball now. For my part, I shall go to the library and discover a good book.'

'Lady Thorndike is known for her reading of improving tomes,' Miss Armstrong twittered, fluttering her fan, but her eyes were cold and hard. 'Treatises on the new farming methods and such like. Lady Thorndike has pretensions of being a bluestocking like her aunt. You will have to take care, Mr Montemorcy, and see that Miss Ravel does not fall under her spell. Bluestockings do find it difficult to find a husband.'

'I had no difficulties.' Henri glared at Miss Armstrong.

Miss Armstrong stared back at her defiantly.

'I fear you're mistaken, Miss Armstrong, intelligence in a woman is something to be prized,' Robert said.

Miss Armstrong's mouth puckered as if she had suddenly swallowed something distasteful. 'My mistake.'

'I like to keep informed, but I'm far from averse to reading popular novels, as Mr Montemorcy is well aware.' Henri took a deep breath and controlled her temper.

'Why should Mr Montemorcy be aware of *your* reading taste?' Miss Armstrong asked, unfurling her fan, but her eyes shot daggers.

'Lady Thorndike has been a guest here for over a week, Miss Armstrong. Such things as a taste for the popular are hard to keep hidden.' Robert's eyes twinkled at Henri, warming her. He caught her hand and lifted it to his lips, brushing it. Warmth flooded through Henri and she pulled away. 'I made sure that *Jane Eyre* was delivered earlier today, Lady Thorndike. It struck me that you might wish to amuse yourself while everyone else was at the ball. Even bluestockings need a break from treaties on cow husbandry.'

'You are such a perfect host, Mr Montemorcy. Not many men would be as thoughtful as you,' Miss Armstrong said, drawing her arm through Robert's and leading him firmly away.

'I do my best, Miss Armstrong.' His eyes sparkled with a myriad of brown, caramel and gold. 'Enjoy the book, Thorndike. It is more edifying than *Cattle Husbandry on the North Yorkshire Moor*.'

Henri stared after the pair for a few minutes as the remainder of the party made ready to leave. Her pulse still pounded. Was it simple kindness or something more that had made Robert send for the book? She had never met anyone like him before—a combination of exasperating stubbornness and the capacity for supreme thoughtfulness. Not what she expected at all. Henri put her hand to the locket that Edmund had given her on her sixteenth birthday, and found the familiar outlines provided little comfort.

Chapter Nine

For the first half-hour, Henri attempted to read, but discovered she was reading the same set of paragraphs over and over, never quite getting beyond the fifth page of *Jane Eyre*. Her mind kept skittering back to the supper party, the things that were said and, more importantly, not said. Miss Armstrong had been too bold by half.

Henri's eyes narrowed and studied the glowing embers of the fire. She should be able to discern her intention. Normally she was fairly astute at understanding the undercurrents.

Then there was the matter of how Robert looked in his evening clothes. Each gesture and facial expression had to be considered and reconsidered again. Had he been humouring her?

When the clock struck the hour, she realised she had been hovering halfway between sleep and waking. Her brain was full of confused images of Robert inviting her into his arms, and then Sebastian and Sophie, or rather Sebastian ruining Sophie at the ball and somehow destroying her friendship with Robert. The thought unnerved her.

Henri sat up straighter, pulled an offending hairpin from her head and allowed her hair to cascade down. Perhaps she should have gone to the ball and endured the looks of pity and questions about her health. Then she'd have been there, ready to forestall any disaster.

She reopened *Jane Eyre* and started with the preface to the second edition. The words—*Conventionality is not morality*—leapt out at her.

Was Currer Bell correct? Had she confused the two?

She read on and slowly but surely this time Bell's words over-powered her and she had trouble believing the book could have been written by a man. There was something that called to her, enabling her to sympathise with Jane's plight with her dreadful aunt. She knew what it was like to have others hate you or never consider you good enough. All she could do was carry on reading and turning the pages, hoping Jane got the happy ending that she richly deserved.

A door closed and she jumped, sending the book crashing to the floor with a distinct thump.

'You're awake.' Robert came into the dimly lit library resplendent in his evening clothes. He had looked debonair when going out to the ball earlier, but now with his stock slightly askew, and his coat thrown over his shoulder, he was even more handsome. The fire cast shadows on his face, giving an intimate air to the room. 'I'd wondered how our modern-day Cinderella-sitting-by-the-fire fared.'

'Hardly Cinderella. It was my choice not to go to the ball.' Henri pointed her toes and circled her feet. Her ankle ached slightly, but the bandages gave it firm support.

The house appeared to hold its breath. Every particle of her was aware of him and how he moved. She found it impossible to look away from his hands. What would it be like to be held in those arms?

'You were missed, Thorndike.'

'I'm sure Lady Winship coped. She'd Miss Armstrong's help.'

'I lost count of the people who accused me of keeping you from your duty, particularly when the garlands collapsed again. They want your sound advice.'

'You're being kind.'

'Far from it. Mrs Charlton accused me of holding you hostage. She desperately wants your advice on whether or not to encourage a junior officer's suit for her middle daughter.'

'And what did you say?'

He gave a conspiratorial smile and took a step closer. 'That you'll be back to your old self soon.'

The warm glow of the oil lamp combined with the fire turned his skin a ruddy gold and Henri was suddenly aware of her tumbled-down hair and the way her evening gown had slipped off one shoulder. She debated whether it would be better to pretend she had not noticed or to do the gown up. She opted for the pretence and raised her chin so that she stared directly into his fire-glowing eyes. 'Where's Sophie and Mrs Ravel? Did they leave the ball early as well? Did anything untoward happen?'

'Sophie remained at the ball under her stepmother's eagle eye. Miss Armstrong and Dorothy appear to have become the best of friends.' Robert tilted his head to one side, trying to assess Henri's mood. Her being downstairs was a gift from the gods. All the way back home, he had thought of how she might look with her black hair flowing free, and the firelight touching her porcelain skin. Reality was a thousand times better than his imagination.

Why had she stayed awake? To ask Sophie about her encounter with Cawburn? Or something more?

Robert pushed the question away unvoiced. This moment was not about questioning her motives as she'd only speak about other people. It was about being with Henri. He had witnessed the frosty reception Sophie had given Cawburn—not quite a cut, but certainly something bordering on it. He had been correct to trust Henri's instincts and to deliver the letter. He had the added insurance of holding Cawburn's paper. On the balance of probabilities, Sophie was safe from the bounder.

'Last seen Sophie was the new belle of Corbridge. Doctor Lumley admirably fought his way through the crush of admirers to bring her an ice.'

'Doctor Lumley? Who is suffering from a propensity to match-make now?' Her voice held a teasing note.

'Any match is Sophie's choice, not mine.' Robert took another step near her.

'Sophie would be wasted on London.' Henri leant forwards and a sudden spark from the fire highlighted the vulnerable hollow of her throat. 'I don't think she wants a title.'

'Practical advice from the matchmaker-in-chief.'

'Practical? You do wonders for a woman's confidence.'

'Far better to be practical.' Robert watched, mesmerised, as the firelight slid over her skin, caressing it. 'Or are you fishing for compliments? Would you rather I say that you were far too vibrant and alive?'

'No, no, *practical* will suffice.' Her tongue flicked over her bow-shaped lips. 'Was the ball not to *your* taste? Is that why you returned early? Did you dance?'

'I danced the opening quadrille with Sophie and discovered I enjoyed it. She will be giving you a report in the morning.'

'Did you stand on her feet?'

'I know the figure, Henri.' Robert took a step closer to where she sat. Every step he danced, he knew he was holding the wrong woman in his arms. The right woman was here in this room.

At his approach, Henri's eyes lit with a sudden deep fire, trans-forming her face. If she had been at the ball, every man would have turned towards her. There was something about the curve of her mouth that promised sensual delights for the right man. Henri's head and shoulders emerged from the froth of lace much as Venus must have emerged from the sea. The vision had played on his brain through supper and the ball, and he'd once absently answered a question from Mr Charlton with the one word—*lace*. His fingers itched to unwrap the complicated layers. And there were a hundred good reasons why he should turn around and say goodnight. But one good reason why he should entice her to dance with him: he wanted to.

'However, as I did the figures, I realised that I also owed you a dance. You've refrained from meddling.'

'And have seen others attempt to do it with far less finesse.' Henri's mouth twisted and he knew how hard and painful it must have been to see Miss Armstrong's attempts earlier this evening. 'And it's only by lack of opportunity. I should never have insisted on that particular forfeit.'

The pulse in the hollow of her throat beat more quickly and he knew she was following his lead.

'I keep my promises, Henri.' Robert waited, silently willing her to take the next step. He intended to have her properly in his arms and see if reality matched his dreams.

'Circumstances intervened; besides, I gave advice about Sophie and my cousin. Some might call that meddling.' Henri kept her voice light as her heart skipped a beat. Did he truly mean to dance with her here in this room? Now, with all the servants asleep or lightly dozing at their posts? The notion was preposterous, but tremendously exciting at the same time.

A tiny sane part of her told her to flee to her room, but she continued to sit in the winged chair and watch him. *Conventionality is different from morality.* The words she had read earlier thrummed in her brain. Conventionality demanded she leave, but she wasn't doing anything wrong or immoral.

'You did not try to engineer a match between your cousin and Sophie—quite the reverse.' His voice deepened and flowed over her. Inside her, bubbles fizzled and sparkled, making her feel wonderfully alive. 'We shall dance, Henri.'

'At another ball.' Henri struggled to keep the disappointment from her voice. She longed to know when and where. Her entire body tingled with anticipation.

'Tonight.'

'There is no music here.'

A dimple played in his cheek, giving a devilish aspect to his countenance. 'And your sole objection to dancing with me now in this room is the lack of music.'

'It's a major one. Without music, how can one keep the time?' The tension in Henri's shoulders eased. He was teasing her now. He knew as well as she did the impossibility of the enterprise. But the image of them waltzing around the room with his firm hand on her waist kept filling her brain. And she knew she had to leave or she'd succumb to the temptation. The trouble was that she did not want to leave. She wanted to be in his arms. She wanted to circle the room to the imaginary violins. For once, she wanted to experience the romance.

Henri made one last attempt to be sensible and rose from her chair. 'Unless you happen to have brought a few spare musicians back with you, I shall bid you goodnight.'

'I can do something better than that.' He gestured towards a small rosewood box. 'Behold your music.'

'Music? From a box?' Henri tilted her head. Had Robert partaken of far too much punch? 'What sort of gullible fool do you take me for? You cannot get music from a box.'

He put his hands behind his back and rocked back on his heels, like a young schoolboy. 'Would you care to wager?'

Slowly Henri shook her head. 'I'm prepared to be amazed. You are far too confident. Demonstrate this musical box of yours and we shall see if it produces music fit for dancing.'

'Very wise.'

He gave a few deft turns of a key. 'It is a musical box. I picked it up in Switzerland a few years ago when I visited the Continent.

My father had a mechanical bird that used to sing when I was a young boy, but I broke it about the time my mother died. My father was very angry with me at the time. The box commemorates my first success. Unfortunately my father died before I could bring it home.'

His first success and he wanted to make amends for something he had inadvertently damaged. The father who had told him to trust logic rather than his feelings. Only his father never knew. Henri put a hand over her mouth. She wanted to gather him in her arms and wipe the vulnerable look from his eyes. 'You never speak of your past.'

'I find it better to live for tomorrow's hope. The future holds much more promises than the past's disappointments.'

'But the past…is important,' she said, trying to keep the fizzing feeling from exploding.

He lifted the inlaid lid and a sweet lilting melody came out of the box, filling the room. Henri laughed, enchanted, and the bubbles seemed to enter her bloodstream. 'The box is playing music. Actual proper music, Robert.'

'You like it, then?' he asked with a note of barely suppressed excitement.

'I have never seen such a thing before, but it is wonderful.' Henri regarded the spinning cylinders. Her body swayed in time to the music.

'And your objection to dancing with me is?'

Henri ran her tongue over her parched lips. 'Can there be any objection?'

Her bare hand fit snugly into his gloved one. It would only be a few steps or once around the room at most. It was not a proper dance lasting a half-hour. But even still, her pulse beat faster.

Robert's hand went to her waist and held her as they slowly circled around the room. All the while Henri was conscience of only him—the way his hand felt against her waist, the sandalwood scent that teased her nostrils and how he moved, his leg brushing against her skirts.

She missed her step and clung to him to keep herself from falling. His arm instantly tightened, pulling her more fully against his body.

'Does your ankle pain you, Henri?'

'No, it is stronger than I thought it would be.' She leant back slightly, putting a little air between them. 'Shall we continue?'

His lips brushed her temple. 'The music has stopped.'

'It has?' she whispered, but did not move away from him. Her entire being trembled. Leave now and she'd regret it for the rest of her life. She wanted to be here, with him.

'It has,' he confirmed and his arm drew her more firmly into his embrace. Her curves hit the hard planes of his body, moulding to him, and he held her against him. 'What shall we do?'

In response, she lifted her mouth and put her arm about his neck. His lips touched hers—warm and inviting. Time stopped. And all her being concentrated on this one point of contact. She parted her lips and tasted the sweetness of his mouth. An intense flame flickered though her. Their tongues touched and tangled. Slowly explored.

All the pent-up demand and hunger of her dreams coursed through her, blotting out everything else. The only thing that mattered was the sensation of his mouth moving against hers. And she knew she wanted to live for the now rather than looking over her shoulder, wondering what some unknown person might think about her behaviour. This wasn't wicked. It was wonderful.

Somewhere in the depths of the house a door slammed, startling her, bringing her back to sensibility.

Using all of her will-power, Henri stepped away from his arms. The cold air rushed around her and she shivered slightly. Of all the mistakes she had made, this was potentially the largest and most life altering. Her stomach knotted in confusion. 'I must…I must retire for the night.'

'As you wish…' He stood, unmoving, neither preventing her from leaving nor asking her to stay.

Henri crossed her arms over her aching breasts. 'What else is there to do?'

A distinct gleam came into his eyes. 'As you say, what else? What else could we possibly *do*? It's late. Your choice.'

Henri knew her cheeks flamed. She had been wrong to turn her head and invite him to kiss her. She was the one who had behaved like a courtesan.

She ran her tongue over her aching lips, trying to remember what she was, trying to recapture that sense that she was destined to die a widow, but it was gone. And in its place brand-new feelings coursed through her, shocking her.

She'd spent her whole adult life being one person and tonight she learnt she'd lived a lie. Her feelings for Edmund had never included dark passion and that wasn't her fault. Desire and temptation flooded through her. And looking under hooded eyes at him, she knew she couldn't risk confiding any of this to him. It was all too new. She needed time to make sense of it, to make sure that she was not going to get hurt again.

He stood there, looking at her. His eyes were dilated and she knew the kiss had affected him as well. But he made no move to recapture her.

'I'm overtired.' Her voice echoed in the silence, far too high and shrill, and she knew she was taking the coward's way out. 'I will retire on my own. Please give my apologies to Sophie and Mrs Ravel. I had wanted to greet them when they returned. The news of Sophie's triumph will have to wait.'

'I'm not keeping you here.'

The firelight threw a shadow on his face. She wished he had protested. Or drawn her into his arms again. Her stomach knotted.

She wanted to lay her head against his chest and listen to the steady thump of his heart. She made herself go and pick up her discarded book.

'I know.' Conventionality might not be morality but she knew it kept her safe. 'I've trespassed on your hospitality. You returned for a reason.'

'You are a guest. You have behaved impeccably. It is I who should beg your pardon.'

'No pardon is needed…on either side.' Her voice sounded breathy to her ears. 'We remain in the utmost civility…as friends.'

'It is good to have you as a friend.' His rich voice filled the room. 'I would hate to miss our discussions. We haven't fully explored the implications of the scientific method.'

Relief flooded through her. He wanted to see her again. He did not think her wanton. And she could think about her response, instead of having the room spinning, pushing her towards him. 'I look forward to it.'

A tiny smile crossed his features. 'Then it's settled. Our acquaintance will continue.'

'I'd like that.'

'Until the next time, Henri.' His rich voice floated after her. 'Sleep well. There is no need to fear—anything.'

Henri stumbled up the stairs, not daring to turn around and see him. If he held out his arms, she'd be in them. Robert Montemorcy was far too tempting. Once she was back in the safety of Aunt Frances's, then she could remember all the reasons why Edmund was irreplaceable. Suddenly Edmund's kisses seemed like watered milk compared to the smooth intoxication of Robert's mouth moving against hers. Henri raised her eyes to the gilt ceiling, trying to get her racing heart under control. This time, she'd grown up. This time, she had learnt her lesson. This time she kept her heart safe.

Chapter Ten

Henri stood in the New Lodge's entranceway, her bonnet set firmly on her head. The carriage wheels crunched on the driveway, coming to a stop just outside the door. Aunt Frances's note this morning was a gift from the gods. It made her decision easy. She wasn't running from her feelings. She had responsibilities and people needed her.

'You're determined to go,' Sophie said with a pretty frown. 'Robert will be disappointed. He mentioned nothing about it at the ball. Did you see him after the ball?'

Henri tied the ribbons of her poke bonnet tighter. 'Why?'

'I'd wondered. I swore I could hear the musical box as I came into the front hall, but it must have been my imagination. Stepmama thought my hearing needed attention. And if you go, Doctor Lumley will have no need to call.'

'An excuse will be found.' Henri forced a smile on to her lips. They'd had a lucky escape. She hated to think what Sophie would have said if she had seen them locked in an embrace, with her pressing her body against Robert's.

Robert had departed because he did not wish to face her. His business was smoke and mirrors to hide what had passed between them. She knew that. It made it easier to carry out her decision. If he was here, she'd have been tempted to stay, but after last night that would not be a good idea. She had to put distance between them and see if the attraction was real or some imagined thing. Far too often the close confines of a visit led to imagined affection. What Sebastian called Country House Fever—a malady of closeness rather than something real and lasting.

'My aunt needs me,' Henri said and hoped Sophie would drop the topic of conversation. 'She sent a note. It is time for me to take up the reins of my old life. My ankle is nearly healed and the supper party and ball but memories.'

Henri allowed her voice to trail away, certain that Sophie would understand the unspoken message. She wanted to return to see Sebastian and discover how he fared.

'Robert will wish to say goodbye.' Sophie made a temple with her fingers, but her eyes narrowed. Henri knew Sophie had not missed the attempt to change the subject. 'His valet is here and he always takes Fredericks if he will be gone for any time. He will be back before nightfall. You could delay your journey another day. And take your leave properly. You'll need to quiz him about his dancing.'

Henri's cheeks burnt as the innocent words conjured up the image of last night's illicit waltz. 'I'm happy to take your word.'

Sophie made a moue. 'Besides, I shall miss you. Do you really have to depart today? It promises to be dull without you. Stepmama is in bed with a headache and I want to discuss every moment of the ball. Did you know Lady Winship's three pugs escaped and ran riot around the ballroom floor before the footman captured them? Apparently they wanted to see Lady Winship dance. And one of the garlands tumbled down in the chase. I laughed so hard that tears came into my eyes.'

Henri looked about the drawing room. The curtains were drawn and sunlight streamed in, but the musical box stood silent in the corner. Passion was a poor basis for anything. Calm considered reflection was best. Her mother's words had kept drumming through her brain all night.

'You have to be a regular caller.' Henri forced her voice to sound light and unconcerned. 'Our At Home day is a Wednesday, but you mustn't stand on convention as we're friends.'

Sophie put her hand to her throat and played with the string of red beads. 'Will your cousin be there?'

'Did Sebastian speak to you at the ball?' Henri asked quietly, pretending an interest in her lace mittens. 'Has he given you an answer to your letter?'

'Matters are satisfactorily concluded. All misunderstandings cleaned up. I repeated what I said in the letter. He understood.' Sophie clapped her hands together and gave a beaming smile. Henri breathed slightly easier. She hoped that Sophie had let her cousin down easily. Sebastian deserved to learn that women did have minds of their own.

'Henri, if you ever need me to come and nurse you, simply send word.' Sophie gathered Henri's hands between hers. Her face took on a very earnest expression. 'I heard what Doctor Lumley said about you overdoing things. If you will be more comfortable in your own home, so be it.'

'I doubt Robert would allow that. It would be far too much to ask of him.' Henri hated how her voice broke over his name.

Sophie gave her a sharp look. 'Robert left the ball early. Did you know?'

'Yes, I did.'

Sophie gave a dazzling smile. 'Then you will understand why Robert would not dare refuse. And why he will want to say adieu.'

'What is going on here? Why is Lady Cawburn's carriage here?' Robert's voice rang out.

Henri's pulse leapt and she struggled to keep her breathing even. Her simple escape plan had been foiled.

'Dear Henri is leaving,' Sophie called out. 'I'm attempting to persuade her that she needs to stay for a while yet.'

'Henri's leaving? Why?'

Sophie cocked her head to one side. 'Is that Stepmama calling? I promised her a tisane for her poorly head. Henri, you can explain to Robert why you are going on your own, can't you?'

Without waiting for an answer, Sophie skipped away, leaving Henri standing in the entrance while Robert came through the front door. Sporting a wide-brimmed straw hat and loose coat, he'd obviously been out inspecting the Roman excavations.

Henri clutched her reticule to her breast, acutely aware of him and the searing kiss they had shared last night. She attempted to get her thoughts in order.

'Aunt Frances sent a note. She needs me.' She fumbled with her reticule, trying to find the piece of paper. 'I'll find it for you.'

He waved an impatient hand. 'And you were going to sneak out like a thief in the night without saying goodbye. Cowardice, Thorndike.'

'We were bound to see each other again and no one knew where you had gone. Something has happened.' Henri's fingers closed around the note and she held it out to him.

She sucked in her breath as their fingers brushed. The merest touch sent her heart hammering against her ribs. She struggled to maintain her poise.

'Then you must go where you're needed, Lady Thorndike.'

Lady Thorndike. Henri's insides twisted and she saw she had hurt him. She hadn't intended to do that. 'She's my aunt. I look after her.'

'She has a son.'

'She depends on me.'

'You are putting your responsibilities first.' He gave her a dark sardonic look. 'Who could fault that?'

'There's no need for sarcasm.' She worried her bottom lip. This interview was proving far harder than she had dreamt possible. 'I thought you'd understand.'

He pulled the brim of his hat down so it shaded his face. 'I do.'

And she knew from the tone of his voice that he'd seen through her ruse. He was well aware of why she was going. But to stay was to risk temptation.

'Everything will be as it was, Montemorcy. Life will return to normal. There won't be a need to wager again.'

He caught her arm and pulled her close. Her body collided with his. His sandalwood scent surrounded her and held her. 'I'll let you go…this time…Henri.'

His whispered words sent an aching thrill arcing through her body. She flicked her tongue over her lips and resisted the temptation to turn her head, meet his mouth and discover precisely how intoxicating his lips were. She broke free.

'The carriage is waiting.' Her voice sounded thick and husky.

His knuckle traced the outline of her lips. 'We'll finish this conversation later. I promise.'

Raised voices in the drawing room greeted Henri when she returned to Dyvels. She breathed deeply, allowing the unchanging scent of beeswax polish, mothballs and old wood to fill her lungs. This was the place she had found refuge and had regained meaning to her life. She liked the constant unchanging rhythms. She knew who she was here. With Robert, she was someone different. Here, she'd become once again Lady Thorndike, instead of Henri. And Lady Thorndike knew her late husband was irreplaceable. Her heart was not going to be touched again or hurt again. She couldn't bear the thought of going through that all-consuming grief again. Never again would one person have the power to reduce her to a gibbering wreck.

'You are home, my lady.' Reynolds bowed and his face betrayed nothing but welcome. 'A most unexpected pleasure.'

'Aunt Frances sent a note.' Henri gave a polite smile.

'We are glad to have you back. There has been a nasty tempest brewing. My lady is in despair. And it was good of you to come...'

The voices in the library became raised again. Henri tilted her head. 'Stormy weather?'

'My lady has discovered his lordship's debts. They are worse than his father's.'

Debts. Henri stood still. Sebastian had promised.

'I see. Thank you, Reynolds.'

Henri opened the door to the library. Both voices stopped immediately. Aunt Francis stood frozen with several pieces of paper in her hand and Sebastian wore his sullen face.

'Henrietta, my dear,' Aunt Frances said, recovering first. She reached for her shawl and placed it about her shoulders. 'You are so good to me. You may deal with this unpleasantness as I fear I'm not strong enough. Sebastian, tell your cousin what you've done.'

She rose and, after kissing Henri's cheek, departed the room. A muffled sob sounded from the hallway.

'How bad is it, Sebastian?' Henri asked after the library had fallen into silence. 'How did you disgrace yourself this time? You mightn't care for Corbridge and its provincial society, but it is your mother's home.'

'It could be worse.' He gave a shrug and began to play with the letter opener, tossing it from hand to hand. 'I simply lost more than I bargained for at the gaming table, but it will be put right. I'm determined to look after Mama and to keep her in the style she is accustomed to. Me! This wagering with strange men for Mama's sake must stop, Henrietta. It was wrong of you.'

'I...I...' Henri put her hand to her throat.

'Dear Mama is worrying over nothing. It won't come to selling this house and her widow's portion is safe. All I did was ask her for a loan just until my rents come through. You would think I had asked her to commit murder.'

'This is the real reason why Robert Montemorcy did not want you to court Sophie—your inability to manage money. He thought you a fortune hunter of the worst sort.' Henri put a hand to her head and sank into the winged armchair. Her ankle throbbed slightly. 'The sale of Chestercamp wiped the slate clean.'

'My money situation is my business, cousin. It is temporary, until the rents come in… A gentleman's debts of honour must be paid.'

'You're becoming exactly like your father, Sebastian, and you always swore you never would,' Henri said with resignation.

'Temporary, Henri. My luck is about to change. I can feel it in my bones.'

She hugged her arms about her waist. She did not know what was worse—Sebastian's debts or the fact that he had hidden them from her. Or that Robert had kept it from her as well. As if she had ever asked for his protection!

'Gamblers always say that, Sebastian, just before they lose it all.'

'A slight setback. I plan on paying Mama back. My creditors are being less than generous. I will recover with the right woman by my side. It is only because I am missing her that I spend time at the tables.'

'And wouldn't this right woman have expectations at being kept in a style that she was accustomed to? Without fear of the bailiffs?'

'No wife of mine would ever want for anything!' Sebastian made a mutinous face. 'Montemorcy had no right to go prying into my affairs!'

'He has every right. Sophie is his ward. He needs to look after her interests.' She closed her eyes.

'You're being ridiculous, Henrietta!' Sebastian looked aghast that she might think differently. 'You're being far too judgemental.

You've forgotten what it is like to be passionately in love. You're far too practical.'

'Your faith in my character does wonders for my self-regard.' Henri shifted uncomfortably. What would Sebastian do if he knew about the kiss she had shared with Robert Montemorcy? Would he use it as a bargaining chip to get what he wanted? She refused to let him. 'But you need to consider Sophie. She wrote to you. She doesn't want to be estranged from her family.'

Sebastian half-closed his eyes and an overly pleased smile crossed his lips. 'How does Sophie feel about me, Henrietta? The truth, now. Did you tell her of my suit and how I long to be with her? We spoke—briefly. That Armstrong person hovered at her elbow, like a determined dragon. It was all I could do to get her to dance with me.'

'Sophie danced with you?' Henri leant forwards, looking for any slight clue in Sebastian's demeanour of what had actually occurred.

'We danced one of the Harlequins. There was time for a few whispered words without the Armstrong dragon descending.' Sebastian drummed a steady beat against the rosewood table. 'Why does everyone assume the worst of me, Henri? My intentions are honourable.'

'And...?' Henri waited for Sebastian's verbal acknowledgement of Sophie's indifference.

'Her guardian doesn't favour my suit and his mind remains unchanged as my prospects remain the same.' Sebastian made a face, but he ceased drumming. 'She has no wish to cause distress to her family. Would I be willing to wait until she reached her majority and then we'd see.'

'Then, it is an end to it. She has more familial feeling than she has feeling for you.' Henri wished she could shake them both—Sophie for hiding behind Robert and Sebastian for ruining his prospects. 'There are plenty of other women...'

'Poor sweet Henrietta.' Sebastian shook his head in a pitying way. 'You have no talent for deception whereas Sophie is a mistress of it. It is her guardian that is the problem. Blast his eyes. Sophie as good as told me that. Without him…she would already be mine.'

Henri stared at her cousin open-mouthed. 'Sophie is an intelligent young woman who is used to making up her own mind. From what I know of Robert Montemorcy, he wouldn't stand in the way if his ward truly desired the match. Take the rejection on the chin, Sebastian. Move on and find a woman who adores you.'

'Are you saying that it's not Sophie? When has a woman ever refused me?' His eyes widened with incredulity. 'You're sadly mistaken, cousin. Sophie adores me. No woman who adores me has ever said no to me.'

'Sometimes no means no, rather than an attempt to be coy.' All of Henri's muscles coiled ready for a fight. He had to understand before he ruined them all. 'The trouble with you, Sebastian, is that up until now, women have fallen into your lap like ripe plums. You've never had to work hard. If you truly wish to have Sophie, then, in light of your debts, you had best do something to deserve her.'

A stunned silence filled the room. A wave of triumph surged through Henri. She put her hand on the doorknob. 'Now that your non-future with Sophie is settled, I do have a busy life beyond your whims and fancies.'

'Miss Armstrong told everyone who cared to listen about her supper party with Robert Montemorcy,' Sebastian said as she was about to leave the room. 'I understand it was quite intimate. Are wedding bells in the air?'

'I was at the *intimate* supper party of twelve. Mrs Armstrong exaggerates the friendship,' Henri said when she had gulped several mouthfuls of air.

'Miss Armstrong has set her cap for Robert Montemorcy. The

entire neighbourhood is aware of it.' Sebastian gave a half-smile and a tiny flutter of his fingers. 'I wondered if you were.'

'Miss Armstrong may very well be interested in obtaining R—that is to say, Mr Montemorcy's hand in matrimony, but I dare say that Mr Montemorcy is well able to look after himself. Miss Armstrong will not be the first woman to have tried.' Henri pulled at the door, which suddenly gave way and sent her flying backwards. Her bottom hit the occasional table with a thump.

'But I thought you would welcome the names of your competition.'

'And you know I have no desire to remarry.' Henri put her hands on her hips. Sebastian was intent on making mischief rather than having guessed her secret. 'Stop trying to pair Robert and me off. It is really most annoying.'

'It is Robert now, is it?' Sebastian gave her a hard look. 'What else has been going on while you have been away? What are you keeping from me, cousin dear? Do you know his antecedents? How his stepmother ran away with the dancing master? And the scandal of his father's suicide? I do. I made it my business to know.'

'Mr Montemorcy rescued me.' Henri concentrated on undoing the ribbons of her bonnet and placing it on the side table, rather than thinking about the ugly rumour that spilled from Sebastian's mouth. Was it any wonder that Robert had given up dancing and decided to concentrate on saving the family's business? And how bitter arriving back in England with the musical box to discover his father dead by his own hand must have been.

Sebastian must not learn about last night's kiss. In his present state, he'd confront Robert, accusing him of seeking to seduce her in revenge for his own thwarted love affair with Sophie.

She bit off each word, making sure that there could be no misunderstanding. 'I recuperated at his house. We spoke a little. Mostly Sophie nursed me. She likes to paint. Terribly artistic. She has done a portrait of me. I shall have it framed and put it above the mantelpiece in my bedroom. And before you ask, Sebastian, I will not lend you any money either.'

'Do not seek to change the subject, Henri.' Sebastian held up his hand. 'Was Sophie your nurse the entire time? Or did you have cause to speak with Montemorcy?'

'Sophie did have to sleep,' Henri said thoughtlessly and then regretted it as Sebastian's gaze became intent. Her cheeks began to burn. She stared at a point somewhere above Sebastian's head and tried not to think of the intimate moments she had shared with Robert. If she did not think about them, she would not mention them, but even now the memory of his touch threatened to swamp her senses.

'He entertained you late at night. Curious. One of you must be aware of how easy it is to ruin a reputation, even a reputation as fearsome as yours, Henrietta. The great tragic widow. Are you planning on becoming his mistress?'

'I refuse to answer your question.' Henri tapped her foot against the carpet. 'You are being improper and impertinent.'

'No.' Sebastian stroked his chin and made a note on a piece of paper. His eyes took on a sly look. 'You are being naïve, Henrietta. Men like that always want something more. You need my guiding hand. If you just lend—'

'Sebastian, where is this conversation going?' Henri crossed her arms. 'I have no need of a lecture about propriety or family feeling or whatever you might think to lecture me on. Your troubles have nothing to do with me. And I will not give you any hush money to stop you spreading rumours. I know where the lines are drawn. I've no intention on crossing them.'

'No one said anything about blackmail. Perish the thought.' Sebastian put his hands on Henri's shoulders. He looked down at her, his deep blue eyes showing injured innocence. 'I'm not the villain here, Henrietta Maria; remember that. I only want to be with the love of my life and for that I need to restore my fortune. I'll do it with or without your help.'

Henri stepped away from him and looked at her cousin closely, truly looked at him. Superficially he was the same handsome man, but there was a hardness in his eyes and she knew soon the years of extravagant living would begin to show. What was worse, he stood there with a superior expression on his face as if she'd give in and help him because she'd helped him so many times before. 'Sometimes I've trouble believing you, Sebastian. Go back to London and leave us alone.'

His eyes widened before his face contorted with fury. 'I'll not be denied, Henrietta.'

'I'm not against you, Sebastian.' Henri held out her hands. 'I want the best for you, but you're behaving like a spoilt child. You're better than that. Grow up and solve this problem yourself.'

Henri snipped off the dead heads off the overblown roses with fierce strokes. Two days of Sebastian's sulking and not a word from Robert. Sebastian kept making barbed remarks and then apologising as he was supposed to try to be an adult. Aunt Frances was not being any use in the matter, retreating to her library and assuming that Henri had somehow wronged Sebastian.

Robert's silence bothered her. Twice she penned a note, only to toss it in the fire. Life would be easier if he wrote first. And Henri hated waiting. Even the various doings of village life held no interest.

In desperation, she tried reading the letters between Edmund and her, but they seemed to belong to another age. She barely recognised the girl who had penned the breathless declarations of love, and had stopped the exercise as pointless after reading the first six. Somehow along the way she'd stopped grieving for Edmund. She knew she'd always treasure his words, but they no longer sent wave after wave of racking pain through her being. As she carefully replaced the letters, she felt embarrassed, as if she was peeking into someone else's life; it was the mundane detail about the dresses, parties and what he had had for dinner that held her interest rather than her overblown expressions of love and devotion.

The whole exercise seemed to make her think more about Robert rather than less—the way his eyes crinkled when he laughed and how his hands felt against her back when they danced, when they kissed. The maelstrom of passion that made her feel alive in a way that Edmund had never done.

Henri gave the roses a fierce swipe with her shears. Did she even have to bow to propriety and convention? Sebastian never did.

'You appear about ready to murder those flowers. What have they done to deserve that sort of treatment?'

Henri missed her stroke and cut through a swathe of buds. Now she was starting to imagine his voice.

'Henri? Has something happened?'

Her heart skipped a beat, but she stared at the beheaded rose for a moment longer, seeking to control her reaction. She had promised herself so many times that what had happened the night of the ball was an aberration. However, she only had to imagine his voice and her pulse raced faster.

'Henri? Are you going to speak to me?'

Henri spun around. He stood there, hands held out, a half-smile on his face. A lock of hair fell over his forehead. Her fingers itched to smooth it away.

'Robert, it's you.' Henri grasped the basket tighter. 'An unexpected pleasure.'

'Sending a note about the other forfeit was unnecessary. I'd promised to call, but there was urgent business at the works.' He touched his fingers to his hat. His face seemed thinner, making his eyes appear more intense.

'How did you know where to find me?' Henri stared at him, perplexed. What was this about a note and forfeit? And more to the point—who had sent it? Was this Sebastian's test of loyalty? Henri rejected the notion. Sebastian had nothing to gain by sending Robert to her.

'Your aunt said that you would be in the garden and encouraged me to find you.'

Henri breathed a little easier. Mystery solved. Aunt Frances was playing at matchmaking. It was very like Aunt Frances to send a note and then leave matters to work themselves out.

'I believe you will find the note was from my aunt.'

'Does it matter? It is good to know that your aunt approves of me.' A faint smile played at the corners of his mouth. 'Unless you have a reason why you and I no longer have any need to be civil, I want to hear how the patient progresses. And Boy wants you to come and visit soon.'

She laughed as the blood started to rush through her veins, warming her all over. Nothing mattered except he was standing there. He'd come expressly to visit her.

'Has the dog told you?'

'It was in his eyes when I told him where I was going.'

'You are exaggerating.' Henri concentrated on a rosebud that was just unfurling its petals to the hot summer sun. She had never seen Robert indulge in light-hearted whimsy before and it amused her. 'That dog does not miss me.'

'Visit and see for yourself. You've made a conquest.'

Henri kept the basket in front of her like a shield and tried to remember all the reasons why seeing Robert alone again was a bad idea and why she should suggest going up to the drawing room where Sebastian lurked. Henri's heart plummeted. The last thing she wanted was to have Sebastian be unbearably rude.

'The flowers need seeing to. I was cutting the dead blooms away.'

'Surely you have a gardener.'

'I like doing it myself. It soothes my nerves to put the border to rights. Then I will attend to village business.' Henri paused, shifting the basket on to her hip, acutely aware of him—where he stood, where his hands were and the exact position of his mouth. Her entire being trembled. What seemed so straightforward in her lonely room was far more difficult with him standing near her, close enough to touch, to caress, to kiss. The longing to be touched swamped her senses. 'The other night...'

The dimple deepened in the corner of his mouth. 'Should I apologise?'

'Yes...no... It should never have happened. I was wrong to allow it to happen.'

'But it did.' His rich voice flowed over her, warming her and making her want to... Henri concentrated on breathing steadily. 'It is fruitless to wish to undo the past, so I will make no attempt to.'

She held up her hand, preventing him from continuing. 'I've no plans to remarry, Robert. I value my independence.'

He lifted an eyebrow and the corners of his mouth twitched. 'Generally people wait until they are asked before refusing an offer.'

Henri's cheeks grew hot and a pang of regret went through her. Robert was not behaving how she expected. Had she misread the situation? Surely any man with a sense of honour would make an offer? It was how things were done? Weren't they?

'I wanted to make certain you understood, before...before you made an offer out of duty. I've no wish to fall out of civility with you, but remarriage is not in my future. Ever.'

Chapter Eleven

'Duty?' Robert stared at Henri in disbelief. Her level gaze met his. She was serious. They both knew all it had been was a kiss, a kiss that no one saw or commented on. True, it had nearly gone much further, but he'd never forced a woman and wasn't about to start with Henri. 'I have kissed other women without them demanding marriage.'

'I wanted to make sure.' Her deep blue eyes were guileless. She made a little gesture with her hand and nearly sent the greenery tumbling out of the trug. She bent to retrieve them and her bonnet slipped forwards, shielding her face from view. 'It is best that everyone understands and no one feels obligations or expectations.'

'I know where the boundaries lie.' Robert stared at the crown of her bonnet. What he felt for Henri was far removed from duty. Passion. Desire. A longing to be with her. But not duty. And passion alone was a good enough reason to be with her.

In many ways, Henrietta Thorndike was more naïve than Sophie. At least Sophie did not believe that a simple kiss would lead automatically to a declaration of intent. However, she would come to see his perspective—what was between them needed to be explored and savoured. Enjoyed while it lasted.

'We kissed the other night. It was wrong. We both know that. My reputation in this village would be destroyed if anyone discovered. They would never believe that we stopped at one kiss.' She stood up and brushed the dirt from her skirt. 'Village gossip can be ruthless, and I am determined to make very clear where boundaries lie.'

'Are you ruined? Has anyone commented?' Robert asked. If someone had seen them, then he would force the issue. Henri's reputation was safe with him. But for now, it was about enjoying each other's company, rather than thinking about society's dictates. 'Will they? You are a widow of twenty-six, not some débutante of seventeen.'

'No.' Her brow puckered and her white teeth caught her full bottom lip. 'No one knows. I am certain of it.'

'Then you're troubling trouble—a very bad thing to do.'

'The kiss,' she said before colouring a dusky rose. 'I mean you're right. As long as we agree on a stratagem, we are safe. Our lives can continue on as they have been.'

Robert watched her mouth. She wet it, running her tongue over it, turning her lips the colour of the unfurled rose she held in her hand. The air between them hummed with energy. 'What boundaries do you propose? Shall we open negotiations?'

Her lips formed a startled O. 'I...I propose friendship.'

'Friendship. Intimate friendship?' he said softly, watching her much as a cat watches a mouse, waiting for her to move towards him. She wanted to, he could sense that. The very air crackled between them. But it had to be her choice or he'd lose her.

'We're both adults.' Her voice was husky as she took a half-step towards him. 'We can control our passions.'

'Do you believe that?' Robert pounced, capturing her unresisting waist. Gently he removed the rose-filled basket from her fingers, set it on the gravel path. 'Do you truly believe it? I never thought you lacked imagination or innovation, Henri.'

Slowly she nodded.

'Liar.' He bent his head so his mouth was a breath from hers.

He watched the way her tongue flicked over her lips, wetting them. The blood surged through him, and he knew he had to possess her mouth again.

'I am attempting to be sensible,' she said, her breath mingled with his.

'And you think this will not happen every time we are alone, and that we won't find reasons to be alone?' He pulled her more firmly into his arms. Her body brushed against his as he claimed her mouth. A long drawn-out sigh emerged from her throat as her arms reached up to pull him closer.

He penetrated the sweet interior of her mouth. Her tongue touched his and retreated, explicitly inviting him to follow, to sink deep into her depths. For a long moment, they stood submerged in each other. His arms crushed the soft curves of her body against him, moulding to him. And he knew he wanted more than was prudent.

'Henri,' he said against her mouth, drawing her breath into his lungs. 'We need to move. Too exposed. Discretion in all things.'

She gave an indistinct murmur and looked up at him with passion-dilated eyes. Not letting go of her waist, he led her into the shadow of the summer-house where they would not be easily spied and kissed the nape of her neck, tasting her sun-ripened skin.

'Too exposed for what?' she whispered, not moving away. Her eyes were large and luminous. Innocent.

'This.' He trailed his mouth along her neck until he reached the hollow of her throat. Her skin tasted of strawberries and sunlight and something that was pure Henri. Addictive and he knew his control was slipping. He wanted her. Far too much. He wanted to take his time and explore all the mysteries. He breathed deep and regained some vestige of self-control.

'When you wish to stop, we stop. But this is going to keep happening. The question is—what are we going to do about it?' he asked, watching her like a hawk.

Henri stood completely still as Robert's words thrummed through her. He desired her. He wanted more. She wanted more. She wanted to feel his touch on her skin. She wanted to touch him. And the desire hadn't diminished in the time they had been apart; it had grown until it threatened to consume her entire being. What she was experiencing wasn't some weak gentle thing, but something powerful and terrifyingly wonderful. This was what it was like to be in a strong and healthy man's arms. And she wanted more.

Logically she should pick up her skirts and run like the very devil was after her, but her feet seemed rooted the ground. And he made no attempt to kiss her further, but neither did he move away. He simply stood there, looking at her with his gold-flecked eyes, as if she was the most desirable cake in the world and he a starving man. The heat from him rose all around her, enveloping her senses. Her skin tingled with anticipation.

'We should walk away. Leave this place now and forget that it even happened.' Henri attempted to make her voice sound decisive. But her entire being screamed that her lips were lying. She was incapable of moving away from the warmth of his body. Tingles of liquid warmth pulsated through her body and she knew her legs could not carry her. 'Never meet alone again.'

'Leave? I have no intention of leaving Corbridge. What happens if we encounter each other in the street, at the haberdasher's or even at a ball? Do we walk away then? Or do we find some deserted summer-house?'

'We must be distant friends.' Henri hated the way her voice trembled on *distant*. She'd miss him. She had missed him in the past two days more than she had thought possible. What she was doing was the correct and proper thing. Surely Robert had to see the futility of them meeting and becoming entwined with each other. Sooner or later someone would find out and she'd be forced to make a choice. But she wondered if there was anywhere far enough away from him that would make her forget his smile, the way his eyes crinkled when he laughed and the touch of his skin.

But, given time, she knew she could. A traitorous voice in the back of her mind screamed that she would not.

'The truth, Henri.' His hands skimmed her arms, sending fresh sparks throughout her. 'Lie to yourself if you must, but forget lying to me. Can you turn your back and go? Can you forget? Because I know, God as my witness, I will remember and I will long to taste your lips again.' He rubbed his thumb against her aching mouth, causing her insides to tremble. 'The truth, Henrietta—are you going to walk out of my arms and not look back?'

Slowly she shook her head. The other night she had been able to walk away from him, but not now. Suddenly she felt more alive than she had in years. It was as though, after Edmund's death, something had died within her as well and she thought that she would never be whole again. But now, with Robert's arms about her, she knew that little bit of her had not perished, but had been merely in abeyance, waiting. Except Edmund had never made this raging ache grow within her.

'I want to stay.' She held out her hands, palms upwards. His fingers curled about hers and pulled her to him. Her body shuddered with an inexorable fever.

'Is that all you want?' he whispered against her hair.

'I want to be here with you and feel your lips against mine. I want to taste you.' She stood on her tiptoes and brought his face closer to hers. His lips hovered above hers, tantalising her with their nearness 'I know what I am doing, Robert. I've stopped lying. You're right. Martyrdom and I are a poor combination. I want to indulge.'

Her hands grasped Robert's hair and held him against her. He groaned and his arms went around her, moulding her body to his.

The flickers of heat flamed, growing stronger with each touch of Robert's tongue against her skin. Every inch of her was sensitive to his touch. It was not right and yet it seemed so right to be in his arms. Perhaps she was like Sebastian—afflicted by an attraction that would vanish once she had bedded Robert. All she had to do was to put aside her womanly notions of convention and manners, and think like a man. This deep brooding was passion, not pure love like she had felt for Edmund. She'd never understood the difference before.

Men had no problems with passion. They simply took their pleasure. She could do this. This was all about their shared physical attraction. Physical need, rather than engaging her heart. She would be able to walk away with her head held high and her heart unscathed when this was done. She would not lose him because she had never had him. They could be discreet with precise planning.

'Stay,' she murmured. 'Please stay with me.'

Her back touched the wall of the summer-house, which supported her as his mouth moved lower. Her breasts strained against her stays as her nipples tightened. He slipped a finger between the material and her skin. Stroked. A convulsive shudder went through her and her back arched upwards, seeking his touch.

The white-hot heat burnt through her body, reaching her soul, and everywhere his cool mouth went, her fevered skin received some relief. However, the instant it had moved on, her skin craved more.

With expert fingers he loosened her dress and exposed the tops of her breasts, which strained upwards, seeking his touch. He brushed the material away, and his mouth captured one dark rose-hued nipple. His tongue encircled its tip, tracing circles on her heated flesh. Nuzzled, sending ripples of pleasure coursing through her. Pleasure that she'd never guessed could exist, but the sort she knew she wanted to give back to him.

Her back arched and her body encountered his arousal. He wanted her as much as she wanted him. The knowledge made her feel powerful. Fire surged through her, urging her to throw away her caution.

'Robert,' she breathed, burying her fingers into his crisp dark hair, exploring its silky smoothness.

He made no answer, but took her other breast from its confines. His breath teased the tightly furled bud, making it contract tighter until the ache thrummed through her. Then he captured it in his mouth, running his tongue over and around the nipple.

Henri's knees melted and she gripped on to his shoulders in an effort to keep upright. His knee parted her legs, rubbing against the apex of her thighs, rocking her body back and forth. The ache in her centre spread outwards. Her world had come down to this one point and the way his touch inflamed her.

She put her hands on his chest and started to undo the buttons, slipped her hand inside. The smooth contours of his chest slid under the pads of her fingers. Her hand touched his nipples and they became hardened points. Her own tightened in response. He desired her. She had done this to him.

'Henri,' he breathed in her ear. 'I want you in bed with me, but I doubt I'll last until we find one. I need you under me, around me and with me.'

Not trusting her voice, Henri moved her hands lower, undid the buttons of his trousers and slipped in. The length of him was hard, but velvet smooth, alive and vital against her fingers. He groaned. His hand caught her wrist.

'You'll unman me.' He titled her chin upwards so she stared into his golden amber gaze. 'What do you want, Henri?'

'This,' she said, giving voice to her desire. 'You inside me.'

She thought back to her sixteen-year-old self. Then it had always been in a darkened room, late at night. She had been a blushing bride, a virgin, and Edmund had sought to gently initiate her. She'd spent years wondering what the fuss was about. Edmund had seemed relieved that she hadn't pursued that side of the marriage with much vigour. She hadn't understood what she was missing… until now.

Henri sucked in her breath. Now at twenty-six, she realised that there had been love, but no passion in her marriage. And she wanted for once in her life to experience the full glory of passion. She could make demands on her partner. She could make love in the sunlight. It felt good to say the words because she could. Because the sensation of his body moving against hers was sending her up in flames.

'Please,' she whispered, willing him to understand why without explaining her reasons.

'Here?' he asked, cupping her face in his hands. His mobile mouth loomed over hers. 'In the open? By the summer-house? Is that what you want?'

'Yes,' she whispered and steeled herself for his refusal. Even though she knew there was little chance of being caught, the risk somehow made it more exciting. Sinfully wicked, but very right. It was something she had never done before and she wanted to experience it. With him. A liquid thrill coursed through her. 'Oh, yes.'

A light flared in his eyes. He cupped her face between his hands and his eyes became deep golden pools, pools she could lose herself in, where she would never come to any harm. 'As my lady requests...'

She raised herself up on her tiptoes and brushed his lips, tasting his sun-ripened skin and the cool interior of his mouth. 'I do. Now, please.'

He lifted her skirts, and she guided his hand to her mound. She held his warm palm firmly against her. His fingers played amongst the curls, slipping in and out, gliding over her innermost surfaces with a sure touch. The ache rose within her like a great crested wave, building momentum as it consumed her.

She undid another button and saw him. Aroused. Ready. A slight moan echoed in the back of her throat.

He understood and drew her forwards, holding her against his erection. He nudged the apex of her thighs. 'Wrap your legs about me,' he commanded in her ear. 'I will support you.'

She did as he asked and felt the length of him fill her. For a long moment they stood, joined, and Henri knew she was experiencing something outside her comprehension, something wonderful. This joining was full of dark passion. Something within him called to the unknown places of her soul and wakened some very vital part of her.

Slowly she began to move her body, giving in to the timeless urge. Her hands grasped his shoulders, holding on tight. His hard muscles moved against her, supporting her as he thrust upwards to meet her. His mouth took her cry, tore it from her throat. Together they moved as one. She heard him groan her name in her ear in a voice that was made husky with desire. Urgency consumed her and she moved her hips with an increasing tempo, feeling him in her, a part of her. And then her world exploded in sensation. Shattered. And she knew a deep satisfaction. She wrapped her legs tighter about him and clung, being one with him.

Robert loosened his arms and reluctantly set her back down on to the firm earth. In the fierce coupling, her hair had come loose and now hung about her shoulders. Several damp tendrils curled on her forehead. He reached out a finger and smoothed them away. Her lips turned up into a secret smile.

Never before had he felt this sense of completeness and belonging to one person. He straightened his clothing as she stood unmoving with an errant curl caressing her cheek, highlighting her aroused mouth. He forced his fingers to button his trousers rather than to draw her into his arms again. They had tempted fate enough today.

With deft fingers, he did up her gown and twitched the skirt into place.

Putting his fingers to his lips, he left her for an instant before returning with her bonnet. He placed it on her head and pulled it slightly forwards. His fingers slowly caressed her cheek. A simple touch, but one that reminded him of the passion they had just shared.

'No one would guess. It amazes me that I never guessed the passion and fire within you. I have been remiss. But I intend to spend time studying it, seeing what you glow.'

'Ah, an application of your famous method and need for experimentation.'

'I find method helps increase pleasure.'

She smiled up at him, her blue eyes deepening to midnight blue. 'It is best. A secret between us two. I'd forgotten how much I enjoy secrets.'

'We ought to go up the drawing room now,' he said, moving away from her, refusing to give in to the desire to hold her again. He'd only end up making love to her. And right now, he had to abide by her wishes and be discreet. He knew that he would spend most of the time away from her plotting how they could contrive to be together and spend longer together. 'Your aunt will be wondering where we are and why it takes so long to discuss a simple picnic.'

'Yes, we don't want an outraged Sebastian.' She gave a little hic-cupping laugh and he knew all was not right between her and her cousin.

'Cawburn wouldn't dare.' Robert thought of the debts daily flooding into his office. The man was in desperate straits. The sooner he retired to the Continent, the better for everyone concerned.

'I don't know what Sebastian will or will not do,' Henri replied. 'I used to know. I used to think he lived by a certain code. He's changed.'

'You can trust me.'

'It's a family matter.' Henri watched him under her lashes. It was incredible to think that a few moments ago she had held his body against hers, that they had been as close as two people could be. But he didn't need to know the horrible things Sebastian had been saying. 'I'll deal with my cousin. I have done so before. He should know better than to try and flim-flam me.'

'I'm here to help.'

'Do you think we can keep this a secret? That my aunt won't guess?' Henri put her hand to her mouth, and explored her aching lips as she searched for a way to change the subject. To explain about Sebastian would mean she'd have to reveal something about herself and how she'd behaved with Edmund and she wasn't ready for that. She wanted Robert to think of her in a good light. 'I must look dishevelled.'

Her entire being cried out for words of endearment, but Robert simply looked at her. She wanted him to say many things, but he was silent.

'You look adorable, Henri,' he said finally.

'Adorable—oh, dear.' Henri attempted to think clearly.

'What's wrong with adorable?'

'If anyone thinks there is something between us, they might try to matchmake and being alone together will become that much more difficult.'

'Always the practical one, but you remain adorable,' he said, trailing a finger down her bare arm.

'We both must exercise self-control.'

'Self-control? My control is lacking where you are concerned.' He gave a heart-stopping smile. 'With you, I lose all sense. My body craves you, and you are a most pleasurable addiction.'

'We will have to plan and co-ordinate. It is far…far too risky just to meet.' Henri kept her back upright. After what they had just shared, she was not going to beg or ask for more. But no words of tenderness or love had passed between them. She could be like Sebastian and her father, and take her pleasure without having her heart involved. To be any other way was to invite heartache and she had had enough of that to last a lifetime. This was all about the physical and not her heart. It was desire and dark passion. And like a fierce fire, it would burn out, leaving nothing but unremarked ash. One never grieved for ash. She shivered slightly and silently hoped that it would last for a long while yet.

'I thrive on risk.'

'You do?' She stared at him in astonishment and her stomach turned over. She started to shiver with cold. Her instincts shouted to trust him, but she worried.

He ran a hand down her arm, sending a cascade of warmth throughout her, banishing the cold. 'The next time we are together, it will be between white linen sheets—when we have time to enjoy each other properly, when you do not have to fear an errant gardener or servant spying. I may thrive on risk, but I know about caution.'

Henri breathed again. 'The next time?'

'Surely there is to be a next time.' His fingers trailed along the edge of her gown.

'As long as we are discreet...' Henri's entire being tensed. How could she refuse him after what they had just shared? But if she didn't, everything she had said over the past ten years about how she could never marry again was a lie. She could not marry and keep her heart safe at the same time. She could not bear to go into that dark place that she had gone to when she beheld Edmund's waxlike face, not with anyone. Not with Robert. 'You know how I feel about marriage.'

The crinkles deepened in the corners of his eyes as if they were sharing a private joke. 'I respect you far too much to go against your wishes. You wish to have your independence and so you shall. But our affair is not a one-time joining. I am greedy, Henrietta Thorndike, I want more than that. And should there be consequences, we will deal with them together. I take my responsibilities seriously.'

Consequences? Children. Her heart panged. Long ago she'd given up hope of ever holding her own child. If she had not become pregnant before, why would she this time? It would be cruel to hope for one. And, oh, so wrong. But she knew in that moment, she did.

'If there are any consequences, I will face them. Alone.'

'We face them together. You are far from being alone; we are friends.'

Henri ran her tongue over her lips. She had thought being with Robert would end everything between them, but it hadn't. It only made her want him more. She swallowed hard and tried to regain control of her emotions. This was about passion, not love. She was not going to get hurt. She remained in control. 'And how long will this affair last?'

'Until we tire of each other.' He placed a kiss on her nose. His hand caught her elbow and held her against his body. 'What is between us has only just begun, Henri. I believe I amply demonstrated that. Let us be truthful with each other.'

She put up her hands and broke free. *Be truthful.* It would mean having to confess about how she had contributed to Edmund's early death, and everything else, and she wasn't ready for that. She could be truthful about what she wanted from him. 'An affair between friends.'

'You shall have your wish, my dear Henri. No one shall hear of it from my lips.' He raised her fingers to his mouth. 'I do not kiss and tell.'

Chapter Twelve

Robert strode along the pathway beside St Andrew's church towards the market square. An affair with Henri. Of all the outcomes he'd anticipated when he received her note about the other forfeit, he'd never expected to discover a passionate Henri, willing and eager to make love in the sunshine. Unexpected, but highly desirable.

It amazed him that they had been neighbours for all this time without him understanding the passion smouldering within her. And it also showed how little her cousin knew her. Cawburn's mockery still rankled. Henri was better than that. She judged people on their deeds, not their pedigree. She was honest and true. He'd seen it in her actions. But would it be better to end it now? Keep it to the one perfect time?

Not see Henri again in that way? Prudent, but impossible.

Even now his body thrummed with the anticipation of encountering her again. And someday, he'd discover why she clung to her past and her late husband's memory so tightly. But he had to keep a cool head. He knew the folly of completely engaging his emotions. He knew when to stop. He would end it before it happened. He always had before. Kept his heart apart. There was no reason why his encounters with Henri should be any different.

'Mr Montemorcy. Mr Montemorcy!' Miss Armstrong signalled

to him from near the market cross. Her violent green dress made her look bilious. 'It's imperative that we speak.'

With a mental sigh, Robert bid goodbye to the pleasurable but vexing problem of Henri. 'Miss Armstrong, what is the matter? You appear distressed.'

The spinster's yellow silk bonnet shook and she withdrew a hand-kerchief from her reticule. 'I have been insulted and you are the only person I can turn to.'

'Indeed.' There was no reason for Miss Armstrong to suppose any finer feeling existed between them. He had proceeded with the utmost care and consideration, but with no special or marked attention. It bothered him that the woman should feel he would be willing to be her protector against the world. 'And who has insulted you? If it's within my power, of course, I will do something about it.'

'Your ward.'

'Sophie!' Robert stared at her. 'What has my ward done? Does her stepmother know?'

'I did my best, Mr Montemorcy,' Miss Armstrong said, wringing her handkerchief. 'But your ward refused to listen to common sense. It comes from the upbringing, I suppose. Perhaps manners are different where you are from and Miss Ravel is simply misguided and high-spirited. But the fact remains that you were in error when you allowed her to go to the ball.'

'Where is Sophie? Have you two quarrelled?' Robert glared at Miss Armstrong. How dare the woman judge Sophie in that fashion! Sophie might be headstrong, but she had behaved in an exemplary fashion at the ball.

'She has gone and all because of the ball.' Miss Armstrong raised a lace-edged handkerchief to her eyes. 'And you are going to blame me. I did my best, Mr Montemorcy. To keep her here and to guide her along the right path. I did my best to warn her of the folly of her actions.'

'I'm sure you did, Miss Armstrong.' Robert retained a narrow leash on his temper. He refused to quarrel with a pillar of the community in the middle of a busy market square. Already several people had turned to look at them. 'Both the Ravels have been grateful for your guidance and hand of friendship these past few weeks.'

'Once you are apprised of the situation, you will understand why we must now be distant acquaintances. I could not possibly ally…' Her tiny mouth pursed as she dabbed her eyes. 'I hope I do not pain you too much, but I felt the sentiments must be expressed.'

'Why would I blame you for my ward's bad manners? And believe me, Miss Armstrong, when I say that I had no expectations of any intimate friendship with you.'

The woman's cheek paled and, for a moment, Robert thought she was going to faint, but she recovered and gave her body a little shake. 'Then it's best it's out in the open. Miss Ravel has endangered her reputation through her reckless behaviour and careless actions.'

Robert shook his head. He had always discounted Henri's assessment of Miss Armstrong as being distinctly unhelpful in a crisis as Henri always wanting to be in charge, but now he saw that Henri knew more than she had let on. 'I apologise for Sophie and whatever trick she has played, Miss Armstrong, and am upset that it has inadvertently caused you distress. But Sophie's heart is in the right place and she will make amends.'

'But you fail to understand, Mr Montemorcy. Sophie has destroyed all chances of future happiness.' Miss Armstrong dissolved into loud sobs and it was several moments before she could continue. 'You're going to blame me for everything, Mr Montemorcy. I know you will.'

'Nobody is going to blame you, Miss Armstrong.' Robert clenched his fists and then slowly reopened them as he counted to ten and regained control over his temper. 'Please tell me what happened. Slowly and without giving in to your nerves.'

'We, Sophie and I, went visiting this morning as dearest Dorothy had a sick headache. Several people expressed a keen interest in meeting your ward after her success at the ball. But your ward is given to forthright views like another I could mention.'

There were no prizes for guessing whom Miss Armstrong meant—Henri. Red-hot anger shot through him.

He wished he had never allowed Miss Armstrong to take Sophie under her wing. The woman was a snob of the first order. He should never have encouraged the friendship, but equally he had no wish to antagonise one of the biggest gossips in the entire north-east. The acquaintance ended now. The woman would never enter his house again. But first he had to discover what imagined crime Sophie had committed.

'What has Sophie done? Who has she befriended?' Robert said, exerting all of his self-control. 'Come now, Miss Armstrong, it cannot be as bad as you fear. The truth now. Without embellishment.'

'Miss Ravel has disappeared!' Miss Armstrong clasped her hands together. 'I fear she has eloped. Eloped with Lord Cawburn! He will never marry her and society will be closed to her. And you will blame me for my part in her downfall, but it was entirely inadvertent.'

'Why do you believe my ward has eloped?'

'Miss Ravel made her excuses after one stop, saying that she remained tired from the ball and wished to return home and check on her stepmother. Not wishing to inconvenience me, she would walk.'

'I would suspect she did.' Sophie's great crime was that she had walked. The tension in Robert's shoulders eased. She had not eloped, but walked home in an outrage at Miss Armstrong's tactics. 'Sophie has a reputation for walking whenever she can. She had a French governess leave because she could not keep up. No doubt she simply wanted to clear her mind. Perhaps something disturbed her.'

He gave Miss Armstrong a stern look.

Miss Armstrong took refuge in her intricately beaded reticule, pulling out another handkerchief and raising it to her eyes. 'I know nothing of that, Mr Montemorcy.'

'In fact, you know very little of my ward or her habits.' Robert forced a smile on his lips. He could imagine the scene. Sophie had finally had enough of Miss Armstrong's heartfelt advice, and there had been a slight quarrel. He had hoped her manners were better, but he would address that failing when they conversed. Whatever the quarrel, it did not merit Miss Armstrong slandering Sophie.

'But I do know that something is far from right. She has eloped with Lord Cawburn.'

He fixed the woman with his gaze and waited until two bright spots appeared on her cheeks. 'Before accusing my ward of eloping, and in particular eloping with a notorious rake such as Lord Cawburn, you must have concrete facts. All you know is that my ward decided to walk back to the New Lodge rather than use your carriage.'

'But she failed to arrive. Your ward is missing, sir, and if she is such a great walker, she should have arrived.' Miss Armstrong twisted her reticule so violently that several beads popped off.

'How do you know this?'

'Miss Ravel's card case had fallen on to the seat in my carriage. I did not see them until I finished my calls. I went straight away to return them and your butler told me she was not there.'

'Then something has happened to her!'

'What do you propose to do, Mr Montemorcy?' There was a greediness about the woman's eyes. He could see her eagerness to depart and confront the next person with her intelligence. Unless he was very careful, Sophie's innocent jaunt in the countryside could lead to her ruin.

'The countryside will have to be searched. However, I suspect that there is a much more innocent explanation. This is the Tyne Valley, rather than London or Newcastle.' He gritted his teeth. Behind Miss Armstrong, a cart and horse rumbled, a girl chased a hoop and the milliner put a fresh hat in the window, little everyday actions that served to remind him that Miss Armstrong was jumping to the wrong conclusion. Nothing had happened to Sophie. When he returned to the Lodge, she would be there full of fun and mischief at the great jape she had played.

'Will you chase her to Gretna Green and demand that she marries?'

'Until we know precisely what has occurred, I would suggest you keep your theories to yourself. You do know what they say about people who spread false and malicious tales.' Robert turned on his heel. 'Good day to you, madam.'

'But Lord Cawburn was there just before she made her excuses.' Miss Armstrong hurried after him. Her entire being quivered. 'And as I was leaving, his man delivered a letter to you. From Miss Ravel, I'd wager.'

'You are speculating, madam. Kindly refrain from doing so. A young woman's reputation hangs in the balance.'

'Where is Sebastian, Aunt?' Henri asked going into her aunt's inner sanctum. 'The house seems strangely still.'

Of all the people she dreaded meeting after her encounter with Robert, it was Sebastian. Unless she was very careful, he would be able to discern in an instant what had passed between her and Robert. When she had gone into the drawing room, she had discovered several half-written letters demanding money and a whole sheaf of bills. She wanted to believe that her cousin was better than a common blackmailer, but she'd not expected the extent of his indebtedness.

Her aunt looked up from some shards of Roman pottery. 'He has gone out. He has decided to do some visiting.'

'Sebastian hates visiting. It will be the post inn.'

'No, he definitely said visiting. My hearing is as good as it ever was. You wrong Sebastian, Henrietta. He does have a good heart and now that he is back here amongst people who love him, rather than in the wicked fleshpots of London, he will settle. Over the last few days, it seemed as if the little boy who used to bring me buttercups before breakfast had come back to me.'

A tiny prickle nagged at the back of Henri's brain. Sebastian was plotting. Sophie. Today was the day she went out with Miss Armstrong. He was going to confront Sophie. Hopefully, this time, Sophie would be firm and actually tell him the truth. 'Did he give any reason for this sudden desire to attend At Homes?'

'I fear he thinks you have become awfully dull and censorious.' Her aunt gave one of her silvery laughs.

'Why have I become dull?' Henri asked lightly.

'He thinks you have made up your mind about him and are determined to see the worst. He wants to clearly demonstrate how he has changed and what a success he can make of his life.' She put down the pottery shards. 'He has sworn that he has given up gaming. And this time, I truly believe he will.'

'It would be pleasant to think that he could change.' Henri tapped her finger against the pile of letters. She had the uneasy suspicion that Aunt Frances was keeping something from her. Once Sebastian returned, she would speak to him about these letters. She refused to allow Aunt Frances or herself to become embroiled in some money-making scheme. It would be better for everyone if Sebastian had a new start somewhere else.

Her aunt reached for her teacup. 'Has Mr Montemorcy gone? I had asked Cook to make cucumber sandwiches particularly.'

'There will be more for Sebastian, then, as you seem to have given up on them.'

'Sebastian keeps saying that cucumber is bad for my digestion. Now, why did Mr Montemorcy depart? Were you unkind to him, Henri? Do try to stay friends with him, Henrietta.'

Henri stilled. The rules for widows were slightly different from those for unmarried women, but even so, she had no wish to cause her aunt distress. As long as she was discreet and did not become the subject of common gossip, she was free to behave as she chose. 'He departed a few moments ago as he has other business to attend to in the village. He only wished to assure himself that I was well and the journey back here had done nothing to harm my ankle.'

Her aunt's gaze narrowed. 'He has brought the roses to your cheeks. You are positively glowing. Male companionship is good for one. If I were twenty years younger…'

Henri ducked her head. 'It's more likely going without my bonnet. The sun always gives me a sprinkling of freckles across the bridge of my nose.'

'Henri, dear, you never go without your bonnet tightly fastened on your head.' Her aunt raised a hand. 'Mr Montemorcy is a good man. You could do worse than encourage him. His company obviously does you good. Your face was becoming quite pinched and sallow. Now, you appear in the best of health.'

Henri placed two pottery shards together. They formed a naked man's torso. The best of health. It was as she feared—what had passed between her and Robert showed in her face. Sebastian would guess, but she doubted Aunt Frances would be that direct. A cold shiver went down her spine. But what would Sebastian do about it? Threaten her or, worse, Robert?

'It must be the rest. I was obviously far too busy before the attack.' She picked up a shard and balanced it in her hand, before adding it to her aunt's current pattern. 'You simply missed it before.'

'No, it is something more.' Her aunt tapped a long finger against her mouth and moved the shard to the side of the vase where it fit perfectly. 'It is long past time that you remarried, Henrietta. You were not born to be a widow.'

'I've no plans to remarry.' Henri put a hand on her aunt's shoulder. 'Edmund is irreplaceable. I don't want another husband.'

'For an intelligent woman, Henrietta, you can be remarkably obtuse. Your mother was a silly vain woman who allowed you to indulge in mawkish behaviour. You make it sound like men are interchangeable cogs. No one is asking you to replace him.'

'But Edmund…' Henri waved her hand. Her insides felt empty. Surely her aunt had to understand that she had no wish to be disloyal. Or any wish to risk her heart again.

'Edmund would want what is best for you. He loved you, by all accounts. If the circumstances had been reversed, would you have wanted him never to experience happiness, pleasure or even contentment again?'

'Mr Montemorcy has not asked me to marry him, Aunt. Nor is he likely to.' Henri crossed her arms. Robert had stated often enough that marriage was not in his future plans. She was not going to beg. 'We are friends and we respect each other, but that is as far as it goes.'

'Then you will hold all the blame for a narrow lonely bed.'

'Aunt!'

'They put Edmund in the grave, not you. You are not some Indian widow who is forced to sit on a burning pyre to prove your devotion. You should take a closer look at Mr Montemorcy.' Her aunt gave her a piercing stare. 'You might be surprised. He does have a rather well-turned calf. Youth is wasted on the young.'

Henri stared at her aunt, shocked. Not only had she noticed Robert's legs, but felt she could comment on them! 'Have you been taking sips of the cherry brandy again?'

'I may be elderly, niece, but my eyes work.' Her aunt gave a thoroughly unrepentant smile. 'And as legs go, Mr Montemorcy's are well worth noticing. And without his jacket on, you can see the muscles in his back rippling.'

Henri rolled her eyes heavenwards and tried to regain control of her breathing. Granted, her aunt was trying to matchmake, but the image she had just conjured up was a powerful one. 'You do get the strangest notions in your head. I shall change and hopefully we can have a suitable conversation over lunch.'

'Yes, your linen dress is showing a few moss stains on the skirt.' Her aunt's eyes danced. 'It must have happened when you were gardening. You should take more care.'

'I did rather too much gardening. I forgot to bring a cloth to kneel on.' Henri brushed the moss stain on the side of her skirt. 'The borders were neglected when I was at Montemorcy's. There is still much to be done. I did not want to miss a single damaged bloom.'

'If you concentrated more on Mr Montemorcy than on your gardening, he might have stayed.' Her aunt popped a cucumber sandwich into her mouth. 'He missed an excellent repast and it will have been your fault.'

'I will remember that.' She kept her shoulders down and her head up. She had to say something and she couldn't explain why it would be a bad idea for her to see Robert alone. Seeing him in company was surely permissible though. 'Next time, Aunt, I will endeavour to make sure Mr Montemorcy stays for cucumber sandwiches.'

'Will there be a next time?'

Henri leant back, remembering how Robert had kissed her nose before he left and how his hand had given her arm a light caress. A warm curl of desire wound its way around her insides. A next time? Her entire being demanded it, even though her head screamed that she should be wary. 'I hope so.'

'Has Miss Ravel returned, Downing? Is Mrs Ravel with her?'

His butler stood in the hallway, looking at him. His face became grave. 'Not precisely, sir. Mrs Ravel is here, but has been indisposed all day with a headache.'

'Sophie is here.' Robert tried to look around Downing's bulk. All the way back from Market Square he kept telling himself that Miss Armstrong's notions were fustian nonsense. Sophie would not be as foolish as to actually elope with Sebastian Cawburn. Doctor Lumley had caught her eye, and she'd learnt her lesson about rakes and other ne'er-do-wells. 'She has to be here.'

'Miss Ravel returned earlier in a dishevelled state, but she has departed again with her basket. I believe she had some visiting of the infirm to do. Miss Ravel seeks to emulate Lady Thorndike by taking an interest in the general populace rather than simply attending frivolous At Homes.'

Silently Robert cursed Sophie. She obviously had decided that she had had enough of Miss Armstrong and her social pretensions. However, it didn't explain the basket. Where had Sophie gone? Had she quarrelled with her stepmother as well? But then why did she not wait for the carriage? He drew a steadying breath. Miss Armstrong had put ideas into his head. He required facts rather than speculation, innuendo and gossip. Calm cool logic and digestion of facts rather giving way to sentiment.

'Did she say where she was going? Or how long she might be gone?'

'No, sir, but she did leave this.' Downing held out a sealed letter. 'With instructions to hand it to you personally on your return.'

With impatient fingers, Robert broke the seal.

The bold lettering stood out. She was sorry to cause him pain, but she had decided her future was best spent with the man she loved—Viscount Cawburn. She trusted that he understood, but by the time he read this, she would be well on her way to being married. She had decided to elope just like dear Henrietta Thorndike had done. *Dear Henrietta Thorndike.* Perfidious exasperating Henrietta Thorndike, who had just happened to utterly and completely unexpectedly melt in his arms this morning. Henri, who had seemed perturbed about a family matter this morning. Dear Henrietta Thorndike, who on the evening of the ball confessed to having meddled, but he had ignored it. Just as he had ignored a hundred other little insignificant details she had said. That she liked to keep secrets, or that they needed to suspend the wager or that Mrs Ravel always had a headache after a dinner party. And last night they had dined at the Croziers'. Cawburn had known when to strike. Isolated incidents? Or part of a deliberate plan?

Robert felt as if someone had punched him in the stomach. He'd thought her a friend. His father had insisted on applying cool logic to women and had warned him about the folly of trusting women. He'd allowed his emotions to cloud his judgement.

'Are you all right, sir?' Downing asked. 'You have turned pale.'

'I'm fine, Downing.' Robert crumpled the piece of paper between his fingers. He didn't want to make a hasty judgement. He needed to weigh all the evidence first. 'Get me Fredericks. And get the carriage ready to go. We leave within the hour.'

'Is Miss Sophie all right, sir?' Downing's face creased with concern. 'She is a great favourite amongst the servants. I did not really think anything was amiss. Lord Cawburn, after all, is Lady Thorndike's cousin.'

'I do hope so, Downing. I most sincerely hope so.' Robert tried to concentrate. Panic would not help matters. He needed to go about the search methodically and rationally.

'And one other thing, sir.' Downing's voice floated down the corridor. 'Cook reported to me that Miss Sophie came into the kitchen before she left. A large cast-iron frying pan has gone missing. Cook thought you ought to be informed. She'd like it returned. It is her favourite.'

'I cannot see what use my ward would have with a frying pan, particularly not if she is eloping. Cook must be mistaken.'

'Very good, sir. I will inform Cook of her mistake.'

'Where is Fredericks? Fredericks! I have need of you!' Robert thundered. His voice echoed up the stairs, mocking him.

'Mr Fredericks is out in the garden. I'll fetch him.' One of the upper-stair maids peeked over the banister at him.

While he waited for Fredericks, Robert withdrew the note from his pocket and rapidly scanned it again, searching for clues as to where the errant couple had gone. His ire grew as he realised the inconsistencies his initial shock had blinded him to. Despite the letter being in Sophie's name, it wasn't Sophie's handwriting. And Sophie wouldn't have called Henri *Henrietta*. Henri's elopement with Sir Edmund Thorndike was not strictly common knowledge and he doubted anyone else would have mentioned it. There was something about the writing that reminded him of Henri's. His stomach did a sickening lurch.

Robert strode to his study, withdrew the note he'd received earlier today asking him to visit Henri from the top drawer of his desk and compared it to Sophie's letter. The same hand. Same author.

He tore through his desk, attempting to find anything else in Henri's hand. A scrap of paper, anything. He came across the notice about the dancing classes. It was similar writing even down to the way the *H*'s were formed. Except Henri had denied all knowledge of the note earlier.

So who wrote them? Cawburn or Henri? Cawburn didn't have the wit. It was Henri who was blessed with the brains, Henri who possessed a steely nerve. But would she do such a thing? His instinct screamed there had to be another explanation, but, furious and desperately concerned, he dismissed it. He could remember his father desperately seeking another explanation for his stepmother's actions and ignoring the obvious. He'd always vowed that in such cases, he'd go with the cold hard facts. The handwriting was far too close. All the notes had to be written by the same hand.

He was seven times a fool to seek any other explanation.

Thorndike was up to her pretty neck. It explained her enthusiastic reception earlier. It explained the note and so many things from her acquiescence to staying at his house to the sudden desire to learn more about the scientific method and logic.

Cold logic rather than emotion. Facts rather than feelings—he'd sworn that when he found out about the manner of his father's death. He was never going to be deceived in the way his stepmother had deceived his father.

Robert slammed his fist against the desk. He had trusted her. He wanted to trust her now, but he had the evidence in front of him. He hated the black pit that had opened in his soul.

Thorndike had used him in the worst possible way. She served as bait and distraction in order to allow the pair to escape. And he had followed along, willingly, each step of the way. He could see it all now and the betrayal hurt far more than it should. He had been a lovesick fool and he'd danced to Henri's tune. No more.

He took a breath of life-giving air. He'd warned her what would happen if she meddled in his private life and now she'd discover the consequences.

Chapter Thirteen

'Sebastian has been gone all day. He is doing more than simply visiting. All the At Homes are finished,' Henri remarked to Aunt Frances as they sat in the drawing room. The late-afternoon sun streamed into the room, giving it a golden glow. Everything about the afternoon seemed to be bathed in this wonderful light. She had never noticed how good it felt to be alive. It was as if she had been asleep for a very long time and now she was gloriously awake.

'That colour suits you, Henrietta,' her aunt said.

'It is simply my old dove-grey gown, nothing special. Lucia put a new lace trim around the neckline, so perhaps that is it.'

'It must be the way you have done your hair. But your eyes seem more vibrant.'

'It must be that. Artful disarray is all the rage this Season in London. Spend hours with a lady's maid to achieve the effect of spending an hour's gardening.' Henri forced her lungs to fill with air and to think logically rather than panicking. She had washed her face and splashed cool water on her wrists, but her colour must still be flushed. First Lucia, the maid she shared with Aunt Frances, and now Aunt Frances had remarked how the gown suddenly suited her complexion far more.

Henri shifted uneasily, uncertain how this new life of duplicity and wickedness would be kept a secret from those closest to her. It had to be or she'd never be received in polite society again. As long as it was not overtly conspicuous, she thought they would be all right. And already her mind was trying to work out how and when they'd next meet.

She had not fully considered the consequences when she gave her mouth up to Robert's on the evening of the ball. But there was nothing morally wrong with what she was doing as neither was married.

It was only now away from him that the doubts and fears hit her. And yet she knew if he came into the room, all thoughts of propriety would fly from her head. Even with Edmund, she had not felt this all-consuming attraction. With Edmund, she had been safe. Her white knight who rode to the rescue. He had been someone she had loved for a long time. He had made her feel as if she belonged, rather than being some unwanted encumbrance. Theirs was supposed to be a love to last for all time. She had planned it that way. Only it hadn't. And even the grief had faded to nothingness. She could barely recognise the woman she had once been.

Robert challenged her. He was stubborn, mulish and inclined to favour getting his own way. But their arguments brightened her day. Henri took a steadying breath. This was not some finer feeling, but passion, and passion always faded. She had watched it happen more times than she liked to count. She had to start thinking with her head, and leave her heart out of it. And right now, she needed to know where Sebastian was and get rid of this vague sense of unease.

'Aunt, you are hiding something. Did you give Sebastian money?' Henri leant forwards and caught her aunt's cold hand. 'Should we send Reynolds out searching for him? Do you think his visiting included a stop at the King's Head?'

'Sebastian is securing his future, but had no wish to worry you.' Her aunt squeezed Henri's hand before letting go. 'He is concerned that you remained unwell. He thinks your nerves were affected in the dog attack. You'll be proud of him. He is taking responsibility for his life.'

A distinct cold shiver crept down Henri's spine. Sebastian taking charge of his life could quite possibly end in disaster; what was more worrying, he had enticed his mother to lie to her. She swallowed hard. Sebastian would not, he could not bring her into his scheme this time. She was finished with rescuing him.

'Is this why you told me he was visiting the neighbours? I am no child to be kept in the dark with a pretty fable. Why doesn't that bring me comfort?'

'He wanted it to be a lovely surprise for you!'

'What have you lied to me about, Aunt?'

'*Lying* is far too strong a word. I prefer—*giving only part of the truth*. There was little point in making you anxious. I agreed with Sebastian on that point. He had to take the risk and not always wonder. If you were well, you'd have agreed. You have always helped out with such schemes. Dear Sebastian has always been grateful…even if he hasn't always said so in so many words.'

Henri crossed her arms. It was bad enough having Sebastian being difficult, but Aunt Frances was concealing things from her as well. Her nerves being damaged! Sebastian told some rather large lies. It was more likely the fact she refused to abandon her friendship with Robert Montemorcy and had given him no help in his attempted conquest of Sophie. Sebastian wouldn't have drawn her into an intrigue without her knowledge. She refused to be ensnared.

'You are treating me like a child of six, rather than a widow of twenty-six.' Henri bit out each word. 'I've never suffered from nerves, not even when Edmund died. And whatever mess Sebastian makes, I will be the one who has to clean it up, just as I always do.'

'But you're so good at it. And you're worrying over nothing. Sebastian will sort it out. He promised.'

'Nerves are for women with far too much time on their hands. To even imply that is grossly insulting.'

'You do him a great disservice.' Her aunt reached for her book and opened it. 'He wants to clear all the debts and start his future free and clear. I thought he ought to be given the chance. He is my only child.'

'His future? He has gone back to London? Or has he gone to the Continent?' Henri's heart lifted. She was not going to have to face Sebastian and his accusations of betrayal if he learnt about Robert. With any luck, he never would.

'He took my carriage this morning and promised to return in three days' time with his fortune made. He even promised to buy back Chestercamp. He was always such a sweet boy. I dare say we can get on with the governess cart or a sedan chair.'

Henri laughed. Her heart suddenly felt light. It made it easier somehow that Sebastian was gone. She had worried that he might ask awkward questions or, even worse, guess. As it was, a few days' grace would enable her to figure out how she would dissemble when the inevitable scathing remark about Robert Montemorcy came. 'I wonder why he did not take his carriage. He knows your carriage is slow and badly sprung. It is liable to break down at any moment.'

Sounds of raised voices filled the library, drowning out her aunt's reply. Henri frowned as her body trembled. One of the voices was Robert's. And something had angered him.

Henri put her hand to her mouth. Fear numbed her brain. Someone had seen them. It only could be that. Nothing else. Her life was about to irrevocably change.

'Out of my way, man!' Robert bellowed. 'I want answers. Answers only Lady Thorndike can give. I will not be deterred by a servant!'

Reynolds blocked the entrance to the drawing room. Around his bulk, Henri could see a desperate Robert. At her signal and with an urbane bow, Reynolds allowed Robert into the drawing room.

Robert stumbled once, straightened his greatcoat and strode into the room. His looming presence made the room seem small.

'Well, Lady Thorndike, what do you have to say for yourself? Are you proud of all that you achieved this morning?' Robert's harsh accusatory words cut through her, stabbing her in the heart. He'd condemned her of a crime, but she was innocent. The only crime she'd committed was to give in to his seduction.

Henri crossed her arms and kept her chin up. She took a steadying breath. No man was going to treat her in that fashion! She was not some strumpet to be seduced and discarded at will.

'You will not abuse Reynolds in that fashion. He is not your servant, but my aunt's,' Henri said, trying for a calm serenity. 'Something is obviously bothering you, Mr Montemorcy, but I can assure you that it is nothing that my aunt's servant has done. Or, indeed, any member of this household.'

'Your cousin and Miss Ravel! Where are they? You must know.' He looked about the room as if he expected to see the pair cowering behind the damask sofa. 'Sophie! I want to speak to you!'

'Neither Sebastian nor Sophie are here. Sophie has never visited this house.' Henri stared at him in astonishment. Sebastian and Sophie were together somewhere? Eloped? Instantly she rejected the notion as fustian nonsense. Sophie would never go willingly with Sebastian, not if she had told Henri the truth, and Sebastian would never force a woman. But Aunt Frances had spoken of Sebastian's plan. Was this it? Suddenly, Henri struggled to breathe. Leaping to conclusions would be fatal. Somewhere, somehow, this coil was a mistake. It would need a steady hand and a cool head to untangle it. 'Jumping to ridiculous assumptions will not solve anything.'

'An officious manner will not deflect me. Surely you can do better than that, Lady Thorndike.' Robert stood, bristling with anger. 'They have run away together.'

'How do you know that they are together?' Henri attempted a placating smile, but the knots in her stomach tightened. Everything seemed to slow down. Sebastian's new scheme. He thought she was involved. 'I think I'd have known if something like this was planned. And I can assure you that neither confided any such scheme to me. Quite the opposite, in Sophie's case. Where is your proof, Mr Montemorcy? Or is it merely some village tittle-tattle gone wrong?'

Robert thrust a piece of paper under her nose and she caught a flash of hurt betrayal in his eyes that was almost instantly masked. 'My ward has run away with your cousin and I want to know what part you played. After all, *dear Sebastian* would never do anything like this without consulting you first, Lady Thorndike. You're the oracle for all things matrimonial. Miss Armstrong also waylaid me with the news! How long have you been planning this?'

Henri took the letter and rapidly read it before numbly handing it to her aunt. All the bright glory of earlier faded to a dull grey. She'd been living in a fool's paradise. She'd been caught in Sebastian's web of intrigue and there was no way that Robert would believe in her innocence.

'Sebastian, what have you done?' she whispered, glancing up into Robert's hard unyielding face.

'No, Henrietta, no! Not this!' Her aunt gasped and rapidly began to fan herself. 'He promised me no scandal. Do you think I would have lent him my carriage if I thought there would be a scandal?'

It was only then the full import washed over her. It was no malicious slander on Miss Armstrong's part, or contretemps with a bored wife. Sebastian was with Sophie. He'd eloped with a débutante. Or worse. This situation had all the hallmarks of a Sebastian-induced disaster, but even Sebastian in his supreme selfishness could not have realised what he had set in motion. How she had fallen into Robert's arms and made love to him. She had behaved little better than a harlot, but it had been her desire for Robert that had driven her, rather than some misguided attempt to give Sebastian the opportunity to elope with Sophie. He had to understand that fact without her saying anything. Or otherwise…

Her insides became encased in ice. Robert and her. He thought she had something to do with it. That she had meddled or, worse still, facilitated it.

An ice-cold hand gripped her heart. He had to believe her innocence. Without trust, where was love? She'd been a fool to think she could experience passion without her emotions being engaged. She did have feelings for Robert but he had none for her.

'Are you willing to give me an explanation now, Lady Thorndike?' The underlying note of passionate anger shimmered in his voice. 'What was your part in this wretched affair? As you said, you were bound to be involved if the pair ran away together, and they've run. You were the one who counselled me not to read her letters. You were the one who advocated Sophie going to the ball where she did dance with Cawburn.'

'I played no part. Sebastian and Sophie both duped me.' Henri held out her hands and willed him to believe. She was innocent on that accusation. She shouldn't have to explain to him of all people. He should understand, after what they had shared, that she couldn't hurt him in that way. 'I wish them well, but this is the first I have heard of the elopement. Believe me, please. You must believe me.'

Robert's features showed a look of immense pain before hardening into a disdainful mask. 'You deny your part. You contend that you had nothing to do with the elopement. And you expect me to believe that.'

'Yes, I do.' Henri clasped her hands together and tried to hang on to that flash of vulnerability, rather than his avenging-angel look. Somewhere inside him that passionate lover of earlier today lurked and had to be listening to her and believing.

She waited, but his look grew colder and more remote. Her words of denial had fallen on deaf ears. Henri attempted to swallow around the growing lump in her throat. He'd no finer feeling for her. For him, it had all been physical need. And for her, it had been an expression of emotion, a desire to be close to him. Despite her vows and declarations, she'd done the unthinkable—she'd fallen in love. The knowledge tasted like ash in her mouth. But in that instant she knew she could never let him know. She couldn't risk being hurt again.

Keeping her gaze on a point above his shoulder, she started again in a voice that picked up strength and purpose with each word that she uttered. 'I'd no idea that they were going to run away together. I thought the romance was dead. Sophie seemed far more interested in Doctor Lumley than an ageing rake, which is what she called Sebastian on the last morning I was at the New Lodge. I told Sebastian this. I told him to grow up and solve his problems on his own.'

She was proud of the way she finished. She waited for his abject apology.

'Your protestation of innocence grows increasingly wearisome, Lady Thorndike.' He grabbed her by the shoulders and held her away from him. His mobile mouth, which only a few hours before had kissed her senseless, was now an angry white line, his eyes hardened points of coal instead of multicoloured pools.

Henri's insides twisted. He believed her guilty without even waiting for her explanation. It was as if what lay between them was irrevocably shattered, leaving only bitterness and resentment. And she knew she would miss that ease and friendship. She was bereft and alone. Unjustly accused. And her brilliant idea of it only being the physical that she cared about was a foolish lie. It had gone beyond the physical for her. She had cared and cared deeply for Robert, and his refusal to believe her hurt far more than it should.

'Why shouldn't I when I am innocent?' she retorted in a furious undertone.

'Innocent? You?' Robert shook his head as he struggled to hang on to his temper. Henri was lying through her teeth and he wanted to know why she cared so little for him. 'It's clear what happened and how you two conspired. The poor stupid man will be so blinded by Lady Thorndike's attention that he will not even notice what is going on beneath his nose. Will not even notice until it is far too late. How do you think that makes me feel?'

Henri twisted in his grasp, but he clung on, wanting her to admit the truth. He wanted to shake her or to kiss her senseless. Anything to get her to tell him the truth. 'You have it all wrong. Now let me go!'

Lady Cawburn advanced towards them. Her widow's cap quivered as she reached for the poker. 'Mr Montemorcy, stop assaulting my niece!'

The words shocked him back to sensibility. He released her, not knowing who he loathed more—Henri for deceiving him or himself for losing his temper.

'Forgive me, my emotions overcame me.'

Henri stumbled away from him. She wrapped her arms about her middle and tried to keep her heart from breaking into a thousand shards. Robert wanted to believe the worst of her.

'I wish I could help, but I had no idea this was going to happen,' she said, blinking furiously. She refused to humiliate herself further and beg. 'I've not left this house all day. You were here earlier. Do you think I could keep something like this hidden from you? I'm dreadful at keeping secrets, truly I am.'

'I know where you were this morning, and that I was with you. You summoned me.' He paused and his gaze travelled slowly and insolently down her, as if he were remembering every curve of her body. A hot flush crept up Henri's body. 'The note purporting to be from Sophie is not in her hand, but in the same hand as the note I received this morning from you, asking me to visit and discuss the proposed picnic.'

'I wrote no note.' A deep chill entered her bones. He had called because a note had been sent in her name, a note written by the same person who had penned the one from Sophie. Sebastian had set her up. He had been the one to play Cupid, not her aunt. This was his doing, everything, and she'd blundered into a trap. 'Show me the note and I will prove it is not in my hand.'

'Compare the two. Compare it with the notice about the dancing classes. Prove me wrong.' He reached into his pocket and thrust the other notes into her hand.

Henri gingerly plucked the papers from Robert's fingertips, being careful not to touch him. Her name was boldly scrawled, including the distinctive *H* she used. Nausea rose in her throat.

'Why would I write about the other forfeit? I had agreed the treasure-hunt picnic needed to be held elsewhere. I understand about the scientific method and what you are trying to achieve. You said to look at facts, and right now you are ignoring them. You have decided that I'm guilty when, in fact, I'm innocent.'

The silence pressed down on her soul, but she kept her head high, stared directly into Robert's eyes and willed him to believe. A myriad of emotions washed over his face.

'My son did send a note over to your house earlier,' her aunt said, breaking the silence. 'He didn't say who wrote it or divulge its contents.'

Robert closed his eyes. A sliver of hope sliced through him. Maybe Henri hadn't behaved badly. All of his instincts told him to fold her into his arms and apologise, but he couldn't, not until he knew for certain.

'One must be logical about these things,' he said finally in a flat voice. 'Logic before emotion.'

Their eyes met for a long moment and then Henri dropped her head and examined the carpet.

'No, you are right,' she said in a voice devoid of emotion. 'The reason why you came over this morning has no meaning now. My mistake, such as it was, was not to ask to see that note then. This entire affair might not have happened if I had.'

Henri was proud of the way her voice remained steady. Inside, her stomach ached with searing pain. Her pleasant dream of a quiet affair with Robert lay in ashes at her feet. There could never be anything between them because of the trick Sebastian had played. If Robert had not come over here, if they had not made love, Sophie might not have been ruined. She knew it and Robert knew it. What might have been was already over.

'What does he intend for Sophie? Marriage to clear his debts?' Robert's voice came from a long way away.

Henri wrapped her hands about her waist. She wanted him to hold her and to tell her that this time she was not alone and Sebastian had not gone too far. That everything would end happily. But long ago, she had given up wishing for the moon. She gave her head a shake and tried to concentrate on the matter at hand rather than what might have been. 'He mentioned that he thought her an angel and the idea of marriage had crossed his mind.'

'I see.' He nodded towards her aunt. 'Forgive the intrusion, Lady Cawburn. I had hopes of finding my ward before her reputation was irreparably damaged. But I see I was led along a false trail.'

Or she was condemned to an unwise marriage. The unspoken words hung in the air.

'You don't see and you are wilfully misunderstanding.' Henri grabbed his sleeve. He looked down at her with cold hard eyes and she released him. 'You are looking at it all wrong, just as you always do. Sometimes you have to trust your instincts.'

'Instinct leads you down false paths.'

'My ideas are better than your blind logic!' Henri cried.

Robert shook his head. He stood in the middle of the room, taking huge gulps of air. His hands clenched and unclenched, but he made no move to touch her. He appeared lost and alone, a little boy instead of the angry man, the boy who had idolised Sophie's father and given him his promise to look after his daughter. The young man whose father had committed suicide rather than face the disgrace of his new wife leaving him for another man. And she knew how seriously he took his responsibility. Despite everything, she wanted to gather him in her arms and hold him. She wanted to wring Sebastian's neck for doing this.

'You never give up. Even now,' he said in a low voice.

Her head throbbed with pain. Logic. She had to think and find a way to see her way out of this tangle. 'I want to know why Sophie lied to me about Doctor Lumley. Why she pretended to be my friend and then implicated me in this. They deceived us both.'

Robert stood there, a muscle twitching in his cheek. Henri watched him with her heart in her throat. He had to believe her or otherwise everything they had shared counted for nothing.

'Why did Cawburn take Miss Ravel in this clandestine manner? Why didn't he court her openly?' her aunt asked.

'His creditors,' Henri answered without hesitation. 'He was being pressed. He'd tried to win the money back at the gaming table and lost heavily. He will have seen her fortune as the only way to free himself. But in his own way, I am sure he thinks he loves her. I truly believe that.'

'He knew what he had to do to stop being pressed. I informed him of the actions required several times,' Robert ground out. 'He refused to listen or take any heed of my advice.'

Henri put her hand to her throat and her knees buckled. Robert was Sebastian's main creditor, the man pushing Sebastian to the brink? She stumbled over to the armchair as her stomach roiled.

'*You?* You hold his paper? Then you are to blame for this!' Henri cried. 'You were the creditor who had pushed Sebastian to this?'

'It seemed prudent.' Robert pulled at his cuffs stubbornly. A faint flush appeared on his cheeks. 'I wanted his situation to be brought home to him. All he needed to do was to clear his debts and the obstacle to my ward would have been removed. He refused. I then asked him to quit the neighbourhood. He refused. I was left with no choice.'

Henri rolled her eyes heavenwards. He'd pushed and pushed Sebastian until Sebastian had had to act. 'I'm pleased to have seen such a master at work. And you said that I'd no business meddling.'

'I took prudent steps.'

'Prudent! When has prudency ever had anything to do with love?'

Robert gave her a knowing look and she knew he, too, remembered those highly imprudent moments in the garden this morning.

Henri started to pace the drawing room, trying to think and to keep her mind from going back to those moments. 'Sebastian is singularly lacking in imagination. He should be easy to find.'

'On that we are agreed, but he has had the wit to arrange a marriage with a very wealthy young lady.'

'Only because his creditors were pressing.' Henri glared at Robert, who developed an interest in the carpet. 'But I want to find them. I want to make sure that Sebastian does the decent thing and that Sophie understands everyone in *my* family will stand by her.'

He lifted his eyes. 'Why?'

Henri held out her hands. 'You seem to feel that somehow I contributed to this débâcle. I want to find them so I can have the pleasure of wringing his neck. This is a thousand times worse than the pugs.'

'Gretna Green is the usual destination in these cases,' Aunt Frances declared. 'We'd best start there.'

'I've already sent my man and Mrs Ravel in pursuit. They've taken the express to Carlisle.'

Henri put her hand to her throat. Mrs Ravel was already speeding her way towards Carlisle. Robert had come here not to find out about Sebastian's whereabouts, but to punish her. But there was something that was not right. A detail… Why would Sebastian borrow her aunt's carriage when he could simply take the train?

'No, Sebastian will not go to Gretna Green,' Henri said, tapping her fingers together. 'Sebastian always has said that he would never elope to Gretna. It is far too plebeian. And Jedburgh is easier to get to from Corbridge if one is going by carriage. He wants you to waste time searching around Gretna Green. And he borrowed Aunt's carriage to go visiting. It is better sprung for travelling. Details are important, Montemorcy. Instinct.'

She tilted her chin in the air and dared Robert to argue differently.

'The logic of your mind always impresses, Thorndike,' Robert said sarcastically.

'You are right, Henrietta. I'd forgotten about Jedburgh,' Aunt Frances said far too quickly. 'Only a month ago, the farmer's daughter and the butcher's son went up there and returned wed. Of course, her mother insisted on a church blessing of the marriage. But it was the talk of the ball.'

'And he will not go to the Continent, not without securing his funds first,' Robert said, stalking about the room. 'But a Scottish marriage is not what I would have wanted for Sophie. They can go through a proper church marriage.'

'But what does Sophie want?' Henri said, crossing her arms and looking hard at Robert. 'Even my cousin is not that insensible to society's dictates. He knows that he cannot just ruin a débutante and he needs her funds. I do hope Sophie knew what she was doing. Did she take anything with her?'

'Apparently a frying pan. Why Sophie would want such an article, I have no idea. Sophie can't cook.'

A frying pan. Henri winced, remembering her conversation with Sophie about men who were unsafe in carriages. 'And if Sophie doesn't want to marry?'

'They will have to be made to understand what is at stake,' her aunt said. 'If this Ravel chit is ruined, then he will do the decent thing…or else.'

'Reluctantly, I agree with Lady Frances. Cawburn will not be allowed to ruin my ward. Either he is stopped or they marry. My promise to Sophie's father compels me.'

'Aunt.' Henri forced her voice to stay even. The frying pan changed everything. Someone had to look after Sophie and make sure that she was all right. Someone had to stop Robert before he compounded his error. 'It is why I plan to go with Mr Montemorcy and make Sebastian understand his position. He has gone too far this time. Even if Mr Montemorcy discovers the pair and they are unwed, Sebastian might refuse out of pure devilment.'

Her aunt gave a reluctant nod. 'That would be dreadful for everyone. I will go and see if Sebastian left any clues in his room.'

She hurried from the room, holding a handkerchief to her face. Henri heard a muffled sob in the corridor.

'My aunt…believed the best of her son. She thought he'd changed.'

'And you would be prepared to leave immediately?' Robert raised an arrogant eyebrow. 'Or are you like other ladies requiring several days of preparation?'

'I can leave within the hour and we can travel throughout the night.' Henri lifted her chin. Several days of preparation! What sort of ninny did he take her for? She could travel as swiftly as any man. Swifter than most. 'Did Sophie leave her maid?'

'She did.' Robert waved a dismissive hand. 'I have already interviewed her. She knows nothing or at least nothing she is willing to say to me.'

'Grace can come with us,' Henri said, concentrating on the practicalities rather than on what Robert had done. 'My aunt and I share a maid and I have no wish to deprive Aunt Frances. Grace can serve me for now. Sophie will be glad of her.'

'You appear to have worked everything out in a very short period, Thorndike.'

'It's my family's honour at stake as well yours, Mr Montemorcy.' Henri crossed her arms. It hurt beyond describing knowing that she loved him and that he hated her—hadn't trusted her enough to give her the benefit of the doubt in this awful situation. 'If you refuse to allow me to join forces, I'll go on my own. I want to clear my name, and I'll take great pleasure in watching you eat humble pie.'

He grabbed her elbow and murmured in her ear, 'One of us will. If you are playing games, Thorndike, you will regret it.'

'Are you a coward, Montemorcy?' she asked in an undertone. 'Or are you worried about something else?'

A muscle jumped in his cheek. 'Nothing. Do you know what you are doing?'

'I can assure you that I'm able to control my desires,' she said with dignity. He should have believed her without question. She'd mistaken lust for something more. And it would be a lesson to her. The only way she knew how to get over hurt was to concentrate on someone else, and the nearest person to hand was Sophie Ravel. But whatever happened after this adventure, she and Robert were finished. Somehow the prospect made her feel unbearably sad. She was not ready for it to end. She wanted Robert to admit his mistake. She wanted to find a way, but happy-ever-afters only happened in fairy tales.

His cool eyes assessed her. 'Very well, you may come, Lady Thorndike, if you're ready within the hour.'

Chapter Fourteen

To Robert's astonishment, Henri was waiting in Dyvels' courtyard with her portmanteau at her feet and a fearsome expression on her face when he returned with the carriage an hour later. And he knew that he had made a grave error. He had been far too ready to believe in her guilt, far too ready to condemn.

'We should have an hour or two before the carriage lamps need to be lit and it never gets truly dark at this time of year,' Henri said as he alighted. She moved briskly towards the carriage and he knew the ultra-efficient Thorndike was back. Somewhere beneath all those layers was the passionate woman he had held in his arms this morning. His desire to reach that woman confused him. He was supposed to believe in logic, not emotions. 'We can make good time if your carriage is fast. My aunt's is cumbersome at best and liable to break down. Sebastian—'

'We need to discuss this morning,' Robert said in an undertone, touching her elbow. She jumped as if his touch burnt her, he noted with grim satisfaction. 'Before you get into the carriage. Too much is unsettled.'

Henri caught her lip between her teeth and turned her head away. Her poke bonnet shadowed her face. 'This morning is best forgotten. An aberration. A mistake I should bitterly regret. Giving in to passion was wrong. Logic shall rule every move from now on. Pray do not refer to it again.'

'But I'm very glad you did.' He kept his back straight, but his heart sank. This was going to be harder than he had considered. He'd hoped that after a few words of apology, all would be well.

'The situation became out of control for both of us.' Her voice became clipped as if she was saying a prepared speech. 'It must never happen again. After we find Sophie and Sebastian, then we shall only meet in public. I'm going on this journey to ensure the proper thing is done. Our friendship such as it was is over, Mr Montemorcy. There's no trust between us.'

'Whom don't you trust, Henri?'

'Please.' She raised a gloved hand. 'I've no wish for a vulgar scene.'

Silently Robert vowed that it wasn't over. He would discover a way to break through her barriers once again. He would find a way back. He wasn't going to lose her now. He reached out and caught her arm. This time, she remained still. 'I can respect your decision. It doesn't mean I agree with it.'

'We quarrelled and that's the end to it.'

'Friends can quarrel and make up. They can forgive. To understand a friend…'

Her eyes widened and he knew that, despite everything, she was far from indifferent. 'Are we even friends?'

Robert took a deep breath as her words cut deep into him. 'I'd like to think so. We have certainly gone beyond mere acquaintances.'

'You did not trust me before. You believed Hortense Armstrong rather than believing in me. Common gossip. And false letters. I told you that I didn't send you a note this morning. You wanted to believe the worst of me and you did.' She lowered her head so the brim of her bonnet shielded her face. 'I deserved better.'

'You did. An honest mistake,' he admitted reluctantly. 'Am I not allowed to make mistakes? Faulty logic. Please understand, Henri,

I gave my word to James Ravel that I'd keep his daughter safe. It was his dying request. James saved my life as a young man. After my father's tragic death, all the creditors were pressing for payment; he alone stood by me and believed in me. And I've failed him in the one thing he asked of me. Believing the worst in you made it easier than admitting my failings.'

Henri pulled away from his grasp, her bonnet trembling. 'We need to leave, Mr Montemorcy, otherwise we will be forced to stop before we find them. I've no wish to sleep in an inn.'

Robert watched Henri's chin slide downwards and then her head jerk upwards as she carefully held her body away from him. Sophie's maid had long since given herself up to sleep. The faint light from the carriage lamps filled the carriage.

'Are you too tired to continue, Henri?' he asked softly. 'Shall we stop?'

She sat bolt upright and hugged her beaded reticule tighter to her chest. 'Who, me? I can sleep anywhere. I swear it.'

'I will take that under consideration. For our next wager.'

He was rewarded with a tiny laugh. He hated the way the sound of her laugh made his heart leap. 'Whatever it is, I'll win. You deserve to lose.'

'You always say that.'

'Because it is the truth, Mr Montemorcy.' She paused, fiddling with the catch of her reticule. Then she lifted her head and her eyes bore into him. 'Why did you do it?'

'Do what?' He stared at her, a thousand different things coursing through his brain. Why had he kissed her? Why had he made love to her? Why had he not wanted to believe in her innocence? Why did he fear what he felt for her? He knew he wasn't ready to give those sort of answers. He wasn't ready to see the contempt in her eyes.

She folded her hands in her lap. 'There was no reason to drive Sebastian towards Queer Street and bankruptcy. I had matters perfectly under control. I've known my cousin far longer than you. I know how he operates.'

His shoulders relaxed slightly. This was about Sebastian, rather than them. 'Did you? Do you think that is the only reason it happened?'

'Sophie Ravel has money and Sebastian was infatuated. But he was managing.'

'On the contrary, he amassed his debts on his own. I merely bought some of his paper as insurance. Unlike your aunt, I am far from convinced that he will do the right thing without persuasion. James Ravel lost one fortune due to an aristocrat fleeing the country. He entrusted me to make sure his daughter didn't lose a second one. I owe him that much. His daughter will not have to live like a pauper.'

'And if Sophie doesn't want to marry him? What will you do to his debts then? Will you explain to everyone that his credit is once again good now that he is no threat to you?'

'The only good thing that will come of it is that some of the ordinary people, the tradesmen who extended him credit to buy his boots, or the tailor who keeps him in waistcoats, won't suffer. Did you think about them or are they beneath your notice?'

'He will pay the money back…somehow.' She ducked her head. 'I suppose something else will have to be sold… I'd thought he'd learnt his lesson. And everything else will go on as it always has. Sophie will suffer no lasting stain.'

'You're wrong. They will marry. They will have to. No one forced her to get into that carriage, Henri. Both you and your aunt were agreed on that. Sophie went of her free will.'

'Sophie is young. If she has thought better of marrying my cousin, then what? Will she be forced to marry a debtor? How far will you go to ensure your promise to a dead man? It is Sophie's future we are speaking about.'

He threw his hat on to the seat and ran his hands through his hair.

'I don't know. I want to prevent the scandal from getting worse. Sophie needs to be protected. She is far too young to know her mind. Someone has to decide what is best for her future.'

She wrapped her cloak about her and moved closer to the window. 'And you know best. Just as you knew best about the notes and who to blame.'

Robert's breath caught. He had to take the risk and explain. 'I was ten when my mother died and all the light went out in the world. My father brought me up to trust the rational rather than my emotions. Then he remarried—a bright young thing and he seemed to love her far more than me. He lavished all sorts of material advantage on her to keep her happy. She died giving birth to another man's child and he killed himself rather than continue. I then fell in love with a woman who I thought would love me for ever, only to discover she was angling after a richer prize. I find it very hard to trust instinct, Henri.' He reached over and touched her hand. 'I made a mistake because I wanted to. Does that satisfy your pride?'

'Pride has nothing to do with it. I know forced marriages don't work and right now I'm praying we catch up with them before Sophie is irrevocably ruined.'

Robert felt as if he'd been punched in the gut. She hadn't forgiven him. Henri should understand. Sophie was his responsibility. His head had been so certain that Henri had been in league with Cawburn even when his heart revolted. And he had long ago stopped trusting his heart. Only he wanted to trust it now and wasn't sure if he could.

'Ask yourself this one question, Henri—if you were faced with the same evidence, would you have acted differently? I gave a death-bed promise to her father. Long ago I learnt to distrust my feelings, but I did go to you and ask. I wanted you to be innocent. It's why I went to you rather than going to Carlisle.'

Henri said nothing, just stared out the window at the darkening sky.

* * *

'There is an inn ahead,' the coachman called, waking Henri from a fitful sleep.

All of her muscles ached. In the enclosed space, her body was more aware of him than ever. Spending time with him in an enclosed carriage might not have been the best idea she had ever had, but she was stuck, and she wanted to prove him wrong. He of all people should have trusted her implicitly. Without trust, there wasn't anything. And yet, a tiny voice nagged in the back of her mind, she knew all about responsibility. She wanted to forgive him, particularly after hearing about his childhood. She wanted to feel his arms around her and his lips against her hair. She'd fallen in love with Robert Montemorcy.

Love. It was not a pleasant feeling. Not like the gentle feeling of wanting to make the world a better place for someone else that she had with Edmund, but a wild untamed thing that howled in anguish because he doubted her. She'd get over it. Someday. She had to. She refused to let him use her weakness against her.

'The horses need a rest,' the coachman called down. 'Good a place as any to change them.'

Henri peeked out through the window. A steady rain had begun to fall. A warm light shone through the darkness and an inn sign creaked in the wind.

'We stop here for the night.' Robert rapped on the top of the carriage, signalling to the coachman.

'Are we in Jedburgh?' Henri asked, stretching slightly. Jedburgh would be fine. They could start looking for Sophie. She wouldn't have to think about the temptation of spending a night in an inn. 'Your carriage is much swifter than my aunt's, I will grant you that.'

'No,' Robert said, gathering his greatcoat around him. He seemed remoter than ever. 'The horses are tired and there is little point in travelling further tonight. Grace has been complaining about feeling ill.'

'I'm sorry, ma'am,' the little maid said. 'I'm not a good traveller. I only need a few moments of fresh air. After that…'

Henri sat up straight and tried not to think about an anonymous inn with white linen sheets. Only this morning, it would have been a godsend, but now everything was conspiring against her. She glanced at the maid and saw a single tear dripped down her cheek. Robert was right. Grace wasn't well. It was one of the things she admired about him. He did think about servants as if they were people instead of objects. 'I thought we were travelling until we caught up with Sebastian. We agreed.'

'Your cousin likes his creature comforts. It's late and this is an excellent inn. I've stayed here on business before. As we have not caught up with Sophie before night fell, they will be marrying with my blessing and in a proper church.'

Her heart sank as she remembered the frying pan. Sophie had meant to send a message, but what sort of message and why hadn't she simply stayed at the house? Somehow, she had to find Sophie before Robert did and find out what had truly happened, what Sophie actually wanted. Then she could decide what was best… when she had all the facts. 'We could go on…after Grace has a breath of fresh air.'

'Why are you intent on proving how strong and capable you are? I can see you're exhausted.' His hand stroked her cheek. It was all she could do not to lean into the touch. The desire to be held in his embrace nearly overwhelmed her. 'We both will need our strength. You can sleep in the carriage, but I guarantee that the beds in the inn will be softer.'

Henri watched Grace's steady breath. The little maid had fallen asleep as soon as her head hit the pillow in the dressing room.

Henri had refused all offers of help from the innkeeper's wife, insisting on looking after Grace. Concentrating on Grace was supposed to be an antidote to the growing anticipation in her stomach. Robert had procured private rooms for both of them.

The worst part was that, thinking about how Robert had accused her several hours later, she knew she could have made the same mistake. Superficially she could see why, but she didn't understand how he'd made the mistake and she wanted to understand. She wanted to go back to that easy friendship they had had before, but it seemed impossible. She'd never had to forgive Edmund for anything except dying.

The feelings that were coursing through her were far too new. And she was lonely without him. The future without Robert was a bleak prospect. Was Robert right? Was it only her pride that was hurt?

'How's the patient?' Robert asked from the doorway. His hair flopped over his forehead and tiredness etched his face.

'Asleep. I gave her a sleeping draught.' Henri schooled her features and held up her bag. If she kept the conversation on Grace, he'd never guess her thoughts and desires. She wasn't ready to open herself up to more hurt. 'I came prepared. I've no idea of the state Sophie will be in. Poor Grace. Her head pained her. No doubt the day's events overcame her. She couldn't have continued on. You were right to stop. I wish I'd seen it earlier.'

'You're admitting that you were wrong. Is this a first, Thorndike?'

She concentrated on the coverlet and winced. 'I'm not perfect. I know how imperfect I am, but it doesn't stop me trying. Far easier to look after someone than give in to self-pity.'

'You always think of others…' He didn't move from the doorway. 'Now it's time for someone to think about you. You need to eat, Henri.'

'I will survive. I had muffins for tea with Aunt Frances.'

'It'd be a shame to let the light supper the innkeeper's wife has prepared go to waste. I had her lay a table in your room.'

The merest mention of food was enough to set her stomach rumbling. She pressed her hand against her gown.

'I was going to sit beside Grace.'

'You need to eat. I insist.'

'Do you?'

'Someone has to look after you.' His eyes danced. 'You weren't made for martyrdom, but you seem intent on trying for it. No one will think better of you if you stay here.'

He caught her hand and raised it to his lips. The warmth radiated throughout her body. She looked up into the shifting browns in his eyes, teetered and knew she was lost.

'You shouldn't have… I can look after myself.'

'It's what makes it so much fun.' He gave a half-smile. 'I asked the innkeeper's wife to make enough for two. You can watch me eat if you like, but you will take a look at it. There is a meat pie.'

His fingers closed around her arm and he led her from the small room to a much larger one. As he promised, a cold supper with salads and a variety of pies and a jug of wine was laid out in front of a small crackling fire. She also noticed the four-poster bed hung with dark blue velvet curtains and piled high with pillows, a feather bed and white linen sheets. Her hand gripped her reticule until the beaded pattern dug into her palm as she remembered his earlier promise. It would be easy to turn in his arms and demand he take her to bed… Even the thought made her breath catch.

'Shall we eat? I'm ravenous,' she said and advanced towards the food. Food to calm her nerves and dull her appetite. It was merely hunger that had given her this giddy feeling. 'You are right. I am famished, but there is far too much for one.'

He gave her a speculative glance and she knew her cheeks slightly flamed, but she wasn't ready to say goodnight. She wasn't ready to be alone with her thoughts.

'It would be wrong to waste a good meal after the innkeeper's wife went to much trouble.'

'Indeed it would.'

'Well, then.' She sat down and gave a nod towards the other chair. She could keep the topics on general subjects; when they were finished, she'd be able to bid him goodnight. She would demonstrate that she was immune to his charms. 'Shall we begin?'

Halfway through supper, Robert covered her hand in his. 'Now are you going to tell me why you are always insistent about looking after others? You are willing to make yourself ill if it means that others don't suffer.'

Henri looked at her barely touched food and withdrew her hand. It would be far easier to tell him about such things than to speak about how much she wanted him. She had thought it was just hunger, but it was a different sort of hunger. She wanted to feel his lips against hers.

She took another sip of the wine and tried to concentrate on the fire.

'I suppose it comes down to my mother.' She began to explain about her mother and her sayings and how the only thing that was important when she was growing up was what her mother wanted. How her mother had needed constant attention and how it had driven her father away, and how she had learnt to manage.

He gave a nod, refilled her glass and motioned for her to continue.

She sneaked another look at the bed, and then back at him and how he looked in his shirt sleeves with his stock ever so slightly undone. She toyed with her piece of pie. There had to be a way of controlling her desire. 'I suppose I ought to explain about Edmund.'

His hand froze in mid-air as he topped up her glass of wine. The wine spilled over the edge before he recovered his composure. 'Only if you want to.'

'He understood me, you see. He had a lonely childhood as well. He was always getting sick and having trouble breathing.' Henri looked over Robert's shoulders towards the glowing coals. 'He had the time to listen to my dreams and he was such a gentle person. When I was fourteen, he became seriously ill for the first time, but his guardian was far too busy. I decided to look after him. At sixteen I proposed. He refused me, but then when he saw how upset I was and how they were going to take me away, he relented and agreed to elope. He needed someone who cared about him, rather than just servants.'

'What did he have?'

'A weak chest. Each time he became ill, it went straight to his chest and he had trouble breathing. The night we eloped, it rained and he caught a cold. We had planned to go to Italy once he was well. The air is supposed to be better there for weak chests.'

'But he didn't get better.'

'I tried and tried, but I don't have Sophie's knack for nursing. Every day, he seemed to get weaker. I wanted him to fight, but he told me that I had to fight for both of us.' She hugged her arms about her waist as her stomach knotted in on itself. 'The only day he ever became angry with me was the day he died. I had brought a vase of daffodils to brighten the room and show him how alive the world was. He thought I was mocking him. He accused me of wanting too much. I told him to stop lying there and to take an interest in life.'

'You had words.'

'An angry exchange. It was so unlike him. I flounced out of the room; by the time I returned, he had slipped away. No one should have to die alone, especially not someone like him.' She put a hand to her head. 'If I'd known… My last words to him were angry and bitter. He deserved better… I shortened his life. Everyone said so.

You asked me earlier why I have a hard time forgiving. I never had to forgive Edmund anything except for dying.'

'Hush.' He came over to her then and raised her up from her seat. His arms went around her and held her. She gave a shuddering sigh and laid her head against his chest, listening to the steady beat of his heart.

His fingers lifted her chin. 'Henri…'

She put her fingers to his lips. 'So you see…'

'What happened with you and your husband was fate. No one's fault. I've seen men have horrible accidents and survive and others die over the most trivial of things. Nobody chooses the time of their death—it just is.' His arms tightened about her. 'And you can't change it as much as you would sometimes like to. Neither can you blame yourself for not being somewhere. You can only look towards the future. Forgiving mistakes means you can be forgiven.'

Just is. The words echoed around her head and she knew he was speaking about his father's death. And she couldn't change that he wanted to protect his ward or that Sebastian had used her name. It just was. Tonight just was. 'Maybe you are right.'

His fingers stroked her cheek, sending a promise of illicit pleasure pulsating throughout her body. 'Trust me. Start living and stop blaming yourself for others' misdeeds.'

'I think I am overtired.' She took a step backwards, away from the seductive safety of his body.

'Shall I call the innkeeper's wife to help you or shall I play the lady's maid?' A wicked smile tugged at his mouth as he leant forwards until they were nearly touching. His breath tickled her ear. 'I do a passable imitation of a lady's maid, Henri. All you have to do is ask.'

Her senses reeled. Tonight would be about them. Not about anyone else. It was about the here and now, rather than the past or the future. And if he left now, she knew that would be the end. They would never have another chance like this one and, despite everything, it wasn't over between them. She wasn't ready for it to end.

He was offering her the choice and she knew there was only one sensible answer. She took a deep breath and plunged into the sensual unknown.

'Stay. I…I don't want anyone else to help me.'

His arms came around her and she felt them work at the tiny buttons on the back of her gown. It gave way, exposing her back to his questing fingers.

'All done,' he whispered against her hair. His warm hand, kneading her bare shoulder. 'Does the maid get thanked?'

She gazed up at him and wanted to drown in his eyes. She deliberately raised her mouth to his. 'Yes.'

His lazy kiss swamped her senses. She stood luxuriating in the taste and texture of him. Slowly she thrust her tongue into his mouth, drinking deep, devouring and dining on the kiss that seemed to stretch for ever. A primitive craving grew within her and she knew it was not enough. She was greedy, a glutton for his touch. She wanted to feel his skin against hers. Needed it to satisfy her longing.

'If you can play lady's maid, I can play valet,' she murmured against his mouth. 'You are overdressed for this feast.'

He gave a soft laugh that rippled across her sensitive skin.

Henri's fingers worked on the stock and, to her relief, she pulled it correctly. The length of cloth undid easily, leaving the strong column of his throat bare. She pressed her lips against it and felt his steady heartbeat thrumming.

Taking her time, she carefully undid the buttons of his waistcoat, pushed it off his shoulders and undid the buttons of his shirt front to reveal his smooth skin. She slipped her hand in, traced the outline of his nipples and heard the sudden intake of breath.

'Insistent?'

'Determined.' She gave a shaky laugh and withdrew her hand. 'There is a difference. Shall I stop?'

'Never.' He crushed her to him, possessively lowering his mouth and reclaiming hers. This time, his tongue ruthlessly plundered her mouth, penetrating deep until she was gripped in the unrelenting maelstrom of sensation.

His fingers trailed down her back, cupped her buttocks and pulled her close. Against the thin lawn of her petticoat, she could feel his rampant arousal, pressing into, moving against her, reminding her of their previous joining. Her body arched towards him, craving that intimate touch.

Slowly, he nibbled his lips downwards until he reached her breasts. His tongue flicked over them, turning them into hardened points. He suckled, sliding his tongue over and around them. She clung to his broad shoulders for support as wave after wave of delicious sensation washed over her.

'Robert,' she whispered when she knew her legs would no longer support her.

He scooped her up, strode across the room and deposited her on the gigantic four-poster bed in her room. The mattress and pillows moulded instantly to her shape. His fingers worked on the front buttons of her corset until it loosened. He gently opened it and pushed her combination down her shoulders and body until she lay naked in front of him. Suddenly she became shy, aware of what she flagrantly displayed, and her hands moved to cover herself. With one swoop, he caught her hands and moved them above her head. 'Don't even think about it. You are magnificent. Allow me to enjoy you. Please.' She heard the raw note of begging in his voice.

She nodded and he let her go.

His fiery gaze roamed all over her, caressing her. She patted the soft mattress. 'Are you coming in?'

'Much more conducive to romance than the hard wooden floor,' he said as, one by one, his remaining garments dropped to the floor until he stood, naked, skin gleaming in the firelight. Perfectly made with sculpted muscles and a line of hair that ran from his belly downwards to his erection. An explicit invitation. 'Tonight is for lingering and enjoying.'

He knelt on the bed and swooped down so that his warm pliable skin touched hers. Covered her.

His fingers skimmed her shoulders, reached her breasts. Slowly and deliberately he traced the outline of her nipples before lowering his mouth to them. Taking each breast in turn, he suckled. Her back strained upwards as her sensitised skin flared with each new touch.

His fingers travelled down her belly inexorably to the apex of her thighs where they paused, hovered. With one finger he parted her folds and touched her.

He hooked both of her legs on his shoulders and his hot breath fanned her inner core, cooling her but making her ache at the same time. Then his mouth touched her, circled. Slid. Glided over her.

She gripped his shoulders as wave after wave crested inside her. She knew she should be shocked to have his mouth on her in that intimate way, but it felt right. Her world exploded into shards.

He slowly moved upwards and then his warm body covered her. She lay within the circle of his arms as the world righted itself. Then she pushed him so he went over on his back and she loomed above him.

'My turn,' she whispered.

Without waiting for an answer she slid her mouth over him, taking time to explore his nipples and the muscles of his chest. To her delight, she felt his body buck under her, strain to get closer to her. She ran her hand down the length of him, following his line of hair and then, reaching his thighs, she cupped him, holding his arousal in her hand. He groaned in the back of his throat.

Taking her time, she positioned herself over him and, lowering herself to meet his upward thrust, impaled her body.

With a single movement he entered and her body opened to meet him. For one glorious instant she stayed there, with him in her. Joined. Complete. Merged. This time her body instantly matched his rhythm. Together they moved, faster and faster. Soaring until the shattering came.

Satiated. Satisfied. Thoroughly spent. Robert looked down at Henri's sleeping face. Her dark lashes made smudges on her porcelain face and he took a moment to enjoy the pleasure of watching her sleep. He ran a finger down the side of her face, and knew he wanted more than this. Already, he wanted her again and he knew he would go on wanting her while he had breath in his body.

It hit him then that he loved her, really and truly loved her. He wanted her in his life for the rest of time. He wanted to share every particle of his life with her. The thought shocked him and exhilarated him in the same breath. He hadn't meant for it to happen and until it did, he'd been sceptical that it could happen. Logic dictated... He paused, his body shaking. Forget logic, this was Henri, and Henri required an entirely different way of thinking.

He tightened his arms about Henri, intending to tell her how much he loved her. Someone had to be the first to say the words. 'Henri?'

Henri blinked her eyes and looked up at him. Her arms came about his neck and held him close. Her emotions overwhelmed her and she tried to puzzle out why being in his arms made her feel so complete. Then she remembered what he'd said about marriage and how he'd want marriage. She wouldn't make that mistake again. She had to remember the limits and not to expect more.

'I'm so glad we are merely friends,' she said with a long sigh, partly to reassure him and partly to remind her heart of the boundaries they'd agreed. 'After all, neither of us wants marriage. We aren't looking beyond tomorrow. You do agree, Robert, don't you?'

Robert swallowed his words. Silently he thanked God that they had not slipped out. One false word and he'd lose her. He should have remembered his father's experience and how emotions could cloud things. Robert knew then that he was not prepared to let her go. He wanted her by his side, but he just didn't know how to keep her there yet. 'What else would we be?'

She laid her cheek against his. He kept his arm about her, holding her close, fearful that she would guess he wanted much more than mere friendship. Words he tried to convince himself meant very little. It was actions that counted and right now Henri was in his arms with her body snuggled next to him.

'I was afraid earlier that you would say something. My mother told me that in time I would want to replace Edmund, but I never have. I still don't. And knowing that you don't want marriage either makes it easier.' She looked up at him with large shimmering eyes, eyes that he couldn't read.

He wished he had never said those words. Marriage to Henri was an entirely different prospect than marriage to an abstract woman. But now was far from the right time. Caution. He opted for a light tone. 'Did you love him very much?'

She brought her knees up to her chest and went very still for a long time. 'He was very good. Edmund was the most beautiful creature I had ever seen but…he never did anything until I asked him to.'

'Spineless,' Robert supplied, giving way slightly to jealousy. At her questioning glance, he shrugged. 'Things you haven't said. You had to force the elopement. Any fool would know that to be offered a chance with you is worth grabbing with both hands.'

'You do wonders for my confidence.' Her voice faltered. 'I think that sort of love was a once-in-a-lifetime love. I'm not sure I ever want to have that sort of love again. Sometimes, it seems like it was so bloodless, so lacking in passion. You and I…we have passion but passion burns out quickly.'

Robert placed a kiss on her temple, silently vowing that somehow she would love him. It would be more than passion between them. But it had to come from her first, not him. He refused to risk the rejection. 'Then we will be intimate friends who can forgive each other.'

'I knew you would understand.' She tightened her arms about him and snuggled down so her head rested on his bare chest.

'Understand. Yes, I understand.' He captured her lips and pulled her body firmly against his, allowing his body to say the words. 'It is the best sort of friendship. And, Henri, I will protect you. We will keep this our secret.'

Chapter Fifteen

Henri woke the next morning alone in the unfamiliar bed. The bed curtains were pulled tight, but a shaft of sunlight peaked through.

Sometime while she slept, Robert had departed. Discreet, but somehow unsatisfactory. She would have enjoyed waking up in his arms.

Henri wriggled her toes, trying to find a warm spot, a tiny place to remind her that last night was not a dream. Nothing. And the more she tried to convince herself that this was a good thing and that she should be pleased by Robert's thoughtfulness, the less pleased she was. She wanted to think that he'd reluctantly left her bed, and that he'd kissed her forehead as he'd done so, but she worried that it had been some half-remembered dream.

'Ah, you're awake, my lady.' Grace came bustling into the room. 'The master just sent me up to see if you were ready. He's determined to catch them today. It's terribly exciting being involved in a chase like this.'

'We'll find them,' Henri said as positively as she dared.

Grace began to lay out Henri's clothes, humming a little tune as she did so. Henri wondered uncomfortably if the maid suspected what had happened last night. Thankfully her clothes were piled neatly on a chair rather than being strewn across the room. Robert had proved a thoughtful maid. She'd have to remember the little details for the next time. *The next time.* The words had a pleasant ring.

Grace frowned holding up the gown Henri had worn the night before. 'Whoever helped you to undress last night should have taken more care. One of your buttons has come loose and the ruffle on your left sleeve is torn. They will have to be seen to.'

'It was my fault. Will it take long?'

'I'm handy with a needle and thread. It will be mended before you have finished your coffee.'

Henri took a sip of the bitter liquid. A life of wickedness was going to mean changes and she was going to have to learn to sew better. She refused to be undone by a simple button or a torn ruffle. But she could understand now how women could be discovered. 'Thank you, Grace. The sleeping powder appears to have worked.'

Grace bent her head, concentrating on threading a needle. 'You're lucky, ma'am. Travel appears to agree with you. I had so wanted to make a good impression on Mr Hudson, the coachman, and we had to stop because of me.'

'We stopped because it was late and folly to continue,' Henri said firmly. She took another sip of coffee, a plot formulating in her brain. Grace and the coachman. 'The closed air of the carriage caused your problems. If the weather is fine, you should ride up with Mr Hudson, rather than down with me and Mr Montemorcy. I dare say you'll find it easier.'

'I couldn't. I mean…'

'With the wind on your face, you should be perfectly fine and then you can ensure that I don't tear my lace when I undress.'

'The wind on my face. You're a marvel, ma'am!' Grace held up the dress. 'There, it is as good as new. No one will guess.'

Henri deftly turned the conversation to hairstyles. All she needed was a cool head and quick wit. The rest was easy.

* * *

Between the jolts in the carriage, which would have sent her flying towards Robert, and her sudden inability to make easy conversation, Henri discovered her confidence misplaced as the carriage rolled down the road towards Jedburgh. She kept thinking of things to say and then discarding them as trite. She had thought that Grace travelling up with Mr Hudson would make things easier, but somehow the silence felt awkward rather than intimate.

'You are awfully silent,' Robert remarked from where he sat on the other side of the carriage with his top hat shading his eyes and his hands lightly resting on his silver-topped cane.

'Am I?' Henri grabbed on to the seat edge to prevent herself from flying into his arms as the carriage hit yet another deep rut. 'I was thinking about young Master Jenkins and his Latin exam. His mother has hopes of him studying for the church.'

'You're a poor liar, Thorndike.' He reached out and pulled her across the gap in the carriage, settling her next to him. 'There, that is better. It won't do to have my best girl tumbling into the dirt. I can't think why Hudson is driving so poorly today.'

A bubble of pleasure grew within Henri at his words. 'Best girl?'

'I spend far too much time around my workers. Do you object? And why do you want to talk about young Master Jenkins?' His arm gathered her close to him. He tilted her chin upwards. 'Why is it important?'

'Because it means that someone cares enough to remember. It is important to be remembered. Little details.'

'But I've been looking forward to doing this all morning. Good morning, my dear Henri.' Robert dropped a kiss on her lips. 'I don't care about young Master Jenkins or that Hudson is making cow-eyes at Grace. I want to know about how you are doing. It was a wrench to leave you.'

'I'm worried about Sophie,' Henri admitted as inwardly she

glowed. 'The fact that she took a frying pan bothers me. When we first discussed Sebastian, I told her that if she wanted to make sure he behaved, she should always have a frying pan to hand.'

'She took you at your word.'

'It would seem so.' Henri concentrated on the horse-hair seats. 'What if that means Sophie doesn't want to marry Sebastian?'

'Will I force it?' Robert removed his arm from Henri's shoulders. 'I have to look at what is best for Sophie in the future. Her father wanted her to take her rightful place in society. He gave both Dorothy and I that charge. I refuse to have her live the life of a *demi-monde* or not be accepted by the best people. Do not seek to bolster your cousin. He will do right by my ward.'

'The best people are not always the most interesting. My instinct—'

He shook his head, rejecting her argument. 'Sophie is my responsibility. Don't interfere, Henri, or it will be the end of our friendship. It is what is best for Sophie in the long term, rather than right now. Meddling, however well meant, has no place and it won't change my mind.'

Henri bit her lip. Despite everything, he remained convinced that she meddled. He hadn't learnt from yesterday.

He gave a husky laugh. 'Henri, stop worrying. All will be well.'

Henri gave a small nod and allowed Robert to discuss his plans for the aluminium experiments. All the while in the back of her mind, she kept wondering what would happen and whose side would she be on?

The carriage lurched slightly to one side. Robert rapped the roof. 'I pay you to drive, Hudson, not to enjoy the scenery.'

'Sorry, sir. Won't happen again.'

Henri heard the muffled sound of a giggle. She raised her eyebrow.

A dimple showed in the corner of Robert's mouth. 'You are an inveterate matchmaker.'

'Unashamed and unabashed as long as it isn't my own match.'

The carriage gave another lurch.

Robert rapped on the roof again. 'You had best stop at the next inn and check the wheel. We don't want it damaged.'

'Right-o. The Bluebell should be on the left in a mile or two.'

Robert ground his teeth and tried to make light of the delay to Henri. Everything was conspiring against him, and Henri's blind assertion that Sophie might not want to marry Cawburn did nothing to ease his growing anxiety.

'We should be back on the road shortly,' Robert said, helping Henri from the carriage. 'Far better to be cautious now, than to be forced to wait later.'

'I hope so. The sooner we know what truly passed between my cousin and your ward, the sooner a judgement can be made. Far be it from me to prejudge what the future might hold.'

He shook his head. It was a straightforward decision. As much as he loathed Cawburn, Sophie would suffer more from being outside society than from being married to him. Her father's will would ensure that. Cawburn had not kidnapped her off the street. Sophie would have to live with the consequences. He could only hope she was happy. As the marriage was inevitable, he toyed with the idea of prolonging the journey to Jedburgh so he could enjoy more time with Henri.

'Henri, is everything all right? Have you seen another dog?' Robert noticed all the colour had drained from her face and she stood as still as a marble statue. He grabbed her arm, preparing to shove her behind him. He'd hoped her fear of dogs had gone, but obviously not. Silently he cursed her late husband. He should have taken more care.

'Look over there.' She broke free, raised her hand and pointed.

'That is my aunt's carriage. I am sure of it. I would recognise the mismatched wheels anywhere. Only my aunt would have one blue wheel and three yellow ones. Sebastian had long lamented the folly of such an arrangement, but Aunt Frances says it makes the carriage distinctive and easy to spot in a crowd.'

'Then they are here.' Robert opened his arms, ready to embrace her. 'Henri, you are a marvel. You found them.'

'I told you that Sebastian would make for Jedburgh. I knew it! A triumph for woman's intuition!' Her face became wreathed in a triumphant smile before her brow knotted. 'I wonder why they have stopped here. My aunt's carriage is slower than Sebastian's curricle, but they still should have made good time.'

'Why ponder the ways of providence?' He linked arms with Henri. Cawburn had not made it to the safety of Scotland. He could ensure that Sophie was properly married, rather than being married through Scottish law. There would be no question about Sophie's marriage lines or tittering behind fans. Sophie would not be ostracised. He'd fulfil his promise to Ravel. 'Shall we go and find the errant lovers, Henri?'

'But we will do this discreetly,' she said firmly, tightening her grip on his arm and holding him back. 'The last thing we want is a huge scandal that will be all over the Borders and beyond.'

He gave a sigh. What did she think he was going to do—go in and haul Cawburn from the bed he was undoubtedly sharing with Sophie? 'I want to protect Sophie's name. There is nothing to be gained by making this a bigger scandal. And there's a slim possibility that Cawburn can be moulded into a good husband.'

'Thank you,' she said, laying her hand on his arm. 'Nothing is gained through complexity. There'll be a simple explanation.'

'I would love to know what it is.' Robert looked down at Henri's upturned face. Her blue eyes were troubled. He wanted to take her away from this, take her someplace where they could be together. Somehow, he knew that whatever happened here, she wouldn't be satisfied. And he refused to give in to her overly simplistic request of waiting. 'I will give Cawburn a chance to explain, before I pound his face to a pulp. And, Henri, he deserves a beating. You know he does.'

'But you will give him a chance to say more than two words.'

'Because you ask, I will give him the chance to say two words.'

The corners of her mouth twitched. 'Thank you. My cousin believes his features enhance his fortune.'

'Without them, he'd be a pauper.'

She did not move away from him, but stood there, looking up at him. Her breath fanned his cheek. Giving in to impulse, he lowered his head and drank from her lips. Her sweet mouth opened and he tasted the cool interior. Summoning all his self-control, he broke off the kiss and put her away from him.

'What was that for?' she asked, bringing her fingers to her mouth.

'For luck. You are not going to deny we need all the luck we can get, are you?'

'I never took you for a superstitious man, Robert. I thought it was all the modern scientific method with you.'

'Sometimes, we can all use a fair wind and sunshine.' His fingers twitched her bonnet into place, making her into the formidable Lady Thorndike again. Robert pressed his lips together. 'Sometimes, all you can have is hope.'

Henri entered the smoke-filled public room with trepidation. She lifted her skirt slightly to prevent it from making patterns in the sawdust-strewn floor. A good part of her wished Sebastian would be there, but the other part hoped he wouldn't. Everything was conspiring against her. With each touch and with every kiss, she fell more in love with Robert and it was becoming impossible to keep a clear head. She knew that if she wanted to keep Robert in her life, she had to be discreet, but discretion was the last thing she wanted to be with Robert.

A variety of farmers, labourers and drovers filled the smoke-wreathed room to bursting. A game of cards was in progress and the sound of voices assaulted her ears. She gave a quick glance around the crowded room and the tension in her shoulders eased slightly.

There in a dark corner with his greatcoat obscuring his face sat Sebastian, morosely nursing a pint of beer. She glanced about the room, but he appeared to be alone; not even her aunt's coachman sat with him. Her stomach clenched. Something had happened. Sebastian never drank alone. Ever.

'He is here, but I don't see Sophie,' Henri said in an undertone. 'Perhaps she did return to the New Lodge. Perhaps we have been on a wild-goose chase. It could have happened, Robert.'

She started to wave to Sebastian but Robert caught her wrist.

'Discretion, Henri.' Robert stepped in front of her, shielding her body from Sebastian's view. 'Quietly. We do not want to startle him. Let me speak to him.'

'But we need to find Sophie. He is our best hope. And if he is innocent, we need to know that as well. Allow me to do this on my own. Sebastian will tell me. You confront him and it will end in tears.' Henri clasped her hands together. Robert had to understand and give way. 'My way is better. I understand my cousin.'

Robert scowled. 'I will give you half a minute to discover Sophie's whereabouts before I make Cawburn confess.'

Henri's heart hammered in her chest. Rather than insisting on his way, Robert was letting her try. He believed in her.

'Sebastian likes to think his ideas are his own. The trick is making him think of the correct idea.'

'Cawburn will do the right thing or else,' Robert said grimly. 'He had best understand that this is no time for his usual behaviour. And, yes, I know all about the pugs and the women he left before that. I dislike leaving anything to chance.'

'Let me speak to Sebastian. He *will* do this for me.'

Heedless of the farmers' stares, she broke free of Robert's restraining hand and hurried over. When Sebastian did not look up, she gave his boot a little kick.

'Sebastian! Where is Sophie, Sophie Ravel? You must know where she is. It is imperative I find her. Immediately.'

Sebastian looked up from his beer with unfocused eyes. 'What are you doing here, Henri? Go away and play somewhere else. Your presence is not required. Run along. You must have something better to do.'

'Run along? Where do you think I have appeared from, Sebastian? The corner shop?' Henri tapped her boot against the sawdust. 'You have caused me a great deal of trouble and this time you will be held to account. I'll not be left holding pug puppies again.'

'Never fear. No pugs were involved in this, cousin.' He leant back in the chair and suddenly his gaze narrowed as he caught sight of the man looming behind her. A strange smile crossed his face. 'You should be more concerned about yourself, Henrietta Maria. I have always been able to look after myself. Come out smelling like your blasted roses.'

'Not this time.' Henri glared at him. 'You're in trouble. You picked the wrong person to manipulate. Sophie Ravel is very dear to me. Answer the question—where is she?'

'It looks from where I sit that you are the one in over her head.' Sebastian rocked back on his chair. 'This is a most intriguing development. You showing up here like this with the current company glowering over your shoulder. Not quite the scenario I had envisioned, but one that presents opportunities.'

Henri ground her teeth and struggled to keep from throttling him. Sebastian was well on his way to being an impossible drunk. Her earliest memories were of her father in these sorts of dark sarcastic moods. She had always hated it. 'You had to expect that someone would come looking for you.'

'Why would you think that? I'm perfectly fine. Perfectly fine. Thank you for asking.' Sebastian took a long draught of beer. 'You told me to grow up and so I have. Can't say I like it much, though. I'm going to make my fortune in the Californian gold fields.'

'Sebastian!' Henri stamped her foot against the sawdust-covered floor. She stepped back and encountered Robert's bulk. 'Robert, you promised to give me time. Go away!'

'You've had your time. I measured it with my fob watch.' He replaced his fob watch in his waistcoat. 'Sebastian is starting to make comments about you. I won't allow it.'

'You will do nothing!' Henri glared at Robert and willed him to go. With him standing there, Sebastian was likely to behave very badly indeed. Things were going to get a lot worse instead of better.

'Goodness me, this sounds like a lovers' spat if I ever heard one and here I thought you were only distant friends, Henrietta.' Sebastian clapped his hands together like an eager child. 'What an interesting development. Deep water, Henrietta, deep water is where you are at. Be careful you don't drown.'

'Sebastian! You are spouting fustian nonsense and flim-flam. No one is impressed.'

'Allow me to handle this, Thorndike. Please.' Robert grabbed Sebastian's lapels and hauled him to his feet.

'Keep your blasted hands off me, Montemorcy. I have nothing to say to you!'

The entire public room echoed with the sudden silence. Henri winced. This little confrontation was about to become public gossip of the worst sort. She could imagine the tale being repeated on every lip from here to Newcastle and beyond.

'Please, Robert. You promised! No violence.'

Robert gave her a quelling look. He shook Sebastian. 'Answer me! Where is my ward? She left with you! Where have you hidden her?'

Sebastian rolled his eyes and made a considering noise. 'I refuse to tell you while you are clinging to my jacket. And I do not believe you'll hit me, not in front of my cousin. You want to keep her sweet, but you are deluding yourself… She's utterly devoted to her late husband.'

An ice-cold finger went down Henri's spine. Sebastian had tried to make a mockery of Robert and was seeking to taunt him. He didn't know about their liaison. He couldn't.

'You have no idea what I will do.' Robert grabbed Sebastian again.

'Sebastian! Robert!' Henri stamped her foot. 'Everyone is staring. You must know where Sophie is, Sebastian. Tell us now and stop playing stupid games.'

'Not until he promises to behave.' Sebastian stuck out his bottom lip. 'It is a point I will not be moved on. I will not answer anything while I am being manhandled.'

'Robert, everyone is looking,' Henri said in an urgent undertone. 'Think! Do you want your ward's business known and the subject of taproom gossip? What happened to no violence and discretion?'

'Very well, Henri.' Robert loosened his hands and put Sebastian away from him. Suddenly, like a tap being turned on, noise filled the public room. Henri risked a breath.

Sebastian rearranged his stock and brushed his jacket, taking so long that Henri was tempted to shake him herself. Sebastian was enjoying prolonging this, making Robert suffer.

'Sebastian, stop playing games or I will hit you.'

Sebastian stuck his nose in the air. 'I refuse to respond to threats of violence. From anyone. And you can't hit straight, Henrietta.'

'You constantly underestimate your cousin, Cawburn. She doesn't issue threats. She gives promises and she makes good on her debts, which is more than I can say for you.'

Henri drew in her breath as she caught Robert's look. A *frisson* went through her, warming her down to the tips of her toes. He believed in her.

'Why should I know where that hellion is?' He gave an angelic smile. 'You may do what you want with her. I'm finished with her.'

Henri stared open-mouthed at him, remembering how he always lost interest once Sebastian had bedded a woman. He had gone far too far this time. She wanted to put her hands over her face and weep for the pair of them.

'You kidnapped my ward,' Robert ground out. 'You ruined her good name. I will not have her becoming soiled goods.'

'She came with me willingly enough.' Sebastian held up his hands. 'Never let it be said that I forced a woman. We even stopped to get her basket. Does that seem to be the actions of a woman forced through violence? My mother's carriage goes so slowly that I suggested stopping at this inn for the night as the wheel came off…and then, well…things began to go wrong. But on my honour as a gentleman, nothing happened.'

Henri crossed her arms. She could easily imagine what the things were and unfortunately from the way Robert's eyes narrowed, she knew he did as well. 'Where were you heading with Miss Ravel, Sebastian? Jedburgh? Where did Miss Ravel think you were taking her? Were you going to marry her?'

'It does not matter now.' Sebastian made an expansive gesture, sloshing his beer over the tankard. 'You were right, Montemorcy, as much as I hate to admit it. Miss Ravel and I would not suit. We have fallen entirely out of civility!'

Robert uttered a low growl. 'You will be going before a priest before you do anything.'

'Robert! We need to find Sophie and get her side of the story.' Henri grasped his arm. 'It will be resolved. Somehow.'

'This is where listening to you has brought me, Thorndike!'

'I know,' she replied quietly and wanted to curl up in a little ball. 'Why didn't Sophie—?'

'I will show you where the lady is. The lady has particularly requested that no gentleman be allowed into her room. She has barricaded herself in.' The innkeeper's wife made a low curtsy in front of Henri and it was clear that she had followed every syllable of the exchange. 'Thought there was something not right about that couple, I did. I said to Mr Mumps, you watch and see if someone does not come for that poor miss. Mr Mumps kept watch all night, he did.'

Sophie had barricaded herself in? Henri raised her head. A flicker of hope went through her. Maybe it could be resolved, but first Robert would have to trust her.

'Can you wait for the priest until you have spoken to Sophie, Robert? Give her a chance to explain her side? Learn the whole truth before exploding?'

The silence stretched and then finally he gave a small nod. 'If this is another one of your harum-scarum ideas, Thorndike, I will never forgive you.'

'I will get Sophie for you and you will see that she is safe and unharmed.'

'Good old Henrietta!' Sebastian shouted. 'I knew you'd be on my side.'

Henri felt Robert stiffen at her side. Silently she willed him to believe in her, rather than in Sebastian's words. Even now, he didn't fully trust her and that hurt. But she would show him.

'I want you to be alive when I return, Sebastian, so I might have the pleasure of tearing you limb from limb. Do precisely as Mr Montemorcy says.' She put her hand on Robert's arm and said in an undertone, 'Trust me. I'm doing this for Sophie, not for Sebastian. Intuition will prevail.'

Chapter Sixteen

'I believe the lady you seek is in there,' the innkeeper's wife said after they had climbed a flight of stairs. 'It is our best room. She refuses to allow anyone in. I told Mr Mumps that he should have made them pay first. And now his lordship is claiming, if you please, that she has all the money.'

The woman gave a small sniff as if she expected better of people who rented that particular room.

'I believe I can find my way from here.' Henri reached into her reticule and took out a coin.

'As you like, ma'am.' The woman gave a small curtsy and bustled off, muttering about people who had too fine a manner.

Henri waited until she heard footsteps on the stairs. Then she tapped on the door. 'Sophie? Sophie Ravel, are you in there?'

'Henri! Oh, Henrietta Thorndike, is it you?' Sophie called out. 'Or am I dreaming? I've so longed for a friendly voice.'

'Yes, dear, it is I.' Henri felt a catch in her throat. She wanted something more for Sophie than to be hiding out in grimy rooms with peeping innkeepers. She wanted to throttle Sebastian. Sophie Ravel deserved so much more. 'And Robert is downstairs.'

'You have come to rescue me?' Sophie's voice sounded very young and uncertain. 'I fear I've made an awful pickle of things, Henri. I thought...I thought I could handle him.'

'Nothing that cannot be put right.'

'You're wrong. I know what happens next.'

Henri tried the door handle, but the door was bolted from the inside. She put her hand on the smooth dark wood and willed Sophie to open the door. 'Why did you go with Sebastian? You said that you had no interest in my cousin.'

'I should never have quarrelled with Miss Armstrong, but she would complain about what a busybody know-it-all you are. And I know what a good heart you have. Everyone says so. Jealous cat.'

Henri took a calming breath. She did things because she liked to make people happy, because she cared about them and wanted to help, not because she wanted to gossip about them. And right now, she was here, determined to help Sophie. 'Miss Armstrong's opinions are of no matter. It doesn't explain why you went with Sebastian.'

'He seemed so understanding. And I wanted…I wanted…well, that is…I thought I ought to see what a man who was unsafe in carriages was really like before it was too late. I'm here and hope never to see his face again and now everyone will say I have to marry him or—'

'Sophie, I'm here to help. You quarrelled with Miss Armstrong because you said I had a good heart. Allow me to prove it. There will be a way around this coil. No one will force anyone to marry.'

The noise of a bolt sliding filled the hallway. Henri relaxed slightly and willed Sophie to open the door.

The door opened a crack and Sophie peeked out. Her normally well-coiffured hair hung down in snakes around her shoulders, her eyes were red, her dress creased and the lace torn. In her right hand, she brandished a reasonably sized frying pan.

Henri stepped back and gestured in the empty hall. 'See, me, Sophie, no one else. You're safe.'

Sophie burst into fresh tears and ran into the hall. Henri held her, patting her back until the sobs and hiccupping subsided. 'Henri, I'm ruined. Really ruined. People will draw their skirts away from me. But nothing untoward happened. I shall become an Example!'

'Sophie, your true friends will stand by you.' Henri held the young woman away from her. 'They always do. We'll find a way around this. Did my cousin attack you? Did you know what he intended? Did he dishonour you?'

'No, he didn't get a chance.' Sophie gave a tiny smile as she raised the frying pan. 'Knowing how to use a cricket bat meant I could swing the frying pan with some force. It took three goes before he finally believed I was serious.'

'Sebastian does rather take pride in his attractiveness to the opposite sex.'

'Did Robert send you, Henri? Does he intend on making me marry Sebastian now? Sebastian said he would and there wasn't anything I could do about it. He...he looked forward to taming me and he was going to spend every penny of my inheritance.' A single tear trickled down Sophie's cheek. 'I won't. I can't. I wanted so much more from my life. You must tell him that for me. You will have to do it.'

'I've no idea what Robert's intentions are,' Henri replied truthfully. 'But he wants what's best for you. He wants the truth.'

'He won't like the truth.' Sophie shook her head. 'I can't tell Robert the truth!'

'Why did you go with my cousin? Why not just go back to the New Lodge?'

Sophie winced. 'I didn't really know how I felt about Sebastian except he made things more exciting and I was tired of being good. I thought...about you and how you met the love of your life and you eloped. You were my age. It was so romantic. I want romance in my life.'

'Sophie...you never knew me then.' Henri sighed. Sophie deserved the truth. 'I may have eloped, but it was not romantic. Edmund was seriously ill. We married so I could nurse him. I had a notion about saving his life and I suppose escaping from my parents. A woman should be a wife before she is anything else, my mother used to say, but I didn't understand what she meant. I think I was too young to understand the different sorts of love.' She closed her eyes and thought of Robert, how he was there for her in the quiet moments and how he challenged her without making her feel small or insignificant. And how the passion flared between them. She wanted to be his lover before anything. With Edmund, she had only wanted to be his ministering angel. Edmund would always occupy a place in her heart, but she wanted Robert with all his faults in her life. 'I do know now.'

'Sebastian seemed romantic and certain of his love. He wanted to make a grand gesture.' Sophie ducked her head. 'It seemed exciting, a man of his reputation interested in plain old me.'

'You are far from plain, Sophie. But what went wrong?'

'When we stopped at this inn and I became worried because I thought surely someone would have caught up with us. Robert couldn't have believed the notes. I thought he'd have asked you. Then Sebastian seemed concerned about his hair, his problems with his coat and getting a pint of beer. He wanted…he wanted… Anyway…I hit him on the head. He refused to believe me about the frying pan. I did warn him, Henri, if he persisted I would.' A tiny giggle escaped from Sophie. 'You should have seen his face and he became ugly, not at all like he had been. It was the last blow to his head that sent him downstairs, shouting about how I was a hell-born fury and how he'd tame the wild-cat. I barricaded the door.'

'He hasn't touched you.' A burgeoning hope bubbled up inside her. Sophie was unharmed and no longer infatuated with Sebastian. 'He hasn't actually ruined you?'

'No, he hasn't. My stepmother always is going on and on about keeping my reputation spotless so the family does not suffer, but how I must marry someone in aristocracy.' Sophie hung her head. 'Adventure is thoroughly disorienting. Like my canary, I prefer my gilded cage. And I left the door open for him. Do you think he will still be there?'

'Your stepmother will do as Robert says. And I am certain that we can convince him. And, yes, I think your canary will be close by.' Henri started to pace the hallway. Her mind raced. She could do this. She could save Sophie, but the words had to come from Sophie. Sophie had to tell Robert the complete truth and trust him.

The young woman's eyes widened. 'Do you mean that? I don't deserve you as a friend.'

Henri put her hands on the young woman's shoulders. 'Take responsibility. Tell everyone the truth, rather than saying what you think you want them to hear, and people will stand by you. It is the character of a person that is important, not the reputation. Reputation is what others think of you. Character is what you are.'

'I don't like myself very much now.' Sophie gave a huge sigh. 'I deserve to be unhappy.'

Henri put an arm around Sophie's shoulders. 'Now, shall we get you cleaned up a bit before you go down? Grace is waiting in the carriage.'

'Grace is here?' A single tear ran down Sophie's cheek. 'Do you think she will clean me up and fix my hair before we go and see Robert?'

'Life is always much brighter when you are properly dressed.'

'Henri, you know my one regret about not marrying Sebastian is that you and I will not be related.' Sophie gave a sad smile. 'I don't suppose after this, there is any chance you might fall for Robert, is there?'

Henri took a deep breath. Fall for Robert? She already had. 'I have no plans to remarry, Sophie. And no one has asked me.'

'Then he jolly well should.' Sophie put a hand on her hip. 'And you should accept him.'

'Whatever happens, Sophie, remember you have a friend in me.'

* * *

Robert glared at Cawburn, who continued to sit at the table, humming a strange tune. Robert wished that he could simply take Sophie and leave, but Cawburn had deliberately ruined the young woman and her prospects. Unless he could find a way around the coil, Sophie would have to marry this man and would suffer. It was something he didn't want. Yesterday, everything seemed clear-cut, but today, it was far from straightforward and he hoped Henri would find a way. He gave a small smile. The man who prided himself on solving his problems had discovered he needed someone else. Henri was fast becoming indispensible to his well-being and that made the current arrangement entirely unsatisfactory.

'Why did you kidnap Sophie?' Robert asked, breaking the silence.

'I didn't,' Sebastian spat out. 'I'd thought about it, but she came willingly enough once I spun a few lines about being like Henrietta. She even wrote the notes, you know.'

Robert flinched, remembering how he'd accused Henri about the notes. 'You seduced her.'

'It was the only way. You refused to let me speak to her alone and I thought she pined for me just as I pined for her. And abduction is far too harsh, Montemorcy, merely forcible persuasion. I wanted her to admit the truth and recognise that we belonged together. How wrong I was about that hell-cat. Now I can't wait to see the back of her. But first I will get my debts paid.' He leant back in his chair and a slow smile crossed his features. 'Oh, yes, I will be rolling in clover. Things always work out in my favour.'

'Pity you haven't read her father's will. Sophie possesses a small allowance, if she chooses to marry without my consent.'

Cawburn's mouth opened and shut several times. 'But…but I have a title.'

'I've never been very impressed with titles. It is more the measure of the man. If you have ruined Sophie, and it becomes necessary for you to marry, then I will be holding the purse strings.'

'You could pay me to keep my mouth shut. Just enough to get my creditors off my back.'

'Blackmailers always return for more.'

'Not blackmail, just a way of helping out.' Cawburn signalled to the innkeeper for two more tankards of beer. He cleared his throat. 'However, you are in no position to judge, not being a man of honour.'

'I refuse to play word games with you, Cawburn.' Robert clenched his fist, counted to ten and unclenched. It was not worth smashing Cawburn's face in. Not with witnesses. 'You should be grateful if I do not set the law on you. Abducting an heiress is not looked on with favour in any county of England.'

'You would not want to do that to your future relation. After all, we are all honourable men here and wish to do the correct thing, the thing society expects from honourable men.' With each repetition of the word *honourable*, Cawburn appeared to grow more self-assured, as if the very word was a magic talisman.

Robert pressed both his palms into the wooden table and took deep breaths. 'Plain English, Cawburn.'

Cawburn gave a laugh. 'I was speaking about your marriage to Henrietta.'

A great rushing noise filled Robert's brain. What did Cawburn know? He had to be ignorant about everything that had passed between Henri and him. He had left before Robert arrived at Dyvels and discovered Henri in the garden. Cawburn was merely clutching at straws and seeking to disconcert him. What was between Henri and him stayed private until she decided otherwise. 'Am I getting married to Lady Thorndike?'

Cawburn raised himself up and put his face close to Robert's. His blue eyes shot daggers. 'You and my cousin have been travelling together. I don't see her maid. And you must have spent an intriguing night together last night.'

The back of Robert's neck crept with ice. He wasn't worried about himself, but about Henri. 'Would you stoop to blackmailing your cousin? She has saved you so many times.'

'I rather thought to keep it between us two. After all, you don't want to know what she truly thinks of you.' Cawburn kissed his fingers. 'I knew there was a silver lining to your interest in her.'

'You overreach, Cawburn. Blackmailing is a dangerous occupation. What's more, Grace has been with us all this time.'

'It is of no consequence—in my time, I have seen enough women who have been bedded. How they look and smile.' Cawburn gave a falsely angelic smile. 'I am doing you the honour, sir, of assuming it was you who bedded my cousin. However, if you are not the man, would you kindly inform me of the man who is?'

Robert stared open-mouthed at Cawburn. 'You seek to blacken your cousin's name? She has protected you all these years. She has looked after your mother while you enjoyed the fleshpots of London!'

'Now, Montemorcy, do you or do you not intend to marry my cousin, Lady Thorndike, now that you have done more than kiss her cheek?'

Robert resisted the urge to connect his fist with Sebastian's face. Cawburn had just given him the glimmering of an idea. He could engineer a convenient engagement with Henri. It would allow them some privacy and he could work on persuading her to accept him for ever. '*If* that was the case, I would intend to marry your cousin.'

Sebastian took another pint of beer from the innkeeper. A strange expression flitted across his face. 'When is the date set for?'

'It is not set,' Robert admitted. The sweat started to drip down his neck. Henri had no wish to remarry, and not to do so left her vulnerable to bounders like her cousin. 'And I merely said "if".'

'I suspected as much. Intentions count for naught, as you once said to me.' Cawburn tapped the side of his nose. 'For a considerable sum, I'm willing to forget the matter.'

'I'm no more receptive to this sort of blackmail than the previous attempt.' Robert leant forwards and caught Cawburn's lapels. 'Do I make myself clear?'

He let Cawburn go.

'Nothing happened between Sophie and me. I had intended to wait until we were married. It was going to live in my mind as perfection itself.' Cawburn wiped his hand across his mouth. 'Now, she will live for ever in my memory as the one who thankfully got away. We would not have suited. Her golden curls blinded me and I mistook her lively manner for a pleasant disposition.'

'You will keep a civil tongue in your head. Particularly in a public place.' Robert resisted the primitive urge to smash Cawburn's head in. How dare he seek to blacken Henri's name in that way! It only served to show that Cawburn had no scruples.

Cawburn stood, swayed slightly and gestured to the innkeeper. 'I require a private parlour. This gentleman is paying. When the women emerge from upstairs, kindly usher them there. Then we shall see who is right.'

The innkeeper tossed Robert a questioning glance. Robert nodded and handed the innkeeper a gold coin. The innkeeper led the way to a well-appointed back room where a low wood fire burned. The room would do. Robert allowed Cawburn in before he blocked the entrance.

'Your private parlour, Cawburn,' Robert said, bowing low. 'What do you think Miss Ravel will say? How will she tell this tale?'

'Do not try to change the subject, Montemorcy.' Cawburn trailed his finger along the edge of a table and inspected it for dust. 'Did you or did you not make love to my cousin?'

'It is none of your business.'

'I will take that as a yes.'

Robert finally lost control over his temper. He reached back and landed a punch square on Cawburn's chin. The man crumpled to the floor. 'You ought to hold your cousin in higher regard.'

'I do hold Henrietta in high regard.'

'Enough to know that she hates the name Henrietta?'

Cawburn fingered his chin. 'You will regret that. Henrietta always takes my side. You will have lost her.'

'Fairly hard to lose what I never had.' Even as he said the words, Robert knew he would fight for her and her right to live her life how she wished it—and make damn sure he was going to be in that life.

'God's nightgown, Sebastian! What happened to your face?' Henri asked, coming into the private parlour. The pair were seated at opposite ends of the room, glaring at each other. Robert appeared as she left him, but Sebastian was sporting a rather large swelling just below his right eye.

'He encountered my fist,' Robert said, rising to his feet. His face was far more shuttered than she had seen it. 'But I believe we understand each other now.'

Henri's heart sank. After all her work with Sophie, he wouldn't listen to the truth. He'd hit Sebastian because of Sophie. He was going to act the same way as he'd done yesterday—leaping to conclusions and expecting everyone to agree with them. The pain in her head threatened to become a full-blown headache.

'Henri, he hit me,' Sebastian said with a petulant pout.

'I dare say you deserved it.' She tapped her boot on the ground. 'It can go with the other lumps on your head.'

'You know about those.' Sebastian winced and gingerly felt the top of his head. 'Why did she have to tell you about those? It is bad enough to have been bested by him, but by a mere slip of a girl...'

'Tell you about what?' Robert sat up. 'What did Sophie do to you, Cawburn? How did she best you?'

'Hit me on the head with a frying pan,' Sebastian admitted, making a face. 'The little hell-cat will get her come-uppance. Nobody does that to me!'

Robert's face froze, but Henri fancied that he was struggling to keep a straight face. She bit her lip and hoped. Surely now Robert would listen to Sophie before he started publishing the banns.

'I have brought Sophie down, Robert. And the missing frying pan. She will explain all. It is really quite simple. Pay attention, as you have a tendency to overcomplicate.' Henri grabbed Sophie by the hand and led her into the room.

'Sophie! Your stepmother will be delighted to see you when we get back to the New Lodge.'

Robert opened his arms, but Sophie held back, clinging to Henri's hand like a limpet.

'Sophie, remember what we spoke about. It must come from you, not me. The whole truth.' Henri tried gently to prise her fingers away. Sophie was going to have to do this bit on her own.

'Henri, you promised to be my ally,' Sophie whispered. 'I might need you to say the words.'

Henri gave the young woman a little push into the centre of the room. It was Sophie's turn to stand up for what she wanted. 'You must, Sophie. Tell your guardian precisely what you do and do not want. He is far from a mind reader. He needs to hear your words. He needs to know how you fought to protect your honour. Without embellishment.'

'I have no wish to marry Lord Cawburn, if you please, Robert.' Sophie moved away from Henri and stood in the centre of the small room. Although she looked young and vulnerable, her voice did not waver and her back remained straight and proud. Henri nodded. Sophie was using the exact form of words they had agreed. She told the whole story from beginning to end. Robert lifted his eyebrow once or twice when she mentioned how she had tricked Henri and then how she had used Henri's suggestion of hitting him over the head with a frying pan.

'I do not believe even after today there is any cause for me to marry him,' Sophie finished, clasping her hands on her chin as Henri had practised with her. 'Lord Cawburn has done nothing to dishonour me. As for a partner to go through life with, Lord Cawburn is far from ideal. I believe I can do better, much better, and Lord Cawburn deserves someone who will love him for the man he is.'

The room seemed to hold its breath, but then Robert burst out laughing.

'I wish I could have seen Cawburn's face when you hit him. Thank you for telling me the truth,' Robert said. 'Ultimately I want you to be happy. Your friends and family will stand by you. And hopefully you have learnt your lesson. And, Thorndike, that was a totally unnecessary gesture you suggested at the end. Melodrama at its worst.'

Henri glared at him. He was supposed to be moved to tears, but the situation amused him. 'Are you accusing me of interfering? You never behave how you're supposed to!'

'It was Sophie's recital of the truth that swayed me, not the gesture. I saw you make a motion to Sophie to bring her hands up. I'd have hoped that you thought better of me than to have to be swayed by play-acting. I wanted the truth and Sophie spoke it.'

Henri's insides ached. Play-acting. Perhaps it was, but it was in a good cause. And he was laughing at her efforts. 'I…I…wanted to help. Details are important.'

'And you did—by telling Sophie to always carry a frying pan!' His eyes softened. 'Thankfully she is not afraid to use it. And there is the evidence of Mrs Mumps. The only person who should be frightened about his reputation is Lord Cawburn.'

'Do you mean that, truly?' Sophie's face broke out into a wreath of smiles. 'I'm not sure I want a Season, either. Far too many rules. I'm beginning to love the country.'

'With your ability to wield a frying pan, Miss Ravel, I do not believe anyone will trouble you if you change your mind about London,' Sebastian said. His face became wreathed in schoolboy innocence, the sort of look that Sebastian used when he was up to something. 'Now, Henrietta, sweet cousin, what are we going to do about your predicament?'

'Sebastian, are you going to tell me why Robert hit you?' Henri put her hand on her hip and attempted to turn the conversation away from her so-called predicament. 'What did you do to annoy him?'

'Henrietta, I am wise to your tricks. I requested this parlour not for Miss Ravel's convenience, but to spare your blushes. You may come down from your high horse and speak civilly to me if you want to keep your present lifestyle. Things are going to change.'

Henri took a step backwards. She glanced between Sebastian and Robert. Robert shook his head. And it crashed over her. Sebastian had guessed. He knew what she'd done.

'I explained this before, Cawburn,' Robert said, moving over towards her. 'Your blackmailing days are over. Lady Thorndike will be marrying me, if it comes to it.'

Chapter Seventeen

Henri stared at Robert. *Marrying* him?

A pulse of warmth leapt through her at the thought of being his wife, but she ruthlessly squashed it. She was not going to marry anyone. She wanted his friendship, not his hand in marriage, not if he didn't love her. It was all decided. They were intimate friends. He hadn't asked her first. He'd waited until Sebastian forced the issue. She wasn't about to marry anyone because someone else proclaimed it necessary. Robert had to want to marry her, and Robert had proudly proclaimed that he wasn't in the marriage market.

'As jokes go, Mr Montemorcy, this is a pretty poor one. I don't need your protection from my cousin.' Henri crossed her arms and regarded Robert through a narrow gaze. They had agreed last night—intimate friendship, not marriage. She refused to become someone's wife because society dictated. It had to be because Robert wanted to marry her. And he didn't. 'You have not asked me, nor have I accepted. This fustian nonsense must cease. Someone might get the wrong idea.'

'As head of the family, I accept on your behalf, Henrietta,' Sebastian said, coming over to her and putting an arm about her shoulders. The gesture was designed to hold her in place rather than seek comfort. Henri shrugged several times, but his grip only tightened. 'I was reasonably pleased that Montemorcy has decided to do the decent thing without too much *persuasion*. That you are far worse than Miss Ravel is self-evident. However, I'm willing to be *persuaded* otherwise if I have made a mistake.'

The back of Henri's neck prickled a warning. Sebastian's easy-going demeanour had vanished and in its place she saw controlled fury. *Persuasion* was a euphemism for money.

'What do you want, cousin?' Henri tried to make her voice sound carefree. Sebastian was seeking to unnerve her, that was all. He wouldn't truly demand money to keep his silence. He had his code. Surely he hadn't sunk that low? Robert had to understand that he didn't need to sacrifice himself for her good name. 'I'd have thought he'd be the last person in the world you would like me to marry.'

'Did you think, sweet cousin, that I can't recognise a woman who has been well-loved?'

Before she could move, Sebastian lunged forwards, caught her chin between his forefinger and thumb and held her face steady. Henri forced herself not to flinch or look away and meet his searching gaze with calm fortitude. Above everything else, she had to stop Robert from making a sacrifice that they'd both regret. She couldn't bear the thought of him resenting being forced into marriage, of losing him slowly inch by precious inch because he had been forced. If Robert married her, she wanted it to be for love.

'Has drink completely addled your mind, Sebastian?'

'Even now, you wear a glow that was not there when I left yesterday morning.' Sebastian gave a menacing glance towards where Robert stood. 'Doesn't she look truly exquisite, Montemorcy? A tasty morsel?'

'You will keep a civil tongue in your head!' Robert ground out. 'There are ladies present.'

'I do beg your pardon, Miss Ravel,' Sebastian said with heavy irony. 'Henrietta Maria, answer the question. Did you spend last night alone?'

'That, Sebastian, is none of your business!' Henri gasped, wrenching her chin away as anger surged through her. Sebastian had to be made to understand that if he persisted in this stupid jape, he would be making her life a misery. 'You have no right! Stop trying to excuse your bad behaviour!'

Robert, to her annoyance, cleared his throat, but she refused to look at him. Who was he simply to announce that they were going to get married without asking her? She wasn't some parcel to be passed around. There was a difference between a loving marriage and a forced one. She knew the difference. She refused to have a one-sided love match. She'd seen how her mother hadn't coped and how the anger and resentment had driven her father away.

Sebastian blew on his fingernails. 'I am, for all you like to forget it, the head of our family. It is my business when my cousin decides to recklessly endanger her reputation.'

'That is rich coming from…from a confirmed fornicator.' Henri crossed her arms and refused to look at Robert. If Robert had wanted to marry her, he had had ample opportunity to ask her. All this morning in the carriage. She would have refused without question, but it would have been out in the open. She didn't want to have a husband because society dictated that she had to have one. She didn't want a husband at all. She wanted a friend and…a lover. She wanted someone who would be there for her always and who thought she was special.

Instead he was being forced into it by Sebastian of all people. Blackmailed. Henri's blood ran cold. Sebastian's debts. He didn't care who paid as long as it wasn't him.

'Is this about money?' she whispered.

'It is different for a man.' Sebastian put a hand on Henri's shoulder, but she shrugged it off. 'Come, Henrietta, what am I supposed to do? Turn a blind eye to your misdemeanours? Allow you to become the subject of common gossip?'

'A joke is a joke, Sebastian.' Henri hated the cold dread that filled her. Sebastian could not be serious about ruining her if she failed to marry Robert Montemorcy. She pushed the panic away and attempted to hang on to rational thought. 'You are not going to tell anyone, Sebastian. Mr Montemorcy is a gentleman. He will keep quiet as well. You are simply seeking to create a storm in a teacup because your own marriage plans went awry and you need money. Your debts are there because you gamble.'

'Your cousin is not joking.' Robert gave Sebastian a deadly glance. 'He intends to use the information to discredit me within the business community.'

'And that would harm your business?' Henri thought of the hundreds of workers who depended on Robert. And all his plans. He created jobs for people. Sebastian wanted to take all that away.

Robert gave a shrug. 'Men do business for all sorts of reasons. But a big enough scandal could hurt.'

'I would never dream of joking about such matters.' Sebastian held up his hands. 'It was your choice to be with Robert Montemorcy. You made your bed, Henrietta, now have the good grace to lie in it. Marriage or else banishment from polite society. You like being good, accepted and helping people, Henrietta. You would be desperately unhappy being bad and wicked. It goes against your nature. You told me to find a way to pay my debts and I have. You, or rather Montemorcy, will pay.'

Henri stared at her cousin in open-mouthed horror. She'd considered him spoilt before, but she had never realised the depths of his depravity. She put her hand to her head and tried to think clearly. Marriage to Robert was not the answer. And she refused to allow Sebastian leave to ruin her life.

'Robert! Mr Montemorcy, explain why it is impossible for us to marry. Sebastian, you are acting exactly like you accused Robert of acting. You did not like it then. Why should I like it now?'

'And quite frankly,' Sebastian continued as if she had not spoken, 'I do not care whom you marry as long as you do marry.'

'Cawburn, you go too far!' Robert said in a furious voice. 'You will stay within the bounds of propriety. We agreed. Henri is not to be bullied. I will not have Henri forced against her will. I take all the blame for the situation. We're engaged and if—'

'Are you saying that my guardian dishonoured Lady Thorndike, Lord Cawburn?' Sophie asked. 'When?'

'I draw a veil over the particulars, Miss Ravel, as you are unmarried.' Sebastian inclined his head. 'Thankfully, Mr Montemorcy showed a particle of common sense. It pains me that my cousin fails to grasp the gravity of the situation.'

Henri crossed her arms and silently consigned Sebastian to the darkest corner of hell. 'All the times I smoothed the ruffled feathers and made certain no outraged husbands followed you. You are the most despicable type of hypocrite, Sebastian English! You will not get a halfpenny farthing from me ever.'

'But I thought marriage was supposed to be the making of people.' Sebastian batted his eyelids. 'I believe it would have been the argument you used with me if I had chosen to dishonour Miss Ravel in that fashion.'

Henri reached out and slapped his face.

'Ouch, that hurt!'

'And that is for a good many other things as well.'

'Cawburn, I will speak with Lady Thorndike in private,' Robert said, stepping between Sebastian and her. 'Violence is not going to solve anything.'

His bulk hid her from Sebastian's triumphant gaze and Henri used the few heartbeats to regain control of her emotions. There had to be some way that she could reason with Robert and make him see. It was marriage in general she was against. She enjoyed Robert's company too much to marry him. She did not want to risk losing him. And there were so many ways she could lose him— death, boredom and even to someone else as her mother had lost her father. Her heart stopped. But she also risked losing him if they did not marry—so was loss inevitable? But which way would hurt less? Was it the hurt she feared? And what about the love she felt for him? Henri tried to concentrate and to think logically.

'I am not sure I should let you, Montemorcy,' her cousin said. 'Your being alone with Henri is what brought us to this impasse, as it were. In good conscience, can I be that derelict in my duty?'

'You will allow me to speak to Henri.' Robert used a slow voice that allowed for no dissent. 'You know *my* intentions are honourable, Cawburn.'

'I'll wait with Grace,' Sophie said. 'There is no need to fear, Robert. I have decided to be the model of decorum from here on out. I have no wish to experience an abduction again. They are beastly uncomfortable and inconvenient. I wonder why popular novels make them seem so exciting. They make you miss your tea.'

'Always the practical one, Sophie. I look forward to the new Sophie,' Robert said with a laugh. 'It will make your stepmother's head rest easily at night. All she wants for you is to be a happy and respectable young woman.'

Sophie stopped and kissed Henri's cheek. Her eyes sparkled. 'I'm pleased we're to be in each other's life after all, but I do think you could have told me before about the secret engagement. When did Robert ask you?'

'He hasn't,' Henri ground out, ignoring Sophie's startled exclamation. 'I have not had the opportunity of refusing the offer.'

Henri practised counting to ten while she waited for the room to empty. Robert, to her annoyance, appeared to be enjoying her anger. When Sebastian left, he shut the door with a decisive click.

'How could you do this to me?' Henri asked. 'How could you declare to all the world that we were getting married? You have not even asked me.'

'You might at least wait for the explanation, Thorndike.' A muscle twitched in his jaw.

'Why? It won't change my answer.' Henri kept her head upright.

She would be dignified. He was being forced into this, just as she had once forced Edmund. Just once, she'd liked to be asked first. 'Forced marriages are always a disaster.'

'We must speak, Henrietta. Sensibly. Without you flying into a rage. Consider for a moment the alternative. Do you truly want that? More to the point, do you think I would have arranged this, any more than you arranged the note? You spoke of trust and trust must run both ways. Do you trust me?'

'Trust you?' Henri froze. He was right—she had behaved precisely in the same fashion that he had. She had chosen the fear instead of waiting for the truth. She swallowed hard. 'Marriage wasn't in my plans. I explained that.'

'Then what is,' he asked softly, 'now that we both know it will be impossible to keep our relationship a secret? Plans can change, Henri.'

Henri thought about the alternative. A life outside the confines of society—one of late mornings, decadent afternoons and sensuous evenings. No longer would she be forced to call on women who were more interested in gossip than people. She could behave exactly how she pleased without trying to be good. She wouldn't have to be interested in what people did. Or have the satisfaction of seeing how her schemes improved people's lives. Conventionality was not morality, but it was comforting.

The anger fled from her, leaving her shoulders bowed down by sadness. The dream that she didn't dare speak was for ever gone. She wanted Robert to marry her for the right reasons, not to save some reputation that didn't matter a jot in the grand scheme of things.

She wanted to beg him to sweep her into his arms and whisper that he had always intended to ask her. Instead he glowered at her and allowed the silence to grow.

'This is a dreadful mess,' she said when her body screamed for her to do something and stop the dreadful silence from pressing down on her. 'There must be a way around this coil.'

'Must there? Your cousin is a determined and desperate man. You were right. I have come to regret harassing him about his debts. Your ideas are at least equal to mine. I did overcomplicate matters.'

'Giving in to blackmail is out of the question.' Henri ran her hands up and down her arms, trying to get some warmth back into her body. She refused to allow Robert even to contemplate such a thing as giving in. 'He'll only come back for more. I wish that I'd seen it earlier.'

'He's been emotionally blackmailing you for years. Telling you that it was your fault about Edmund's death. It is why you helped him, isn't it?'

'Yes. No. I wanted to stop feeling so alone. Sebastian needed my help.' She looked at her hands. 'I suppose you think me foolish.'

'No, I think you have a generous heart, my dearest Thorndike. The most generous heart I have ever encountered.'

Henri put a hand to the side of her head. *His dearest Thorndike.* 'This situation is nothing either of us wanted. You should have done everything in your power to prevent it. There was no need to kiss and tell. Particularly not to Sebastian.'

Something went out of Robert's eyes. Henri squirmed slightly. She had not meant the words as harshly as they came out of her mouth.

'Your cousin guessed without me uttering a single word. I declined to answer his questions as any gentleman would.' Robert's gaze travelled slowly up and down her and she remembered what it was like to have his skin touching hers. 'Henri, your eyes are sparkling and a certain lustre hangs about you. He asked a specific question, I answered as best as I could without lying. I refused to lie, Henri, even for you.'

'But he intends to blackmail you.' Henri clasped her hands together to prevent them from reaching out towards Robert. She was filled with the nearly overwhelming desire to lay her head against his chest and have him hold her.

'Whatever you decide here, Thorndike, my reputation will not suffer in the long term.'

'But...' Henri turned towards the glowing coals and tried to marshal her thoughts. He had not asked her to marry him this morning. It was only now when Sebastian demanded and, somehow, it hurt far more than it should. She wanted his offer of marriage to come from the heart, not to be forced through circumstances. Marriage with love was difficult enough. She knew that from her experience with Edmund. Without love and forced to because society dictated—she shuddered to think. 'But it could affect your business in the long term. You said as much to Sebastian.'

'To be known as less than honourable in my private life...' he gave a shrug '...what happens with my business has no bearing on your future. It has already weathered the scandal of my father's death. It is you he wants to control.'

'But our coming together was supposed to be an interlude.'

'Henri? Are you going to say that our coupling was meaningless?'

'Yes,' she lied, hating that he had guessed and longing for him to deny it. 'I had assumed it. It was supposed to be our secret, something that had no bearing on our real lives. I never expected anyone to guess. I thought I had planned everything precisely.'

'Why would you think that?' He looked genuinely astonished. 'Why would you think so little of yourself?'

'Isn't that how all men think? Coupling is a purely physical act with little meaning for the rest of one's life. One has to apply cool logic.' She watched the glow of the fire and tried to control the sudden fluttering of her stomach. 'Certainly it was how my father thought, and my cousin thinks. Edmund even... Logic.'

'Logic has nothing to do with it. You taught me that. All men are not your father or your cousin. And I cannot claim to speak for the rest of humanity.' He came and stood behind her. His hands lightly skimmed her arms. 'I can only speak for me. Being with you was the most incredible experience of my existence. You are the most intriguing woman I have ever met. I want you in my life. You showed me that there are some things that can only be seen through the heart. A generosity of spirit can do far more good than cold logic. And I'm not too proud to admit it was a lesson I needed to learn.'

The warm curl in her stomach grew. Henri concentrated on the fire, rather than giving in to her impulse and turning. If she turned, she'd be in his arms and kissing him. But it was wrong. What they had shared was supposed to be just a passionate interlude. He had never mentioned love and she knew she needed that reassurance if they were going to marry.

She gave a shaky laugh. 'I thought passion was a bad basis for marriage. It has no part in a rational well-ordered life.'

'I am quite willing to be proven wrong, Henri.' There was a rich warm laugh in Robert's voice. 'Will you take the risk?'

'Are we opting for a long engagement?' Henri relaxed slightly. She was an idiot of the highest order. She should have understood what Robert was doing before jumping to conclusions. They would be engaged for a little while and then decide quietly that they did not suit after all. The interval did not have to be long, but it was the perfect solution. 'Long engagements prevent mistakes happening.'

'I am opting for marriage with you or nothing.'

'Don't force me to do this. Don't force yourself into something you will regret. Maybe not today, but tomorrow or the next day. Marriage was not in your plans or mine.'

Robert listened to Henri's words as tears shimmered in her eyes. He was about to lose her. Last night he'd agreed that they were merely friends, but today the very real prospect of a future without her stared him in the face. If he was going to lose her, then he would lose no matter what he did or said. He who took so many risks in business was afraid to take this risk in his private life? Henri had taught him that life should hold more. He wanted to give her that commitment because she deserved the security.

'Would you make me into a hypocrite, Henri? First a liar and then a hypocrite. How little you know me.' Robert traced the line of her jaw. She turned her face away. His heart clenched. Had he already lost her? 'I already told you that we were going to be together again. I promised white linen sheets and long lazy mornings. I want to be more than your friend, Henri. I want to be your lover. For now. For always. For always is a long time, Henri.'

'And you don't break your promises.'

'Not promises to beautiful ladies.' His hands reached out and turned her towards him.

'I am grateful you think me beautiful,' she said carefully. An insidious tendril of hope curled about her insides. 'No else does. Everyone in my family has always commented on my faults.'

'Then they are blind.'

'My nose is too large, my mouth too small, my figure is less than fashionable. I do know my faults.'

'Which are?'

'I'm headstrong, bad tempered in the morning particularly, and inclined to want my own way.' She started counting off her faults on her fingers and he knew he had to take the final risk.

'You have forgotten arrogant, stubborn, high-handed and one last thing…' He gathered her unresisting to his and tilted her chin towards him until her sapphire-blue eyes looked directly into his.

'What is that?' she breathed.

'Utterly and completely lovable.' He bent his head and his mouth caught her bottom lip. He allowed his lips to say the words that he did not dare say, slowly and quietly, showing as well as telling her his feelings.

A long drawn-out sigh emerged from her throat and she twined her arms about his neck. 'Lovable? No one has ever called me that before.'

He smoothed her hair back from her temple. 'I'm selfish, Henri, I want you in my life for the rest of my life. Not because of Sebastian or anyone, but because I want you there when I wake up and when

I go to bed. When I look up from my food, I want you there across from me. I want to hear your voice. I want to touch your skin. I want you.'

'As your wife?'

'I can't promise an easy life as we are both far too set in our ways,' he admitted, 'but it would never be dull. Life without you would be an empty shell. I will even allow you to have treasure-hunting picbeetnics wherever and whenever you want and if that isn't love, then I don't what is. But, yes, I want to marry you. Marry me and stay by my side always.'

'Wherever I want?' A tiny smile touched her lips.

'I'm a man of deeds, not words, my dear. Pretty poetry doesn't spring easily to my lips, but then I suspect you would deride it as a pile of mush.'

'Sometimes I like mush, but grand gestures do just as well.' Henri laid her head against Robert's chest, listened his steady heartbeat and tried to make sense of his words and the feelings that swamped her. He thought her lovable and beautiful. He wanted to marry her. 'And if I wanted to be wicked?'

'You will find being wicked inside a marriage is far easier.' He waggled his eyebrows. 'We still have a lot to explore for when you are married. The wagers can be much more interesting. With the right person, it is far more fun to be married, and, Henrietta Thorndike, you are the right person for me. I love you deeply and passionately.'

'You do?' She captured his face between her hands. Her heart was so overflowing that she found it difficult to speak. 'I don't want to lose you, Robert. I can't bear the thought of losing you.'

'Then you'll marry me.' There was a note of hesitation in his voice. 'Say the words, Henri. Say them for me.'

She took a deep breath. Her insides did a dance all of their own. It was exhilarating and made her feel wonderfully alive. Their marriage would not be perfection, but it would be full of passion. 'We'll marry. I adore a challenge.'

* * *

The wedding day which seemed to take for ever to arrive, went by in a flash. It did not matter that a steady drizzle came down all that morning, or that St Andrew's was distinctly cold for a late August morning. All she noticed was how crowded the church was and how many people stood in the church yard as she came in on Doctor Lumley's arm. Aunt Frances sat in the front pew, wiping her eyes, but Sebastian had long since departed for the Continent, one step ahead of the debt collectors after Robert provided him with money for the passage. To Henri's great surprise, Sebastian had returned the money once he arrived in Venice with a note about how a gentleman always repaid his debts of honour to other gentlemen.

The coloured light from the stained-glass windows gave the church an enchanted air as Henri stood beside Robert, listening to his deep voice recite his vows. His fingers curled around hers tighter when he promised to worship her with his body. The rest of ceremony went by in a dream

Just before they went out into the church yard, when they were in the quiet of the entrance porch, he stopped and turned towards her.

'Problem?' she breathed.

'First this, Mrs Montemorcy,' he said, bending down to cover her mouth in a heart-stopping kiss. Slow, sweet and a seductive promise of what the night would hold.

When he lifted his head, she struggled to take a breath. 'And that was for…?'

'To remind you of all you have been missing during this inordinately long engagement of ours.'

'You were the one who refused to elope,' Henri reminded him with a smile.

'The village would never have forgiven me. Everyone has contributed to this wedding.' He gave a mock sigh. 'There is a problem, though.'

'Problem? What sort of problem?' Henri tried to crane around him. In the build up to the wedding, what had she missed? She had wanted a perfect day…no, she admitted, she had wanted Robert and that the rest didn't matter.

'Teasdale, Melanie Crozier and Miss Armstrong have nearly come to blows. Each is claiming responsibility for the match.'

Henri shook her head. They were all mistaken. 'Let them if it makes them feel better. All I know is that I am devotedly glad that the match did happen. But this matchmaking is becoming infectious.'

Henri tucked her hand in the crook of her husband's arm and prepared to go out in the special light of a Northumbrian August morning. The rain had stopped, and the entire world appeared festooned in diamond-studded sunlight.

And she knew that it didn't matter that the flower arrangements were lopsided, that Miss Armstrong had burst into noisy sobs during the last hymn or that Lady Winship's pugs had suddenly burst free of their mistress and were now tumbling about her skirts, making it difficult to walk. The perfection of the day was in her husband's smile, the way his hand felt against her back and the love and joy that surrounded her. Perfection came not from outward things, but from within. It came from loving and being loved and she knew that the day would live in her memory as one of the most perfect ever.

'I love you, Robert, my dearest friend,' she whispered.

'And I love you, Henri.' He kissed her again to the obvious delight of the crowd.

HISTORICAL

Novels coming in June 2011

RAVISHED BY THE RAKE
Louise Allen

The dashing man Lady Perdita Brooke once knew is now a hardened rake, who does *not* remember their passionate night together…though Dita's determined to remind him! She's holding all the cards—until Alistair reveals the ace up his sleeve!

THE RAKE OF HOLLOWHURST CASTLE
Elizabeth Beacon

Sir Charles Afforde has purchased Hollowhurst Castle; all that's left to possess is its determined and beautiful chatelaine. Roxanne Courland would rather stay a spinster than enter a loveless marriage… But Charles' sensual onslaught is hard to resist!

BOUGHT FOR THE HAREM
Anne Herries

After her capture by corsairs, Lady Harriet Sefton-Jones thinks help has arrived in the form of Lord Kasim. But he has come to purchase Harriet for his master the Caliph! Must Harriet face a life of enslavement, or does Kasim have a plan of his own?

SLAVE PRINCESS
Juliet Landon

For ex-cavalry officer Quintus Tiberius duty *always* comes first. His task to escort the Roman emperor's latest captive should be easy. But one look at Princess Brighid and Quintus wants to put his own desires before everything else…

HISTORICAL

Another exciting novel available this month:

LADY DRUSILLA'S ROAD TO RUIN

Christine Merrill

Mad dash to Gretna!

Considered a spinster, Lady Drusilla Rudney has only one role in life: to chaperon her sister. So when her flighty sibling elopes Dru knows she has to stop her! She employs the help of a fellow travelling companion, who *looks* harmless enough…

Ex-army captain John Hendricks is intrigued by this damsel in distress. Once embroiled with her in a mad dash across England, he discovers that Dru is no simpering woman. Her unconventional ways make him want to forget his gentlemanly conduct…and create a scandal all of their own!

HISTORICAL

Another exciting novel available this month:

GLORY AND THE RAKE
Deborah Simmons

An unsuitable job for a lady!

Miss Glory Sutton has two annoyances in her life. One: the precious spa she's determined to renovate keeps getting damaged by vandals. Two: the arrogant Duke of Westfield— the man assigned to help her find the perpetrators.

Oberon has no interest in this independent, troublesome woman! And Glory couldn't be less interested in the enigmatic rogue!

As they get drawn deeper into the mysteries of the spa, they too must reveal their secrets in order to uncover the truth. And then, perhaps, the legend of the waters will come true!